JESSICA

Mary Francis Shura

Bridget Lavoie
— This is an awesome
book!!

SCHOLASTIC INC.
New York Toronto London Auckland Sydney Tokyo

ISBN 0-590-33242-2

12 11 10 9 8 7 6 5 4   0 1 2 3 4/9

JESSICA

A *SUNFIRE* Book

SUNFIRE

Chapter One

JESSICA Findlay had galloped the mare Dancie at a marvelous clip through the dry Kansas prairie grass all the way from home. If she hadn't been going visiting, she would have loosened her long, taffy-colored hair and let it blow in the wind, as she had since she was a child. Lacking that, she had sung at the top of her lungs all the way, startling the prairie dogs from their burrows. But she *was* going visiting, and as her stepmother Melanie so gently told her, she was also going on sixteen and must start behaving like a lady.

"Sixteen," she groaned aloud, pulling Dancie into a walk. She didn't want to be sixteen and have to make some decision about her life. It didn't make sense that the passing of a single day, even if it was a birthday, could change a girl from being a child in her father's house to a grown-up. It would be different if there were something she really wanted to do more than just stay with her father and stepmother Melanie and the boys.

If there was such a thing, she certainly hadn't thought of it. Should she marry Roy Blanding, who was as dull as unsalted porridge and who wore her out, trying to think of something to talk about? Should she perhaps try to get a job, maybe as a maid in one of those fancy English houses over at Victoria as her friend Agatha had done? She had been good at school, maybe even good enough to get a job teaching as a lot of "young ladies" in Kansas had done. She groaned. Her best friend Rachel was the lucky one. Her parents owned the general store in town where Rachel had helped out since she was little. And Rachel held the job of postmistress, too, which earned her twenty-four extra dollars every year.

The afternoon heat laid a haze on the Kansas prairie. Jessica peered through that undulating light, looking for the trees that would mark the Sanders place. The hot, dry wind that had blown steadily all that summer of 1873 pressed her muslin dress tight against her legs as she tugged the mare to a halt to stare at the Sanders place. If it wasn't for that half-grown stand of trees, she would be at a loss to find the place. There were a lot of dugouts like the Sanders house scattered around the countryside. Sometimes a family was lucky enough to have a hill that could be shoveled out to make a generous room underneath. With no such hill available, Sanders had simply dug deep into the bank. There were no windows, and the wooden door had been set deep in the wall of sod bricks.

Jessica lifted the heavy blonde braid from her neck and waggled it to let the breeze reach her dripping flesh. Something was wrong. No plume of smoke rose from the chimney pipe thrusting above the roof. If that young couple had really moved in, as Rachel assured her that they had, they had to have a fire going. How else could they heat water and cook?

The door was set so low that any grown, person would have to stoop down to step into the room hollowed from the earth. How could anyone stand to be down in there without fire or light? The hooded wagon in which Will Reynolds had brought his bride west stood a few yards from the door. The canvas flaps were closed, and the wagon tongue lay on the ground like something exhausted. A silent hawk swung above the prairie, gracefully riding the warm drafts of air. There was no other sign of life.

Will Reynolds must be off somewhere, getting water or provisions to settle into this place he had bought from Sanders. But surely his wife would be at home. According to Rachel, she was about to have a baby.

Rachel hadn't seen the wife, really. She had only caught a quick glimpse of her through the open flaps of the wagon. Rachel had reported a violet-colored bonnet that looked like velvet, and dark hair pulled back from a doll-like face. Mrs. Reynolds had sat outside in the wagon staring straight ahead while her husband bought their supplies at the general store.

Jessica slid off Dancie and dropped the reins a few feet from the door. It was spooky there with only the breath of the wind moaning through the trees. Jessica decided that *bleak* was the word she would choose for this lonely place.

She set her basket down to knock at the door. As quickly as she had put it down, she snatched it up again. Fine kind of present that would be, to bring a basket of food with ants clambering up from the bottom.

When no answer came to her knock, she rapped again, louder. She wished she could shake off this feeling of being watched. There was not so much as a chipmunk in the clearing and yet her flesh crawled. She broke the silence with a call. "Mrs. Reynolds. Mrs. Reynolds!"

Dancie nickered in reply. Jessica looked around. Alongside the wagon sat a wooden box of strange tools and a fancy Eastern plow. The wind rose, whining through that stand of trees that Sanders had set out before he'd given up on finding water.

No one ever really called a man a quitter when he gave up and went back East. Certainly no one blamed Sanders for packing it in. It was bad enough that he had drilled three times without finding a sign of water. But then, his wife Margaret had sickened and died, leaving him with nothing but the ceaseless wind and the howling of coyotes for company.

There were simply Kansans and then there were other people, Jessica thought. Sanders had proved that he wasn't a Kansan by going back to Chicago. She had seen more than one wagon headed East bearing the slogan, "In God we trusted. In Kansas we busted." Sanders was only one among many.

After knocking again and calling into the silence, Jessica stood, undecided. It had been a long, hot ride from home, and it would be a long, hot ride back. Worse than that, her stepmother Melanie would be disappointed not to have greeted their new neighbors properly with a bit of fresh foodstuffs for their table.

As she turned to mount Dancie, she saw a cloud of dust moving toward her across the prairie. She shielded her bright, blue eyes to watch the horseman approach, moving close enough to Dancie to be able to pull her rifle from the saddle if she needed it.

The horse and rider approached swiftly, wheeled, and stopped a few feet away from her.

Jessica knew that this was Will Reynolds from Rachel's description of him.

"Skinny as rain," Rachel had said. "Tall and bone-skinny with wide shoulders. His clothes scream that he's a greenhorn, and he doesn't waste smiles on strangers."

Jessica had discounted the skinny part.

Rachel had been crazy in love with Walt Brannon since she was old enough to tell a boy from a girl. Walt was built like a steer ready to market. As a consequence, Rachel considered any man who wasn't thirty pounds overweight to be nothing but a bag of bones.

This man *was* slender and tall, with dark brown hair and eyes. His horse was loaded with double saddlebags, probably carrying water. The prairie dust had paled the color of his dark pants. He was studying her intently and was frowning.

"Is there something you want here?" he asked, glancing at the covered basket in her hand.

Jessica shook her head, feeling a flush of color rising in her face. It was a wonder that people bothered to have mirrors at all. It only took the studying gaze of a man like Will Reynolds for her to see herself more clearly than she wanted to. Her homemade muslin dress was faded from sun-drying, and her boots, sticking out from under her skirt, were white with dust. As for her bright hair, it had worked free of the braid to tumble around her face like fringe. Her bonnet was surely askew after that gallop. It would be so much easier to answer him if he would just take his eyes away for a minute.

"I'm Jessica Findlay," she told him, "your neighbor from down the way."

When he looked quizzically in the direction she pointed, she found herself stammering.

"It's about three miles, but we're the closest neighbors." She lifted the basket toward him. "Mellie, that's my mother, sent some things to welcome you. I couldn't find your wife. . . ." Her voice trailed off. He wasn't helping. He wasn't helping at all. That was just plain rude after her coming all that way.

"That's very nice of you," he said, "but we have everything we need."

She stared at him. "I didn't bring this because I thought you needed anything. This is just the way we do things out here." She was annoyed at him, but she was furious with herself. What was there about that cool, handsome face that made her words come out in a rush? "It's our way of telling you that we are happy to have you as neighbors."

"That's very kind of you, I'm sure," he repeated. Instead of taking the basket, he turned, unloaded the saddlebags, and loosened his horse's saddle. "Thank your mother for her thoughtfulness." He glanced again at the moist sweat spots on Jessica's dress and her dusty boots. "And your effort in coming here."

"Aren't you going to take these things?" she asked in disbelief. "Mellie makes the best bread anywhere around here. I made the jam myself, and there are fresh eggs. Surely your wife —"

"I am sure that my wife joins in my thanks for your good thoughts," he interrupted. The saddle was off and across his arm. "Now, if you'll excuse me."

7

The annoyance had turned to anger. Jessica drew herself up sharply. "And would you also give your wife my personal greetings, since it appears that I will not be allowed to do so for myself?"

"I will be happy to do that," he said. Then suddenly, he frowned. "I hope that you haven't taken offense. My wife is timid and not feeling well. I wouldn't want you to construe my protection of her as rudeness."

He was walking away, leaving her there with the basket in her hand, the horse clopping along behind him.

"Well, I do," she called after him.

He turned and stared at her. "You do what?" he asked. Jessica couldn't believe that anyone so remarkably handsome could be so boorish.

"I do construe you as rude," she told him. "There aren't very many of us out here, you know. We give and take, and none of us could manage any other way. I think you ought to let your wife decide if she wants some nice fresh bread and jam with eggs that would cost you an arm and a leg if you bought them at the store."

As Jessica spoke, she was startled to see the flaps of the canvas on the wagon stir as if someone were in there, watching and listening to this horrid scene. His face had hardened, and the single step he took toward her seemed threatening.

"Look here, Miss Findlay, I have stood and listened to you deliver this lesson in manners.

I now find my patience wearing thin. I have been gone from my home for several hours. I would like to be able to look in on my wife without being further harassed by you." He paused before stiffening his chin at her. "I might just add that it is not likely that I will ever behave like you Kansans do. I have had a flood of unsought advice forced on me since the moment I set foot in this place. I've been told that everything about me is wrong, from the tools I use to the clothes I wear. Now you have worked over my etiquette. I wish I felt grateful."

The flush that had begun in the embarrassment of his intent gaze had become a rage of color, hot behind Jessica's cheeks. Let well enough alone, she cautioned herself. Instead, she glanced at the fancy toolbox beside the wagon and at the smart leather shoes he wore.

"If you can break this sod with anything less than an iron plow, or keep a rattler's venom out of your blood with those shoes, maybe you can give us Kansans some lessons."

Turning, she straightened her back and marched to Dancie's side. She felt his eyes on her as she hooked the basket over the pommel of her saddle and mounted the mare, her eyes blinded with angry tears.

Rachel had said he was a greenhorn. He was worse than that. A lot of men had come to settle as greenhorns and turned into frontier men that you were proud to name as friends. Not this one. Wait until the day that he needed something from some of them. Then he would learn to talk out of the other side of his mouth.

She was grateful for the cloud of dust that hid her from his eyes as Dancie galloped away. If she never saw Will Reynolds or his timid wife again in her life, it would be too soon.

The sun was blazing toward the horizon when Dancie trotted around the fence to the stable yard. The barn owl that nested in the sycamore tree west of the house was already swaying above the meadow, a slit of angled white against the reddening sky. Jessica's father, hearing the mare's approach, came from the stable to open the gate.

"Well," he said, "you didn't visit very long."

"You might even say that I didn't visit at all," she said tartly, sliding onto the baked ground with a thud. "Not only that, but that rude greenhorn wouldn't even accept the things that Mellie and I packed in the basket."

"You mean he turned down fresh bread and eggs?" he asked.

"And my damsel plum jam," she told him.

"What about his wife?"

"Timid," she reported, tugging off her bonnet and shaking her wet braid loose. "He calls her timid, but she was out there in a wagon peeking at me through the canvas flaps while her husband told me to take my charity back home and not try to teach him manners like everybody else in Kansas had already tried to do."

She should have expected that sudden roar of laughter. Patrick Findlay had one of the more notable tempers in the county himself, but when Jessica showed even a smidgen of fire, rightfully come by from him, he always found it funny.

"Go on and laugh," she told him hotly. "You didn't ride all over the prairie to be treated like so much barnyard manure." She kicked a cow chip with her boot as she spoke.

Her father's expression turned sober. "You sure you didn't say something to set him off? You didn't startle him or anything?"

"Well, maybe I could have startled him," she admitted. "I had been banging on that door and yelling for his wife."

As she spoke, Jessica lifted off Dancie's saddle and slapped her gently on the rump. The mare set off for the water trough in that distinctive dancing gait that had earned her her name.

Jessica's father laid his arm across her shoulder and smiled down at her. "So he was coming home and saw, from a distance, a horse and rider there in that shimmery haze where he had left his wife all alone. That would scare any man until he could see that it was only my beautiful Jessica with a basket of goodies."

She grinned but shook her head. "I'm not kidding you, Papa. That is a spooky place. It feels dead. There were mole runs where Sanders had his garden. There wasn't a sign of smoke coming out of that chimney. And all the time I stood there banging on the door and calling her name, that woman was cowering inside that wagon without a breath of air, watching me. Doesn't that sound a little crazy to you?"

"Well . . ." he hesitated thoughtfully. "I understand that she's barely a woman, only about your age. Her husband is only nineteen."

He stopped at the well and began to wind the bucket up from its depth. The rope creaked and groaned against the wet stones. He lifted the full bucket, set it on the stone ledge, and stared off to where the red of the sky was being laced with deep purple stripes.

"Once that might have sounded crazy to me," he admitted. "Now just thinking about it brings back hurting memories. Your mother was like that when we first came out here. She couldn't stand to look at the prairie because it stretched so far that it brought tears to her eyes. The first time she tried to go into a dugout like that one, she flew right back out, crying." He paused. "She said it was like walking down into your own grave. I thought about those words a lot the winter she died, with the snow piled against the sod and no light coming in anywhere."

Jessica dropped her eyes. It wasn't often that her father talked about her mother. To Jessica, her mother was more music than picture, a voice singing softly, a laugh rising in a distinctive curve of sound.

Her mother had died of malaria the year Jessica was to turn three. For the next couple of years, Jessica had stayed with friends and neighbors. Then her father had married Melanie and had the two boys who were even now yelling from the house for Jessica and her father to hurry.

"Hold up there, boys," her father called. It was a wonder that they heard his words with Jerry's dog, Major, adding his own bark of greeting to the boys' voices. Ignoring the clamor, Patrick Findlay took Jessica by her slender shoulders and looked into her eyes.

"Pretend that you're a city girl instead of a Kansan, born and bred as you are. Say you came here from a wooden house, not log like ours, but real fancy wood or maybe even brick with windows everywhere and curtains white against the light. Say you had traveled all those long, painful miles with only a young husband to talk to and the fear of a first baby coming. Ask yourself what the dark step down into a dugout would make you think of."

Jessica's throat ached for the memory of her mother that she saw in his eyes. "Maybe she'll learn to love Kansas because her child is born here," Jessica whispered. "Like Mama did."

"Maybe she will," her father replied. "But in the meantime, let's give those young people a lot of room."

The boys had lost patience and were running toward them from the house, Jerry in the lead and Tad following. Jerry, at ten, thought himself too much of a man for a wide-armed hug, but he shouldered his father hard before fitting himself in under his arm. Tad, being only seven and full of mischief, would have caught Jessica and thrown her off balance except that Jessica remembered the basket in time. She thrust it up above her head, yelling, "Eggs, eggs!" to warn him off.

Melanie, at the door, frowned at her words. "You brought the eggs back?" she asked, clearly confused.

Her father spoke before Jessica could. "She couldn't find anyone to accept them," he said, touching his wife gently on the shoulder as he passed into the house.

Jessica echoed her father's words in her mind. He was giving the young couple room, not telling the true story because it might turn Mellie's mind against them at the start. Mellie accepted his words with a nod, grinning at Jessica as she took the basket.

Jessica, with Tad's arms tight around her waist, smiled back at this woman whom she loved both as mother and sister.

If Jessica had to choose a word for Melanie, it would have to be restful. Melanie was Kansas-born like Jessica herself, but different in most other ways. No matter how carefully Melanie shielded her face from the sun, her complexion was a warm, deep olive. Her thick, straight hair was as dark as her expressive eyes. Her lips always curved a little upward, even when she wasn't really smiling. Although Melanie's boisterous sons could be horribly demanding, at least in Jessica's opinion, Melanie never raised her voice to them in anger. Instead, she prodded them with teasing questions until they were smiling, too.

The golden welcome of lamplight streamed from the open door of the log cabin. The air was rich with the scent of smoke from the cook stove, blowing on the breath of the ceaseless wind.

Beyond the sheds where the horses and cows were housed lay the chicken yard. Beyond that was the fenced plot where two grave markers rose from the grass, one for Jessica's mother and the other for the baby girl that Melanie had lost between Jerry and Tad. Jessica thought of a frightened girl in a violet-colored bonnet, cringing in an airless wagon, terrified and alone. A girl like her mother had been all those years ago.

Pity the girl that she didn't have a husband who could hold a candle to Patrick Findlay. Pity enough for that.

Chapter Two

THAT August, with no rain and the grass dried to a sickly yellow, the two cows, Daisy and Brindle, had given milk stingily. Although Melanie churned as always, butter disappeared from the Findlay family table. Jessica didn't realize at first what was going on. Then the truth struck her. Of course, Melanie was saving the butter to trade for white sugar at the store in town. There was never enough money for special treats like real sugar, but if you were lucky enough to have something to trade, like good fresh butter or eggs, you could get what you wanted.

When Jessica realized what was going on, she protested at once. "I don't need a sugar cake for my birthday. Your molasses cakes are wonderful, all those great spices."

Melanie had shaken her head firmly, catching her lips together in what Jessica always thought of as "Melanie's stubborn line."

"No one will remember eating unbuttered bread for a couple of weeks," Melanie told her. "But I would never forgive myself if you had anything but a sugar cake for your birthday."

With Jessica's birthday party coming up on Sunday, Jerry hitched the bay horse to the buggy for a trip to town. Not until they were all ready to go did Jessica pull the butter up from the cool depths of the well to wrap it for the trip. She smiled to herself as she folded the wet cloths around that great lump of butter. You'd think that anyone going on sixteen would take a sugar cake for granted. Instead, she found herself imagining how delicious that cake would taste, richly golden from the endlessly beaten eggs, perfumed by the vanilla bean that her father had bought for Melanie from a passing peddler.

It was always exciting to go into town. For one thing, Jessica would get to see Rachel. Unless the store happened to be unusually busy, Mrs. Landers would give Rachel time off to have a private visit with Jessica.

And every trip to town managed to yield some new excitement for the boys. The old courthouse in Hays, which had been located just in back of Paddy Welsh's saloon, had burned down. A new one, all of stone, was being built. Until it was finished, the old courthouse cellar, with only a timber and dirt roof laid over it, served as the jail. Sheriff Ramsey kept his prisoners there, chained to a post in the ground. Sometimes a famous gunfighter or a cattle rustler would be there, glaring back at the curious boys.

There was the usual argument about who would drive the buggy.

"How will it look?" Jerry challenged her. "What's everybody going to say when they see a girl driving me along in a buggy?"

Melanie laughed indulgently from the doorway. "Wouldn't you get there quicker if Jessica drove?"

"Only because she makes me plod along like an old man."

"I've seen you give that horse his head," Melanie reminded him. "Don't you think your sister wants to live to be an old woman?"

Tad, already in his seat, was springing with eagerness. Jessica sighed and took the seat beside him. "This is all my fault for letting you drive the very first time," she reminded Jerry. "Let's go before I have a lapful of melted butter."

Soon they were even too far to see the flutter of Melanie's dishcloth as she waved to them from the doorway, keeping a firm hand on Major to keep him from following. Jerry turned to Jessica. "Someday, maybe I will make you glad about teaching me grown-up stuff."

A quick lump rose in Jessica's throat. Why was she getting so softhearted about these ridiculous boys lately? She leaned and patted his shoulder. "I'm glad now," she told him. "And proud, too."

She realized that she was also glad that they didn't have to pass the Sanders place where their new neighbors, the Reynolds, were. In the days that had passed since her meeting with Will Reynolds, her annoyance at him had slowly abated. Then the hurt had all come back again, green and fresh, when Jessica had heard her father and Melanie talking about the new people. She remembered the conversation almost word for word.

"I invited that young Reynolds couple to come over after church and celebrate Jessica's birthday with us," her father told Melanie. "I really urged him to take this opportunity to meet all their new neighbors."

"That was a good idea," Melanie said.

"I must have thought better of it than he did," Patrick Findlay replied. "He thanked me but said he was sure they couldn't make it."

"Why do you suppose they are keeping themselves so private?" Melanie wondered aloud.

His tone was soothing. "Some women don't like to be seen in public so soon before a child," he reminded her. "And you can't blame Reynolds for having his back up a little about Kansans."

"What did we ever do to him?" Melanie asked, astonished.

"Not us. Sanders," Jessica's father explained. "When Sanders sold him that place, he stopped a little short of telling the whole truth. Reynolds came out here thinking that the only reason Sanders had pulled out was because his wife had died."

Melanie turned in disbelief. "Sanders didn't tell Reynolds that he hadn't been able to locate water on that place yet?"

"Not a word about it," her husband said glumly. "That boy is hopping mad now that he knows how many dry holes Sanders had dug. I hate it when people go back East and give all of us out here on the frontier a bad name."

"Maybe we can help make it up to Will Reynolds," Melanie suggested. "Ours is the closest water and we can share."

"We can go only as far as he lets us," he reminded Melanie. There was no point in reminding her that so far, that had been no distance at all.

The traffic was getting heavier at the edge of town, and Jessica concentrated on Jerry's driving. Jessica could read Jerry's nervousness in the sweat stains on his shirt. She leaned and touched his shoulder. "Almost there. Good driving."

He nodded importantly, as if what he was doing was too demanding to permit him to reply.

The single main street of the town was crowded with buggies, horses, and clusters of visiting people. In among the wheels and hooves, the town dogs darted this way and that. By the time Jerry found a hitching post for the horse and buggy, a fine sheen of sweat shone on his face.

It was true that the streets were only paved with buffalo sod, and that there were settlements of tents and dugouts within seeing distance of Old North Main Street, but the air stirred with activity. Work on the handsome new courthouse had drawn a bunch of loiterers, and another group of men with handsome horses clustered around the door of the outfitting store. Since Hays was the end of the Kansas Pacific Railway, it had grown rapidly in the six years since its founding. The town was the outfitting station for all wagon trains following the Smoky Hill route to the West.

Once in a while that bunch of men got so rowdy that a burst of their laughter even drowned out the music pouring through the swinging doors of Dalton's saloon and Faro house. Someone at church had said that there were seventy-five places that a man could buy liquor right there in town. This had sounded like a ridiculous number, but Jessica could see seven of them from where she stood without craning her neck.

Jessica turned at the sound of horses' hooves behind her. Tad and Jerry had run down the street, but she hoped they wouldn't miss seeing the band of young Indian braves passing quietly along the street in single file. It wasn't proper for a girl to straddle a horse, and Jessica probably never would have tried it if it hadn't been for just such riders as were passing now.

Everyone knew that she could ride side-saddle with the best of them. No one but the prairie birds and a curious groundhog or two knew that she could also gallop bareback and swing to the ground on one side and then the other just like an Indian if she wanted to.

She pulled her eyes away from the sleek black braids and glowing skins of the young men with a sigh. Now, see? That was just the kind of foolishness that she would have to give up when she turned sixteen and a woman.

"A decent woman at that," she added to herself as a couple of dance-hall girls passed her, leaving a trail of flowery perfume in their wake. The minute that self-satisfied expression registered in her mind, she was annoyed at herself. Why did she have to parrot everything she heard from other people? How did she really know that those girls were indecent? Maybe they didn't have any other way to make their living except to dance in those wonderfully bright clothes they wore, scarlet petticoats flounced with ruffles, hats so sweeping with feathers that it was a wonder that they could swing those bright little parasols as they walked.

What made her the most cross, if she wanted to be honest about it, was the way the sound of the street changed when girls like that walked by. The men dropped their voices and sometimes laughed among themselves in a low, ugly way. The decent church women of the town were almost as bad. They drew themselves up and stared along their noses at the saloon girls as if they were not looking at other human beings at all but at freaks in some traveling show.

In her own opinion, there were some men who ought to be stared at that way and even driven off the plains. When she had been younger, even ten like Jerry, immense herds of buffalo had still roamed near Hays. Even when they passed in the distance, their hooves beat a thunder you could feel through the soles of your boots.

But that was before the hide hunters had come. Back in 1871, two years before, a Kansas hide dealer named DuBois had sent a shipment of buffalo pelts to Germany. When a German craftsman developed a way to treat the hides to make clothing, the mass killing of the buffalo had begun. For the price of three dollars a hide, two million buffalo had already been slaughtered by greasy, filthy men who prided themselves on how many animals they could shoot down in an hour. And not for food, either. They shot and skinned the buffalo and left the carcasses to rot, filling the prairie air with the stench of death. People looked down on Indians, but you never saw an Indian kill an animal for anything but food.

Jessica stopped there in the street, grinning at herself. What a silly she was! Here she was in town with this rare chance to look around and have fun with Rachel, and instead she was marching along delivering a lecture to herself. With that grin still on her face, she glanced up. One of the dance-hall girls had turned and seen that private grin. She had stopped. Meeting the girl's eyes, Jessica forgot the scarlet petticoats and the reputations to match. Why, this was only a girl about her own age with stuff smeared on her face to make her look older and fancy. But the makeup couldn't hide her eyes, bright with curiosity and hunger for friendship. Without caring who saw it, Jessica grinned at her before turning off to go down the street. Whatever that girl did, at least she wasn't guilty of going out to massacre helpless animals for a few dollars to spend on liquor in a saloon.

The friendly black barber who ran the shop on the corner was named White. He had a roaring business, according to Jessica's father. He was kept busy cleaning up and shaving the cattle herders who had sometimes spent months on the trail without the touch of hot water or a razor. He stopped sweeping his stoop to tip his cap to Jessica as she passed. She had meant to look into Sol Cohen's clothing store and study the windows of the jewelry store, but a glimpse of Roy Blanding up the street changed her mind.

Roy was not a man to miss in a crowd. She saw him well ahead, his head bent in conversation. Seen off like that, she conceded that he was almost as fine-looking as his mother claimed him to be. He was tall and built like a man who has thrown calves and worked the fields all his life. She had to admit that the way his deep auburn hair curled out from under the rim of his Stetson did that expensive hat of his a favor. Even Jessica's father conceded that Roy was "up and coming."

Sometimes when Jessica got really annoyed at Roy, she felt guilty about it. But it wasn't only that Roy was dull company or that the thought of having Mrs. Blanding as a mother-in-law made her blood run cold. There was something about Roy that scared her, and she didn't really know why. When they all had been kids in school together, she had heard some of the other boys refer to him as a bully. This had been hard for her to believe when he had always been so very gentle with her. Still, sometimes when he was talking about someone he didn't like, the meanest look came into his eyes. For no reason at all, the word she would choose for Roy then was *ruthless*.

Even at that moment he was standing with his shoulders squared in a threatening way and his voice, even from that distance, sounded rough and challenging.

Because she wanted this afternoon to be perfect, she ducked into Landers' General Store with her bonnet angled so he wouldn't see her face and come over to talk to her.

Chapter Three

IT took a minute for Jessica's eyes to adjust to the dimness of the store. It took longer than that to get used to the rich mingling of smells that filled her head. The sharpness of dill warred with the smoky odor of hams hanging from ceiling hooks. Onion and sassafras, vinegar and sauerkraut vied with the smell of carrot coffee freshly roasted for the pot steaming on the stove.

Rachel was busy with a customer. Jessica studied the glass case of ribbons while she waited for her friend.

When Rachel was free, she grabbed Jessica in a hug and immediately asked, "Have you met the Reynolds?"

"I met him," Jessica told Rachel cautiously, "but not his wife."

"Rosemary," Rachel filled in. "His wife's name is Rosemary Reynolds. Isn't that a name to go with a velvet bonnet? You did want to trade this butter in for white sugar, didn't you?"

At Jessica's nod, Rachel put the butter on the scale. "There will be plenty for your cake with a little to spare." She continued chattering as she began to measure out the sugar. "That Will Reynolds was in here early this morning looking for someone to dig a well hole for him."

"I hope he found someone," Jessica said. "Once the baby comes, they'll need twice as much as before."

Rachel shook her head. "He really is a city boy, that one. He said he didn't want to pay for any dry holes that didn't produce water. Dad advised him to call in a water-witch first to be sure of the spot. Reynolds drew himself up about three inches and said that he wasn't superstitious."

Jessica stared at her. "What does superstition have to do with it? Doesn't he know that every well around here was found by a dowser with a forked stick?"

Rachel shrugged. "He'll learn. Give me your shopping list. If we get through fast enough, maybe Dad will give me time off for a visit with you."

"I have to keep an eye out for the boys," Jessica warned her, handing over Melanie's carefully written list. "They are the reason I got here so late. Jerry insisted on driving the buggy. I only let him do it if he takes it easy. The minute the horse gets up a little speed, that kid imagines that he's turned into Buffalo Bill Cody."

Rachel laughed softly as she placed a bag of buckwheat flour into Melanie's basket. "He's really yearning to be a man, isn't he?"

It was on the tip of Jessica's tongue to say that Jerry was doing more yearning than learning. A glance at Rachel's face silenced her.

In a community that small, everyone was known. Rachel was even better known than most of the girls because of her work in the store and as postmistress. Jessica had heard more than one comment made about her friend. The older people in town usually referred to Rachel as "the youngest Landers girl . . . the plain one." Others were even less kind than that. They said she was the town pump for gossip and that you could slice a bear steak with the edge of her tongue.

It was true that all of Rachel's older sisters, now married and gone, were prettier than Rachel. It was also true that Jessica herself had lain awake many nights wondering if Rachel would be as free with Jessica's secrets as she was with the confidences of other people.

But I love her, Jessica told herself. *She's my friend and I love her no matter what. And if that Walt Brannon had half a head, he'd marry her like she wants him to.*

"Now," Rachel said, her eyes sparkling, "let's see if we can finagle some play time."

Mr. Landers, glancing at Jessica, grinned

broadly. "It's not hard to figure out what you two are up to. Pour Jessica a lemonade on me, Rachel. But you two stay close. If a big crowd comes in here, I'll need you."

"Thanks, Papa," Rachel told him. She poured two glasses of lemonade and handed one to Jessica to carry. "We'll be right upstairs."

Rachel plopped down beside Jessica on the blue-patterned love seat. "Now, let's talk about your birthday. Turning sixteen must be the most exciting thing in your life. I'm counting the days until I am. Three months and seventeen days exactly." Before Jessica could find words, Rachel looked over at her with a frown. "Something wrong, Jessica?"

Jessica nodded, afraid to speak for the sudden threat of tears behind her eyes. "I don't know what's gotten into me," she admitted. "I can't stand the thought of my birthday. All these years it seemed exciting to be getting nearer to the time that I would be a grown-up and set off on a life of my own. Now that it's right on me, I don't like the idea at all. And even worse than that, everything seems different all of a sudden. I see Dad and Melanie in a new way. Instead of losing my temper at Tad and Jerry for being so pesky, I think about leaving home as a married woman or being off somewhere working. Just the thought of being way from them and not seeing them grow up makes me want to cry." Those treacherous tears were heavy on her lashes as she groped for a pocket handkerchief. "I don't want things to change. I don't want to have to marry Roy Blanding. I just want everything to go on the way it always has."

Rachel was silent, staring at her fingernails as if she couldn't see them. "It's not the birthday, it's Roy Blanding. If there were someone that you loved the way I do Walt, you would feel different."

"Who will I ever meet?" Jessica scoffed, wiping her nose on the edge of the handkerchief that she had meant to save only for show. "I never see anybody that I want to see twice, much less look at for a lifetime."

"Looks aren't everything," Rachel reminded her. "Love changes your eyes as well as your heart."

Rachel had brought out the new dress she was finishing to wear to Jessica's birthday party when they heard the steps on the stairs.

"Jessica," Mr. Landers called up. "There's a gentleman here to see you."

Even as Rachel and Jessica exchanged a startled look, a couple entered the room. The man was wiry with a gray mustache and a completely bald head. "Miss Jessica Findlay?" he asked, looking from one girl to the other in confusion.

Jessica stepped forward, identifying herself.

"Ah," he said, offering her his hand. "I'm Alec Reiner, and this here is my missus."

Mrs. Reiner dragged her attention from

the wicker canary cage hanging in the big front window to nod at Jessica.

Having performed this introduction in a rush of words, Mr. Reiner seemed struck dumb. Rachel leaped to Jessica's aid.

"Won't you sit down?" she asked. "I'm Rachel Landers."

"Ah," he nodded. Then, having perched on the edge of a chair with his hat between his hands on his knees, he found his voice again and spilled out his errand in another tumbled flood of words.

"We're out by Pfeiffer," he said. "The missus and me have three young'uns and there's a passel more nearby. We have been needing a school out there for a long time now and decided we'd just do something about it. I've asked around everywhere to find a teacher who would take on those kids. Every place I ask, they tell me about Patrick Findlay's daughter Jessica." He paused. "That is you, isn't it?"

At Jessica's nod, he went on.

He was nodding, too. "Everybody I asked had a good word for you. They even said you were good at both numbers and reading." He paused, apparently impressed by this. "We came in today to get directions to your place, fixing to ask you about taking on this job. When Landers said you were right upstairs here, it seemed like providence."

He stopped and fixed Jessica with a solemn look. "So that's what we're asking. Would you come and teach? You'd stay with us, sleeping in with our Dulcie. There's a sod house for the school, warm and dry. Likely a lot more children would come from that Russian settlement out there. If we supplied you board and room and you charged a dollar a month for each student, you could lay a little money by?"

This last came like a question.

Rachel's eyes were wide. As postmistress, she had to meet the post twice a week, sometimes in the dead of night when it was storming. She sorted that mail and got it delivered somehow. For all this she earned two dollars a month. Clearly, Jessica's job offer looked like a bonanza to her.

Mr. Reiner was waiting, his forehead wrinkled with hope.

"It's very flattering to be asked," Jessica said slowly. "But your offer comes as such a surprise that I would have to think about it. And in any case, I couldn't possibly accept without talking it over at home. I'm the oldest in our family and have always helped my papa out with the work."

Mr. Reiner nodded as if he understood. Then he rose, clearly encouraged. "We'd like to get started early in September. You could get back to us with what you decide to do."

Jessica nodded. "I'll need your address to let you know."

Rachel found paper and pen for Jessica to write down the man's address. Mrs. Reiner nodded again as they left, having said not a single word.

When the sound of the footsteps was gone

from the stairs, Rachel grabbed Jessica and whirled her around. "A real job," she cried, "and all that money!" Then she paused, her eyes suddenly sober. "You realize how important a school is to that man, don't you? If he could write, he would have put down his address for you. He doesn't want his kids growing up like he did, without schooling."

Jessica stared at her. Suddenly, the faceless kids in the sod school seemed a cloud of responsibility rolling down on her.

"You'll be wonderful," Rachel assured her, "just wonderful."

"I have to ask Papa," Jessica reminded her. "I believe I won't ask until after this birthday. He's been funny about it this year. His eyes even get damp when he talks about my becoming a lady."

"I will really miss you," Rachel said. "First Agatha goes off with her fancy British folks, and then you —"

Before Jessica could reply, Mr. Landers called from below that Tad and Jerry were there.

"I'll be right down," Jessica answered, picking up her basket and hastily pulling on her bonnet.

"This would take Roy Blanding out of your hair for a while, too," Rachel said softly as they started down the stairs.

Jessica stopped and stared up at her.

Indeed it would. It really would, and she hadn't even thought of it. She almost skipped the rest of the way down the stairs.

Chapter Four

JESSICA'S sixteenth birthday fell on a Sunday. She slid from her bed an inch at a time to avoid disturbing her brothers, who were sleeping across the room. Instead of the usual surge of joy, she felt those hateful, hot tears pressing behind her eyes as she put on her everyday dress and boots.

She had gone to bed the night before, fighting tears, and here she was, waking up the same way. She must never let her father even guess that he had sent her to bed the night before with such a heavy heart.

He had read under the lamp until a flutter of moths had gathered around its chimney. When she leaned to kiss him good-night, he had looked up with a smile. "Off to bed, then? And to think that you will wake up a real young lady."

She had only been able to nod and escape to cry herself silently to sleep.

Jessica let herself outside quietly.

She saw that first slender strip of light. The sun did not so much rise as push the darkness back with surging masses of color. As the cock that ruled the hen yard began his clamor, Jessica trembled on the shadowy steps, clutching her knees hard against her chest.

She didn't want to be sixteen. She didn't want her father to treat her like a young lady. She wanted him there beside her with his arm across her shoulders, telling her the story of her birth just as he always had.

Jessica felt her heart leap at the creak of the door behind her. Without looking, she knew it was her father. The heaviness of his tread trembled the warped planking of the porch. Wordlessly, he let himself down beside her. His arm was a warm weight across her shoulders as they both stared at the boiling color in the east.

"It had been a long night for your mother and me," he began in that exactly proper tone.

Relief swelled her lungs with air. Her tears spilled onto her cheeks. Her father stopped, confused, and turned to look into her face. "Jessica, is something wrong?"

"No, no, Daddy," she breathed. "Everything is exactly right. Tell me again how it was when I was born." She couldn't see his face at that angle, but she felt his concern lessen as he patted her shoulder.

"And it was cold for an August dawn," he went on, with that wonderful tone of surprise.

Later there would be presents, always a book from her father and a dress made by Melanie in mysterious snatches of time. The boys would each have something handmade that would be brought forth with much giggling and squirming.

Jessica liked birthday presents better than any other gifts she ever got. At Christmas, sometimes a neighbor would pack a special trinket under the tree for her. This never happened on birthdays. Birthday presents were special private gifts, to come only from one's family, most intimate friends, or, if one were engaged, one's husband-to-be. But even without presents, this was already a perfect birthday.

Once the sun got a foothold on the sky, the day came swiftly. Daisy lowed for the milk pail, and the chickens began to scratch and quarrel behind their fence. Still her father sat silent, as if waiting. Finally he spoke. "I'm still wondering why you cried," he told her.

She nestled hard against him. "I think the word for it is *joy*." At his chuckle, she whispered, "Let's surprise Melanie by fixing breakfast. Just to get her used to having another woman in the house."

While her father revived the coals in the big iron range, Jessica started breakfast.

Breakfast was well begun before Melanie wakened in the room beyond. She flew into the kitchen wearing only her faded blue duster over her underclothes.

"My goodness," she cried at the door. "Whatever is going on here? Did I oversleep?"

Jessica giggled at this tumble of questions. Her father, at the door with a fresh bucket of water, boomed with laughter. "Didn't know how nice it would be to have a grown-up daughter in the house, did you?" he asked her.

Melanie paused, stared at Jessica, and then flew across the room to hold her close. "Oh, happy birthday, Jessica, happy, happy birthday." She drew back and grinned. "When I smelled that bacon cooking, I thought it was a dream."

Jessica turned the thick slices of salted pork and laughed. "No dream, just a surprise because Dad and I both woke up early."

"Big day around here today," her father said. "Don't you think she should get her presents right now?"

"Before breakfast even?" Melanie challenged.

"Well," he conceded, "maybe just until then."

Jessica slid the iron skillet off to the back and piled the crisp meat high on one side. As the bacon fat cooled, she broke eggs into a saucer one at a time before slipping them into the skillet. Instant lace ruffled around the edges of each egg as it struck the bubbling fat. She felt warm inside, not from the fire her father had laid but with tenderness for her father and Melanie. A special birthday, in spite of all her fears.

After breakfast was cleared away, the boys pressed Jessica into a chair with her presents. Jessica was conscious of her father's nervousness as she unwrapped his book. *Great Expectations*, she read on the front and looked up at him with delight.

"I don't even know what it is about," he admitted. "But the name was just right for our Jessica."

"Just don't wear it out before I get to it," Jerry said, peering over her shoulder as she flipped the pages. Jessica grinned to herself. Jerry, too, was a reader and was openly resentful at how well-worn her books were before he got to them.

"Open my present next," Tad insisted.

The corn-shuck doll he had made for Jessica was tall and stiff. She leaned to the left, supported by her broom. The smile Tad had painted on her face was lopsided, too. "I adore her," Jessica told him, grabbing him for a hug.

"But where will she live?" he asked, concerned.

"By my primping mirror," she assured him.

He grinned and ducked his head down inside his shirt collar. He knew that only special treasures were kept on that shelf. Jessica was overwhelmed at the delicate tooling that Jerry had done on a new bridle for Dancie, and Melanie had somehow again managed to find enough secret time to make her a dress.

But oh, what a dress. It was of sensible

cotton, of course, but it was from a bolt of calico from Landers' store that she had fingered longingly ever since they got it in. The deep, sky-blue background was sprinkled everywhere with clusters of white flowers whose centers were a deep rose color. Melanie returned her hug with a bear hug of her own. Then the family left for church in a great rush. "It's a good thing we don't have a birthday here every Sunday," Jessica's father teased. "Preacher Allen don't much like latecomers." He grinned at Jessica, nervous in her new dress. "Even if they come as fresh as a flower garden like our little lady here."

Jessica found it hard to keep her mind on the minister's words during the service. The music part was fine. She sang as loudly as she dared, harmonizing with her father's deep baritone at her side. The rest of the time she looked down at her dress. Had she imagined that the same rose color tinted her cheeks when she glanced in the mirror? She felt elegant and beautiful in her new dress and not stodgily grown-up at all.

She thought about teaching school away at Reiners'. This dress would be perfect for a schoolteacher to wear to church, pretty without being too fancy. Maybe she could use some of her teaching money to buy shoes. Boots made a lot better sense in both summer and winter, but she hadn't grown for two years, and boots did look pretty heavy sticking out from under such a flower garden of a dress.

Outside, blinded by the sunlight, Jessica practically stumbled into Roy Blanding's waiting arms. "Hello, there, Birthday Girl," he said. "You're as pretty as a spotted pig in that getup. I'd be proud to take you home."

"Thanks, anyway," Jessica told him. "Papa's waiting and he's in a big hurry."

Roy looked over at Patrick Findlay resentfully. "You're a big girl now. Just tell him you want to ride home with me."

"But I don't," she told him, trying to keep the crossness out of her voice as she pulled her arm away from his grasp. "Melanie needs my help at home." Then, at his frown, she reminded him, "You'll be along in a little while with your folks, won't you?"

"It's not the same," he growled. "I brought my own buggy special."

"It's too bad you didn't check with me," she told him, jumping up into the Findlay wagon beside Jerry. She was careful not to look back at Roy as her father pulled away. That sullen look on Roy's face was one Jessica feared the most. He did unexpected things when he was in that mood.

On the way home in the buggy, crammed between Jerry and Tad, Jessica tried to imagine herself teaching school. There were parts of it that sounded wonderful. She could read stories aloud, as she had to the boys when they were younger. She could play games with them when they had finished their lunch. And, oh, what a lot of singing they would do, with herself singing as rollickingly as she wanted to with only the students to hear. As soon as her birthday party was over and the guests were all gone, she would talk it over with her father and Melanie.

Once at home, everyone was busy. Her father and the boys had barely finished setting planks on sawhorses to make tables out under the trees before the first buggies pulled in.

"Happy birthday" was shouted more times than Jessica could count. Everyone within driving distance was there. Mrs. Logan, in her rust-colored bonnet with her genial husband in tow, drove in with Agatha Williams' parents. Mrs. Williams caught Jessica in a hug and sniffled in her ear, "How I miss our Agatha. I'll tell her every single thing that happens at your party in my next letter."

Jessica kept an eye out for the Landers' buggy, but Rachel's great love, Walter Brannon, got there first. He swung his mother down from her seat with a wide, good-natured grin and went directly to look over the collection of good food that was accumulating on the table. The blacksmith, Baber, came with his daughter Sara, who was two years older than Jessica and had always privately been Jessica's ideal. Sara played the organ at church, and piano for the important musical functions such as voice recitals and visiting theatrical troupes.

Regal was the word Jessica had chosen for Sara. She wasn't what you'd call a pretty girl, but she carried herself with a graceful pride that suggested power. She had a reputation for a biting wit that scared a lot of people away but only attracted Jessica, who really admired people with the courage to speak their minds.

In no time at all, the tables looked dangerously overloaded. Platter followed platter of crisply fried prairie chickens. Someone brought a huge boiled ham ringed all about with crusty spiced apples. Potatoes and pickles and applesauce bowls were squeezed in along with baked summer squash sweetened with molasses.

Melanie had an especially tender greeting for Mary Huffman, whose skill with sickness seemed close to magical. Mary Huffman had come when Tad was born. Afterward, she had nursed Melanie through a flu that sent Jessica's father to his knees in prayer more than once. Jessica had long ago decided that the word for Mary Huffman was *authority*. And it wasn't the kind of authority that bossed people around.

Preacher Allen arrived with his family just as the Blandings drove up. It would have done Jessica no good to try to avoid Roy Blanding's mother. She came toward Jessica with arms widespread. Mrs. Blanding had a way of enfolding Jessica that made it appear that Jessica was already a part of the Blanding family.

Chattering without pause, Mrs. Blanding took her basket from Roy to unpack it at the table. Jessica tried to escape, only to find

Roy blocking her way. To her horror, she realized that he had a wrapped package in his hand.

"No, Roy," she whispered, "not here."

"And why not?" Mrs. Blanding asked, turning. "Why shouldn't Roy bring you a little trinket on such a special birthday?" The nod with the word *special* seemed to imply some great significance.

"Not now," Jessica pleaded again. "Not with everyone watching."

Roy probably wouldn't have gotten the message, anyway, but Tad's seeing the package ruined all chance of it.

"A present," he cried. "Open it, Jessica, open it."

Jessica felt her cheeks redden. She wanted to sink into the ground. How dare he hand her a present in front of all her friends, who had known better than to do that? Presents were private things between family members or people pledged in marriage. A birthday party was for celebrating life and friendship, not for rewarding the person who had it. He was spoiling her party for everyone, and she had no way to stop him.

The crowd in the yard fell silent as she tugged at the ribbons. When she saw the box, she gasped and looked up at Roy.

"You can't," she cried. "It's too much."

"Slides," Tad was crying. "Dad, look at all those slides for the stereoscope.'"

Jessica's father looked no more pleased than Jessica felt. Not only was this a bad time to offer a gift, but this gift was too costly to be suitable. Even before her father spoke, Tad was off to the house to bring back the stereoscope in its wicker basket to try out the slides.

"Now listen, Roy," her father said quietly. "This just is not suitable." Although he spoke quietly to avoid embarrassing Roy, his effort came to nothing. The guests were clustered around as Mrs. Blanding spoke firmly, instructing Patrick Findlay in the raising of his own daughter.

"You can't possibly object to Roy's gift," she said. "There's nothing personal about it. You might say it is more educational."

Jessica saw her father's face redden dangerously as Tad fished a slide from the box and pressed the stereoscope to Jessica's eyes.

Jessica wanted to be a mile away and still running. Lacking that, she wanted the paper back on the box and her friends visiting in careless little groups as they had been. Instead, she let the dark hood of the stereoscope cover her eyes and bring the three-dimensional scene to life. The picture made no sense to her. Roy had done a cruel thing in bringing her a gift that cost more than most of her neighbors saw in hard money in a year. His gift seemed to diminish her father's book, her delicious new dress, and the boys' presents. Hands reached for the stereoscope as she took it from her eyes. As she passed it on, he saw her father's face, stormy with anger.

But he touched her shoulder gently. "Best see if you can help your mother," he said. "It's time to have grace before the meal."

Rachel arrived just as Preacher Allen blessed the food and began the meal. Jessica was glad that Rachel had missed the scene with the present. Rachel and Roy had argued before. The result was not anything you could call friendly. As it was, Roy glued himself to Jessica's left side the rest of the day while Rachel stayed on her right, with both of them trying to ignore the other. After the men carried Melanie's piano out on the porch, Sara Baber played everyone's favorite songs until the sun tilted down in the west.

Families had begun to gather up children and talk about packing their buggies for home when a cloud of dust boiled on the horizon to the west.

"Now, what do you suppose that is?" Jessica's father pondered, shading his eyes with his hand as he walked toward the road. The other men rose and joined him as the single horseman galloped up to stop only a few yards from the house.

"Reynolds," Jessica's father said, recognizing his young neighbor. "Is something wrong?"

As little as Jessica cared for Will Reynolds, she felt her heart go out to the desperation in his face. He was hatless, and his thick brown hair had blown every which way in the wind. A long smudge of dirt darkened one side of that handsome face, and his eyes were those of a wild man.

"Help," he gasped. "God in heaven, I need help. My wife —"

Melanie and Mary Huffman moved forward. "The baby?" Melanie asked in that serene voice.

He nodded, looking around frantically. "A doctor," he said. "There has to be a doctor."

"There's a doctor, all right," Mrs. Blanding said, her tone almost jesting. "Trouble is, he's forty miles away, if not more."

Melanie seemed not to have heard her. "Water," she told her husband. "Mary and I need water. If you'll saddle and load the pony for me. . . ."

He nodded and turned away before she finished the sentence.

"But we have to have a doctor," Will Reynolds repeated, his tone turning desperate.

Mary Huffman walked over to the horse and lifted her hand to Will Reynolds. "Give me a hand up," she ordered him. "Take me to your wife at once. The others will be along."

He looked startled past words as she swung sidesaddle onto the horse behind him. Jessica heard her firm, low command, "Now go."

The horse wheeled and left as it had come, in a cloud of dust colored by the coming sunset. Melanie left less than five minutes afterward with the saddlebags of water bouncing against Dancie's flanks.

Chapter Five

ALL sense of celebration swirled away in the dust of Dancie's hooves. The guests, their voices hushed by private memories, packed up quietly and left.

At last only the Landers and Blanding buggies remained. With the tables down and Melanie's piano back inside, Mrs. Landers looked around.

"Now, if there is anything more at all that we can do...."

Patrick Findlay shook his head. "Nothing, and I thank you for the help. And for being here to celebrate the day."

"I'd be happy to stay," Rachel volunteered. "Surely there's some way I could be of help."

"Thanks for offering," Jessica told her, "but Dad and I will do fine."

Jessica's father nodded. "I'll ride over there in a bit. But that young mother couldn't have better help than she's got right now in Mary Huffman and our Melanie."

Mr. Blanding rocked from heel to toe, clearly restless at the delay. But his wife still lingered with Roy at her side. At Patrick Findlay's firm statement, Roy's father took a determined grasp on his wife's elbow. "We'll be going along, too, then," he said, "with our prayers there for that young family."

Roy hung back only a moment before following his parents to their rig.

The moment Jessica and her father were alone, he turned to her. "If you see to the boys, I'll start the evening chores."

Seeing to the boys was easy enough. After setting a pitcher of cold milk and a plate of leftovers between them, she changed into her everyday clothes to help her father.

Between them, the stock was fed and the chickens locked away from predators in record time. Her father was in the barn finishing the milking, and Jessica was drawing fresh water for the night, when Major began his furious barking.

Before she could round the house to investigate, Roy Blanding was off his horse and walking toward her. Her annoyance at him early in the day returned in the embarrassment at being caught in that stained work dress with her boots freshly soiled from the stable. Her hair, which had been braided early in the morning, had escaped in pale tendrils that she had to blow from her eyes in order to see what she was doing.

Major's barking had brought the boys to the door to see what was going on, and in the dark stable door, Jessica's father appeared, watching.

"Jessica," Roy said, stopping a few feet from her. He turned shy the way he always did when they were alone. As always, she was startled that a man who was almost arrogant among his fellows should turn uncertain and stammering in her presence. "I came here today meaning to ask you something," he finally said. "Since I didn't get a chance then, I came back."

"This is not a good time," Jessica told him, setting down the water bucket to brush an escaped curl out of her eyes.

"How can you say it's not a good time when you don't know what I came to ask?"

"Because it's not a good time for anything," she told him. "Melanie is off with that young mother. Dad and I have a lot of things to do and" — she faltered — "I'm just not up to answering any questions."

Her father came from the barn to join them. "Is there something we can do to help you, Roy?" he asked as formally as if he were a clerk in a store.

Roy reddened under his gaze and ducked his head. "I guess not, Mr. Findlay," he replied. "Nothing that can't wait for another day." Then, tipping his Stetson to Jessica, he said, "Many happy returns on this joyful day." He backed away a few steps before turning to mount his horse.

"Well," her father said, turning to Jessica, "thanks to your good help, I can go over and see how our women are doing."

"Has it been a long time now?" Jessica asked.

Her father frowned. "Hard to say, since we don't know when she started. But don't wait up for me. I'll stay to do what I can. Melanie can ride back with me, but we need an extra horse there for Mary Huffman."

Jessica watched him ride away, noticing that he was carrying another set of saddlebags full of water for the Reynolds house. It was funny the way he acted about Roy Blanding. He had teased her ruthlessly about every boy who had tweaked her pigtails since she was a child. Yet Roy could do some foolish thing, such as coming back today, and her father wouldn't even mention it. She shivered at the thought. She'd heard some of the women at church talking about how they wanted their daughters to marry well. That seemed an unlikely ambition for her father to have for her. Yet he certainly stepped easy around Roy Blanding. What other reason could he have to act like that?

Night fell swiftly after her father left. Stars spilled into the sky in great white masses, fading the moon that rose as cold and curved as a mowing scythe. Although the boys were too tired to play, they were also too restless at having their parents gone to settle down. Finally, she read aloud to them by her father's lamp. Jerry lay on the floor, pretending to play with Major because he considered himself too big to be read to. Tad curled in her lap, his head heavy against her shoulder and his bony little elbow digging into her ribs. When she suggested they go to bed a little after nine, they only begged to have Major stay in with them for the night. She realized how bleak they felt with both Melanie and her father gone, but she hesitated, anyway. The only reason they got Major in the beginning was to protect the chickens from coyotes and wolves at night. She finally relented, telling herself that one night could surely do no harm.

Jessica knew she should go to bed herself but couldn't force herself away from Melanie's chair by the window. From there she would be able to see her father and Melanie coming home whenever Rosemary Reynolds' ordeal was over.

She had been there a long time before she remembered the candle. Whenever there was buffalo fat, she and Melanie rendered it to make candles for that window. With the nights so dark and the prairie so vast, the lives of many wayfarers had been saved by such candles.

She drifted off to sleep and awakened chilled. Tiptoeing in where the boys were sleeping, she pulled the patchwork comforter from her bed to bundle in by the window. Major, at Jerry's side, blinked up at her, thumping his tail in quiet greeting.

She didn't get any kind of rest at all.

Strange ticks and creaks sounded in the log walls, and the barking of the coyotes seemed closer than usual. Major snored, an uneven rhythm rumbling from the other room.

When a squawking clamor came from the chicken house, she leaped up in horror, conscious that they were unprotected with Major in there snoring by Jerry's bed. Staring from the window, she saw only pale moonlight dusting the chicken-house roof and the white gravestones in the burying yard beyond.

Then it was light beyond the window. For the first time in her life she had spent a whole night in a house without a grown-up. The thought was astonishing. But that was what wives did all the time when their husbands had cattle drives or business in some far place like Abilene or Dodge City. And as it must be to other prairie wives, the morning work of the ranch called her from the chair to stretch, splash her face with cold water, and start the chores.

Now she was sure that Rosemary Reynolds had been in labor too long. Horrifying stories, half heard from whispering women, flooded into her mind. She had to stay busy enough to drive those phantoms away.

The moment she opened their door, the hens spilled, glaring, from the poultry house into their scratching yard.

She tried singing to keep her spirits up. By the time she got all the way through her favorite song, not missing a single verse or any of the choruses, she had all the milk that

Daisy and Brindle would let down to her. As she passed through the barn to take the foaming, fresh milk to the strainer, she stopped abruptly, her song falling silent in her throat. Then it hadn't been a dream. The wagon was gone. Someone had come in the night, harnessed a horse, and driven the wagon away while she slept. Panicked, she walked as fast as she could with the swinging milk pails out into the sunlit yard.

As she stood there, blinking into the sun, she saw two horsemen coming from afar. That would be Melanie and her father, with Mary Huffman on Dancie. She raced to set the milk pails inside the door. They would need hot coffee and something to eat after that long night. By the time she had stuck a pan of leftover cornbread into the oven and set the coffeepot over the flame, Major exploded into barking alarm behind her. She caught at his collar and pushed the door open, gripping the ruff of hair that bristled on his neck.

Melanie was there all right, and so was her father. But the rider of the second horse was Will Reynolds. He semed to be a shadow of himself, his skin as sallow as pewter and his eyes buried in his head. Without even glancing her way, he dismounted, then turned and reached up to lift a small bundle from Melanie's arms. When Melanie had dismounted and stood beside him, he laid the burden carefully in her arms.

Jessica braced herself weakly against the

door frame. She saw her father bend to touch Melanie on her shoulder in that gentle way, as Will Reynolds swung up into his saddle again. The two men turned without a word and rode off.

Jessica was at Melanie's side in a moment. Melanie's face had been frozen in a mask of control. As her eyes met Jessica's, her face crumpled. She began to weep wordlessly, her slender body helpless against the force of her silent sobs. The bundle in her arms twisted and began to wail in a faint mewling voice.

A sudden dizziness forced Jessica to fight for her balance there on that level, unmoving ground. *No*, she wanted to shout. *No*, as if she could shout breath back into the lungs of that timid doll-faced girl whom she had never even met.

Instead, the truth settled on her as a sudden inescapable weight. Rosemary Reynolds was dead.

It took all of Jessica's strength to lead Melanie, a step at a time, into the house and to the low rocker by the window where Jessica herself had spent that long night of waiting. There didn't seem to be anything to say. If there had been, Melanie seemed to be stripped of strength to reply. Jessica poured steaming coffee in a stoneware cup and carried it to the sewing table at Melanie's side.

Melanie shook her head, her tears dropping to make dark stains on the collar and bib of her dress. Jessica ignored her gesture and slid her hands in under the crying child and lifted it against her own chest.

"My boys," Melanie said after a moment. "Are they all right?"

Jessica nodded for fear the child would wake again. "Still sleeping," she whispered after a minute.

Melanie took a careful sip of the coffee before resting her head on the back of the chair. After a long time, she began to speak. Her voice sounded unfamiliar, and her mind seemed to switch without warning back and forth between the child in Jessica's arms and the night just past.

"We'll need fresh milk," she said heavily. "He'll waken and be hungry." Her eyes flew open to stare at Jessica. "In the wagon. The baby was coming in that wagon out there." She shuddered as she spoke. Only after cradling the hot mug in her hands a long time did she find her voice again.

"In the wagon, Jessica." She repeated, as if Jessica had not understood the enormity of what she was saying. "The baby was coming in that wagon out there, because the mother, poor little thing, was afraid to go down into the dugout. And the wolves." Melanie's eyes widened in the horror of remembering. "Somehow the wolves must have known she was going to die, because for a long time they just stood in a ring at the edge of the light, staring."

"Then," Melanie went on, "just before dawn, they started coming closer, creeping low on their haunches with their teeth bared. Thank God your father was there to keep them at bay, your father and that poor young man."

Then astonishingly, just as Tad did when he dozed off during a lullaby, Melanie's head rolled loosely to the side, and she dropped into a sleep so deep that she barely seemed to be breathing.

Jessica stared at her helplessly for a minute before realizing that the child in her arms was stretching and twisting again, as if in pain. Dragging a stool with her foot, she set it near the cook stove where the air was warm. With the child on her lap, she carefully turned back the wrapping blanket and looked down into his face.

Not since Tad was born had she seen a baby this new. She had been nine then, and her memories of those first days were hazy. She didn't remember that Tad ever looked so pale and pointed. A crop of delicate dark hair leaped from this baby's head in all directions, like the bloom of the Scotch thistle that had grown in all the barren places during this summer of drought. He had no eyebrows at all, and his neck folded in moist wrinkles under the tiny point of his chin. Only his eyes were beautiful. As he stared up at her, his forehead creased as if he were trying to understand some message hidden in her eyes. Now that his arms were free of the blanket, they waved restlessly in the air. His hands, with delicate fingers, were like tiny, moving stars.

Melanie had said he would be hungry. Jessica glanced at the fresh pail of milk just inside the door and wondered how they could possibly feed him. As she watched, the baby began to make sucking motions with his mouth, puckering his lips with such strength that his tiny cheeks drew in.

His steady, unblinking stare brought pained memories of herself in those lonely years before her father married Melanie. She remembered chilly nights in strange houses. No matter how dim the lamplight, her young eyes caught the differences between the gentle hospitality she received and the lingering delight with which a mother looked into her own child's face. Nobody deserved to be motherless.

With both of her hands firm under his back, she lifted him so that his warmth lay against her heart. He nuzzled a little as his head found the hollow of her neck. His hands tucked down on his chest like a bird folding its wings. Then he sighed and closed his eyes.

Softly, so that no one else could hear, she hummed Tad's favorite lullaby to him as he slept.

Chapter Six

THE mysteries of that night were only slowly explained. Any other time, Jessica herself would have pressed for understanding. As it was, questions yielded to decisions that could not be delayed. Like a spring storm boiling out of the southwest, Rosemary Reynolds' death and the life of her son swept away all other concerns.

His name was James. James Ogden Reynolds. This Jessica learned when her brothers, still groggy from sleep, stood in the door of their bedroom, staring with confusion at their mother sleeping in her chair and Jessica cuddling the child by the fire. With a finger at her lips, Jessica cautioned them not to disturb Melanie. This effort was wasted. Melanie awoke with a start and would have risen if Tad had not run to hurl himself onto her lap.

Wiser in years, Jerry put the pieces together at once. At Jessica's side, he stared silently down at the baby.

"He's a little boy," Jessica told him, displaying the child in her arms so that he could see his face.

"But he's all right?" Jerry asked. At her nod, he ran his tongue along his lips and frowned. "Does he have a name?"

Melanie answered from across the room, speaking the baby's name carefully as if it were new and strange to her lips. *James*, Jessica's mind echoed. That was a good name. It was strong, as a man of Kansas needed to be. It was solid, to match the steady gaze of those deep blue eyes.

"Where's Papa?" Jerry asked.

Melanie sent Tad away, rose, and straightened her dress. "He'll be along anytime now. He's with Mr. Reynolds."

Tad had joined Jerry at the baby's side. "Is he going to take him back?" Tad asked. "We could sure use him here."

Melanie smiled, touching Jessica's shoulder as she passed to the stove to start breakfast. "He is pretty nice, isn't he?" Then, after a pause, "Would one of you fellows like to check the chicken house for fresh eggs?"

The two boys raced each other for the door as both she and Jessica had known they would. Before they returned, Major began barking his warning that a stranger was riding into the yard.

Mary Huffman accepted the mug of coffee from Melanie and sank gratefully into a chair. "It feels good to be in your quiet kitchen," she said. "Now we must put our minds to keeping this little fellow alive."

At Jessica's concerned look, Mary shrugged. "You must realize how many babies are not saved, even with the best of starts." Jessica nodded, remembering the lines of little gravestones that marked most of the family cemeteries.

Mary Huffman rose and came to lean over Jessica's shoulder to study the child. "Has he had anything to eat yet?"

When Jessica shook her head, Mary Huffman straightened, hooked her hand on her chin thoughtfully, and stared at the baby. Then, with a brisk nod, she turned to Melanie. "We need fresh milk, a little water, some sugar or honey, a clean lamp wick, and a cream pitcher."

Melanie pushed the skillet to the back of the stove and went to rummage in the cupboard. Jessica rocked back and forth on the stool as she watched the women prepare the child's food. Mary didn't ask if Jessica wanted to feed the child. She simply handed her the creamer. The woven cotton lamp wick was already a rich creamy color from soaking up the warm milk. The baby groped with his lips only a moment before closing his mouth around the wick.

Jessica heard the door open but kept her eyes on the baby. He was sucking so hungrily that a froth of milk bubbled at the side of his mouth. He pummeled so fiercely with his tiny fists that Jessica was afraid he might dash the creamer from her hand.

Some quality in the silence of the room made her look up. Will Reynolds stood beside her father in the still-open door. Although some color had returned to his face, he looked gaunt and older as he stared at his son. He crossed the room wordlessly and leaned over his child.

"He's a beautiful little boy," Mary Huffman told him. "And a hungry one, too."

Her words broke the spell. Will Reynolds looked up at her and then at Jessica, as if freshly roused from a dream.

"You've met my daughter, Jessica," Patrick Findlay said, "and my wife, Melanie. Come and sit, Will. I smelled our breakfast cooking clear out at the barn."

Will Reynolds had the grace to flush as he nodded to Jessica. "Miss Findlay and I have met," he agreed, echoing his host's words.

Jessica was startled to see Reynolds' eyes linger on hers overlong. He seemed to be trying to say something to her without words. Was it an apology for his rudeness that other day? Was it thanks for her care of his child that morning? Neither of these seemed reasonable because, as he looked away, his eyes swept her, her everyday dress soiled from the chores of the barn, her heavy boots that she hadn't cleaned since tramping through the mire of the yard. She felt herself flush, relieved when he had looked his fill.

Patrick Findlay would hear none of his

protests but placed Will Reynolds beside him on the bench by the long table. Even from there, with a mug of hot coffee between his hands, Reynolds could not take his eyes from his son.

When the child's hunger was satisfied, he pushed the lamp wick out of his mouth. Jessica, remembering Tad's babyhood, lifted him to her shoulder and patted his back until he burped.

"He should sleep for at least a couple of hours," Mary Huffman said, taking him from Jessica. Then, pausing, she looked at Will Reynolds. "Would you like to hold him a minute?"

Jessica had never seen a man's face change expression that swiftly. It was all she could do not to chuckle. But his expression of instant terror was quickly followed by a frown of concern.

"He's sturdier than he looks," Mary Huffman assured him, laying the sleeping child in his arms.

Only when Jessica and Melanie had the breakfast plates filled did Will release his child to be laid, still sleeping, in the lined basket that had been Tad's first bed.

Jessica studied Will covertly as she ate. While he was no less handsome than she remembered, he looked different, like a man who had visited a strange country and returned changed in hidden ways.

The mystery of the missing wagon was explained as Patrick Findlay tried to persuade his young neighbor that his wife's coffin might better be moved to the church or to the Findlay home than to Reynolds' own place.

"But it's our home," Reynolds insisted, locking his jaw in that stubborn way. "That was Rosemary's home and mine," he paused. "And Jim's." Jessica had the feeling that the sound of his son's name startled him. "My son and I want her there with us."

Patrick Findlay nodded. "That is as it should be. And I've the tools, so that the grave can be dug at your place in any spot you choose. But surely it will take some time for your families to get here from Chicago so that a service can be held."

"We have no families," Will Reynolds said swiftly. Then he paused. "There's only my Aunt Floss. She had made plans at her work to come out and take care of Rosemary and the baby. . . ." His voice trailed off, and he shook his head glumly. "I can't imagine her getting away on the spur of the moment like this. Of course I will wire her and urge her to come the first possible moment she can."

Jerry and Tad, having finished their plates, were bouncing with eagerness to leave the table. Patrick Findlay nodded to excuse them.

"You're welcome to have your wife lie in this house if you've some objection to the church," he told Will Reynolds.

Jessica was startled at the directness with which Reynolds raised his eyes to her father in challenge. She didn't know any man who would dare to confront Patrick Findlay that boldly. Certainly, none who had ever seen him when his temper was aroused would. Yet this Will Reynolds, who was hardly a man at all at only nineteen, was looking at her father in that bold, straight way that had challenged her.

"If you've some objection to my wife lying in her own home, I'd like to hear you explain it," Will Reynolds said.

From the corner of her eye, Jessica saw Melanie turn away as she always did when there was unpleasantness in the air. Jessica herself felt that old fury at Will Reynolds swell behind her throat, begging to be let out in words. He was more than rude, he was bullheaded. What was he thinking about to carry on like this with the man who had seen him through the darkest hours of his life — a man who had given him friendship and protection, and God only knew what else in that wagon.

It never failed that every time Jessica thought she had her father completely figured out, he would surprise her by behaving in a way she hadn't predicted. Without even that tightening of the flesh around his eyes that warned of rising temper, he answered the young man.

"This is not an objection but an opinion only," he said, his voice very calm. "There are two places at your home where your wife could lie. The wagon in which your son was born is disqualified for reasons we both remember from the night past. As for the dugout, I personally would hesitate to take my wife in death to a place she did not wish to go to in life."

During that long moment of silence, Will Reynolds seemed to be lost in his own thoughts. His face was without expression, a handsome mask that concealed what was going on in his mind. Then the young man nodded and rose.

"I appreciate your giving your opinion," he said. "More than that, I think you are right. I'm really grateful that someone is able to think more clearly than I can at this moment."

Then, leaning across the table, he offered his hand to Jessica's father. "I thank you for your honesty. And I'll appreciate the loan of those grave-digging tools. As for the church, I have no objection to my wife resting there until the service. And clearly I have disturbed your household more than any stranger has a right."

"A man goes from stranger to neighbor and friend in the change of his living space," Jessica's father told him. "As for the household here, we are grateful for the chance to pay old debts."

At Will Reynolds' confused look, Patrick Findlay nodded. "Our Jessica has a mother she can't remember. Neither of us will ever forget our debt to those families who nourished her before Melanie and I were married and gave her a home of her own."

"Oh, but I mean to keep my son at home

with me," Will Reynolds protested.

"I wish you good fortune in that," Jessica's father said. "But until your aunt comes, you will need to make some arrangements for the child's care. I know that our Jessica would be happy to help out by taking care of the boy until other arrangements are made."

Jessica stared at her father in astonishment. What was he saying? *Happy to help out by taking care of the boy?*

Jessica's amazement must have shown on her face. She was conscious of Will Reynolds' deepening frown and her father's quizzical look. "That is true, isn't it, Jessica?" His tone was that heavy one that demanded agreement.

"Well . . ." she hesitated, remembering her halfway promise to Mr. Reiner to come and teach school, "of course I would be happy to help, but —"

His eyes were dark and puzzled on hers. "But what?" he challenged her.

"You know I want to do everything I can to help our neighbor, but —" Jessica tried again.

"There can be no buts," Patrick Findlay said firmly. Then, as if Jessica were not even there, he turned to Will Reynolds. "You see, Will, they have much in common, your newborn son and my daughter. Both of them were born in the first flood of light of an August dawn. And both, at least for a while, must depend on the love of strangers. Jessica can only be grateful to be able to give to another child what was freely given to her."

Jessica turned away to hide the quick tears rising behind her eyes. How guilty her father made her feel. But not even that guilt, nor the pity she felt for the helpless child, changed the resentment that welled in her. Had she become a grown-up in words only, that her father could announce without even asking her that she would give up — what? — weeks, maybe, or months, to care for a child. And it wasn't even as if this were the child of a friend. Nobody in her life had ever been so cold and rude to her as this Will Reynolds. How could he dare let her father push her into this when he had seen her resistance as clearly as her father had? But he dared all right. She knew it the minute he looked away like that.

"It will only be until my Aunt Floss gets here from Chicago," Will Reynolds said, as if that helped.

Mary Huffman, at last free to go to her own home and rest, had been right about little James. Two hours had passed almost to the minute when he stirred. He stretched and whimpered before wailing so furiously that Jessica flew to warm his food. Never mind that his father was rude and bullheaded and hateful to her. Never mind that he knew she didn't want to take on this job; it was hers. From the look on her father's face, Jessica knew she was trapped until other arrangements could be made. And although it was not the fault of the baby that he had been thrust on her like this, she wasn't even sure that she liked him, either.

The day of Rosemary Reynolds' funeral came hot and dry as most days had come that long, arid summer. By the time they were all in the buggy, ready to start for church, moist patches marked the back of Jessica's dress.

Having no pew of his own, Will Reynolds had accepted Jessica's father's invitation to sit in the Findlay family place. Naturally, heads turned all around the church when Will took his seat at Patrick Findlay's side. Inside the church he looked even taller than he had before. His city clothes were immaculate and were really conspicuous in the congregation. As much as he was rude and ill-natured and bullheaded and a half a dozen other things that Jessica could think of, he was a remarkably good-looking man, even with his face stone-hard and cold like that.

He barely glanced at any of them as he entered and then sat with his head bowed, listlessly staring at his folded hands with that wide gold wedding band gleaming in the light.

The last thing Jessica wanted to do in the whole wide world was walk past that open casket and look in at little Jim's mother. She pleaded with a glance at Melanie, who tightened her lips, reached out for the baby, and sent Jessica forward with a firm look. Jessica's father, sensing her reluctance, rose and went with her.

She wasn't prepared. In spite of everything, Jessica wasn't prepared for the heartbreaking beauty and apparent innocence of the girl who seemed to be sleeping inside that lined pine box. She was wearing the velvet bonnet set back on hair as brilliantly black as the hair of young Indian maidens. The arch of her brows seemed to express astonishment at being there, so eternally quiet, with folded hands as curved and graceful as her son's had been against Jessica's chest. Rachel had said she had a doll-like prettiness. No doll was ever so subtly formed, so delicately colored, that even the faint tracing of veins on her closed eyelids matched the coloring of her barely closed lips.

It would not do to cry. Jessica studied the lovely girl carefully. She wondered about the time when the baby would be old enough to ask about his mother. There could be pictures, for all she knew. There might even be pictures that did justice to Rosemary Reynolds' fragile perfection. Jessica hoped that there were. The only picture she had ever seen of her mother as a grown-up was so dark and dim that it might have been anyone staring back from that brown cardboard.

At the pressure of her father's hand on her arm, she turned away.

The neighbors had brought a funeral feast as they followed the wagon carrying Rosemary Reynolds home to the freshly dug grave beyond the dugout that everyone still thought of as the Sanders place. Clearly, Will did not know how to react to this outpouring. Jessica's father stayed at his side, protecting him, Jessica thought, as much from Will's own stiff responses as from the shock of unexpected bounty.

The day was beastly hot. Heat rose in shimmering waves from the baked earth around the dugout. The soles of Jessica's boots were so hot that she might have been standing on a stove.

She had been there only a few minutes when Melanie took the baby from Will's arms and brought him to Jessica. "It's too hot for the little thing out here," she told Jessica. "I think you should take him inside where he's out of the heat."

Jessica had no time to protest. Her father was watching, as was Will, as she ducked her head and stepped down into the dugout. It was cool there, as Melanie had suggested, but it was also dark and musty-smelling, and her friends were outside, visiting and having lunch together.

She had stood there in the darkness only a moment before Will Reynolds entered, shutting off the light altogether for that moment that he blocked the doorway.

"If you'll wait there just a moment, Miss Findlay," he said, "I will make a light."

The match flared in the darkness, illuminating the intensity of his face as he lit a lamp. Then, without even glancing at her, he turned away and came back with a low rocking chair.

"Then there is this, Miss Findlay," he said.

To Jessica's astonishment, Will produced a finely carved wooden cradle that he and his wife must have carried all the way from Illinois for their child. Folded in the cradle were fine linen sheets. When he tucked them in the cradle, perfume rose from their folds.

"There," he said with satisfaction. "That should take care of everything. Would you like anything else, Miss Findlay?"

What could she say? That she would like to escape the musty dugout and the child at her side?

"Nothing, thank you, Mr. Reynolds," she told him. He didn't look back as he left. It was probably a good thing. There was nothing he could do about her anger at the situation she was caught in. But just caring that she was trapped like that might have helped.

Rachel, missing Jessica outside, found her and brought her a cool drink from a stone crock of lemonade that Mr. Baber and his daughter Sara had brought. Rachel, being Rachel, couldn't look at the sleeping child without her eyes turning watery. "If Mom and Dad didn't depend on me in the store, I swear I'd just drop everything and take care of that little darling until that aunt gets here from Chicago."

"I guess I'll get along all right," Jessica told her. "Somebody has to do it."

Rachel's eyes were suddenly watchful. "I heard Mr. Reynolds tell my mother that it might take his aunt a month to get here."

Inwardly, Jessica groaned, but she only shrugged, touching the cradle with a careful toe to keep it rocking. "I will do it as long as I need to."

"But what about Mr. Reiner and that schoolteaching job?" Rachel asked.

Jessica shrugged again, not meeting her friend's eyes. "It was my mistake not to talk to Papa about that right away. It might not have made any difference, anyway. But I'll write to Mr. Reiner at once. I need to tell him that he must find someone else."

"But you'll never see a chance to make that much money again," Rachel told her.

Jessica, hating the thought of having to write and give up that job, hadn't even noticed her father and Will stooping in at the low door.

"What's all this about a lot of money?" Jessica's father asked in a confused tone.

"Nothing, Papa," Jessica said swiftly. "Nothing at all."

"I should think not," her father said. "With this drought, the only people making any money are the hide hunters who are butchering the buffalo and the men who gather the buffalo bones to send back East."

"And maybe water-witches," Will added. At Mr. Findlay's startled look, the young man nodded. "If I am going to stay here with my Jim, I need water." He glanced toward the door. "Your neighbors out there finally persuaded me."

"They're your neighbors, too," Patrick Findlay reminded him.

Will crossed to the cradle and studied his son a moment before turning back to Patrick Findlay. "Yet, in spite of that, I have another favor to ask. Would Miss Findlay find it any harder to care for Jim here than over at your place?"

Jessica stared at him in disbelief. Did he think she was suddenly deaf that he couldn't ask her himself? Even as she expected her father to turn to her, Will went on speaking.

"It would mean a lot to me if she could do that," he went on. "It's our home, his and mine. I'd like him to get used to it from the start."

"She and the boy would have to come back to our place at night," Jessica's father told him thoughtfully.

Reynolds nodded. "That would be fine. I just want him in his own home all day and not causing an upset at your house."

Jessica looked up to see Rachel's eyes steady on her own. Jessica tried to look threatening in case Rachel was thinking about telling everyone in town that she had been forced to give up a really good paying job as a teacher to be nursemaid to Will's baby. From the way Rachel looked away, Jessica felt that she had made her point. From the way Rachel went back outside, without Jessica getting a chance to speak to her privately, she suspected that Rachel would do exactly as she pleased about it.

Chapter
Seven

IT took Melanie on the warpath and a nest of snakes to convince Will that Jessica and the baby couldn't stay in the dugout until it had been put into proper condition. Unfortunately, the process entailed another confrontation between Jessica and Will, which left Jessica even angrier at him than she had been before.

In truth, Jessica hadn't paid any attention to the condition of the Reynolds' place that afternoon of the funeral. She had been annoyed at having to go in away from her friends and infuriated at Will and her father for acting as if she were a piece of furniture to be moved around at their will. With only a single smoky kerosene lamp breaking the gloom, she hadn't realized that the shapes in the corners of the room were not furnishings but piles of trash abandoned by Sanders when he packed up to go back East.

But Melanie had studied the room with the eye of a practiced frontier housewife. It was just as well that Will refused their invitation to come home with the Findlays when the burial was over. Although Melanie was uncommonly quiet all the way home, once in her own kitchen, she simply exploded with words.

"I don't know where you two stand on this," she said hotly. "But I don't intend to see Jessica and that baby go back into that place until it's made fit for human beings."

"I guess I didn't pay much attention," Jessica admitted.

"It didn't take much to see what a job of work needs to be done there. And that young man is as independent as a hog on ice. He's just determined to do everything on his own without having any idea what needs being done. Why, not even the pack rats could clean out that place."

"And what about furnishings?" she asked before anyone had a chance to reply. "Until he gets that wagon unloaded, there's no way to tell if Jessica has everything she will need to care for that child."

Jessica saw her father's shoulders shaking with silent laughter as Melanie banged the pots and pans.

"Now, Mellie," her father began in a soothing tone. Melanie, turning as he spoke, saw the twist of a grin on his face and flared up anew.

"Don't you 'Now, Mellie' me, Patrick Findlay. The walls of that place are shedding dirt faster than five women could stay ahead of with hickory brooms. I had sense enough not to ask him if he wanted help. I just told him that Jerry and I would be over bright and early tomorrow to help him clean up the place and move in. And what do you think he said? Just guess."

His answer was a roar of laughter as he crossed the room to catch her in a teasing hug. "Would you listen to this woman, Jessica?" he teased. "Why, she's got as bad a temper as a born Findlay, and she's only married in. Now, let me guess that Will told you that your help wouldn't be needed since he could do fine without it."

Sudden tears filled Melanie's eyes. "He's such a nice young man and so grieved over the loss of that beautiful little wife of his. I hate to go on like this about him, but I never saw anybody so...." Her voice trailed off in frustration.

"Stiff-necked," Jessica filled in. "Rachel said that Will was stiff-necked, and she was absolutely right."

Patrick Findlay sighed. "Be that as it may, Melanie's right about the place, too. We need to figure out a way to help him get set up without losing his friendship over it."

"In that case, I'm the one to do it," Jessica told him. "I have nothing to lose by telling him he is only allowed to be bullheaded stubborn about one thing at a time. If he wants me to stay there with his baby, let him clean the place up. He's going to be lucky to get Jimson home, anyway, before his aunt comes, if he won't accept any help."

"You think that sounds friendly?" Melanie asked, staring at Jessica with astonishment.

Jessica grinned at her father. "Maybe not friendly, but it's pretty much what he expects from me, anyway. It would be a shame to disappoint him."

"I must have missed something somewhere along the line," Melanie mused.

"Nothing of great importance," her husband said. "Let Jessica give it a try. And say," he added after a minute, "what did I hear you call that little fellow? Jimson?"

Jessica felt herself flush. "His name bothers me. James is too grown-up and formal, and Jim sounds like a pesky boy. Then I remembered that weed with the waxy white flowers that are shadowed with lavender. His eyes look like that when he sleeps."

"Jimson," her father repeated, going over to look at the sleeping child. "That nickname could even bring him some good Kansas luck. There's not a weed in this state that grows any faster nor hangs on any harder when it gets its roots down."

Dancie's hooves raised a great curtain of dust as Jessica, with Tad on the saddle behind her, galloped toward the Reynolds place. Jessica had been so tied down by the child that she could barely wait to settle him for a nap and get out of the house. She had every intention of going there and coming back the longest route she could think of, just to get some time to herself.

Then, just as she thought she had gotten away free, Melanie insisted that Tad come along "for appearance's sake," which could only make the trip take longer.

"This is a wild-goose chase if I ever ran one," she told herself. "Wait and see. I'll make this whole ride over there for nothing. He'll be rude, and I'll have to take off to keep from shooting my mouth off like I did that first time."

By the time she recognized the swelling on the prairie that was the Reynolds dugout, she felt heavy with dread. She reined the pony in and approached at a walk, with Tad staring curiously from behind her. Little had changed since that first time she had come to call on the Reynolds. That miserable wagon still stood where it had before. But now a pile of broken pottery and dirt had appeared beside it.

"Hey," she called, hoping that her voice sounded friendly. "Anybody around?"

She had called the second time and slid from the pony's back before Will, stooped almost double to pass through the low doorway, emerged to blink at them in the sudden light. The moment he recognized Jessica, his face turned pale, and he hurried toward her, frowning with concern through the smudges of dust on his face.

"My child?" he asked hastily. "What's the

matter? What's wrong? Nothing has happened to him, has it?"

Jessica shook her head quickly. "He's fine," she assured him. "He's just wonderful. Nothing to get upset about."

Even as she reassured him, Jessica felt terrible. There. She had gone and done that awful thing again. She had started off on the wrong foot with him by turning up where he didn't expect her and giving him a scare. He didn't have to be that jumpy, she told herself defensively.

Tad slid off the pony behind her. He picked up a stick and began to poke at the dirt. After only the barest glance at her brother, Jessica turned her attention back to Will.

Will's expression turned suspicious. "Then why are you here?"

Now that was *really* a hospitable thing to say. It was almost as charming as his greeting that first time, when he had asked, "Is there something you want here?"

She shrugged, as if racing across the prairie right after breakfast was something she did every day. "I thought I'd drop by to see how things were going," she told him. "Between feedings, of course. I thought I could help."

He had stiffened again, his eyes level and cold. "I told your mother I didn't need help."

"I know that," she admitted, "but since you have never set up a house in a place like this, I thought maybe you could use some —"

"Some advice, Miss Findlay?" he asked coldly.

She glared at him, furious at his tone. If he had not interrupted her, she would have said help. But having been interrupted, she didn't care whether he had any help at all from anyone.

So she shrugged. "It's hard for me to tell which you need more, advice or decent manners."

He stared at her. "I guess that was a civil remark," he told her.

"Out here we fight fire with fire," she told him.

"We do the same where I come from," he told her. "But I don't remember being the one who started this exchange of insults with you in the first place."

"Well, of course, I started it," she said blandly. "I rode clear over here in the August sun just to insult you with the offer of some welcoming gifts from Melanie. I would apologize for that, but I might choke on my own words."

"That was different," he said. "I didn't know anything about Kansans then. I only knew that I didn't want to be in debt to anyone. But I am now, aren't I? You really have me in a bind, and you know it. There's no way I can take care of that baby and do what else I have to do. I know how you feel about him and about me. How do you think I feel having to take your charity, bitter as it is?"

Jessica wanted to protest that it wasn't that bad, but he had turned away again, in that cold way he always did. But he didn't leave. Instead, he just stood there for a long minute. When he turned to her again, she felt as if he had just caught his breath for a new attack.

"All right," he said. "Let's have your advice and get it over with so I can go back to work. This place is a mess, full of old trash and leaking dirt. I plan to shovel all the refuse out, scrape down the floor, and cover it with some rugs that we" — his voice faltered — "brought from Chicago. Is that what you were going to advise me to do?"

She flushed and nodded, unable to meet his eyes. If his tone had not been so unpleasant, she would have ached with pity for him. Rachel was right. He did look too thin in that cotton shirt with its sleeves rolled back on his dust-stained arms. The dark shadows that she had first noticed beneath his eyes the night of his wife's death had deepened. Had he eaten? she wondered. Had he even been able to sleep in that wagon he had shared with his lost wife?

"I don't want you to think that I'm not grateful for what you are doing for my son," he said, his tone still angry in spite of his words. "But the quicker I can get this place fixed up, the quicker my aunt can come and relieve you."

Jessica's face stung at this open hint that she was keeping him from more important things. Where was all the fine courage she had felt when she talked to Melanie and her father the night before? With it gone, she seized on his words as an opening wedge.

"I didn't come to fight with you, and I didn't come for thanks," she told him. "But Melanie and I did think about your aunt who's coming. She'll need things fixed up to take care of the baby. We thought maybe we —"

"When my wife and I started this journey out here, we knew the baby was coming," he reminded her. "I have everything Floss will need. Thank you very much, but if you'll excuse me, I need to get back to my work."

When he turned and walked away, Jessica was struck dumb.

"Why, you. . . ." she whispered. Then, betrayed by that sudden rush of angry tears, she turned and mounted Dancie. "Tad," she called urgently. "Come on, let's go."

"Coming," he called happily. Then, as he reached Dancie's side, he called up to Jessica. "Would you please hold these for me while I get up?"

She nodded absently and took what he handed her, her eyes blinded with tears. Only when the crisp bundle of snakeskins was in her hand did she realize what he had been gathering.

"Tad," she said, struggling to keep her voice calm. "Where did you get all these?"

He grinned up into her face with pride and delight. "In that trash over there. Did you ever see so many?"

"Never," she breathed. She turned and stared back at the open doorway of the dugout thoughtfully a moment, before speaking to Tad. "You wait here for me. I'll only be a minute."

"But my skins," he cried, reaching out for them possessively.

"You'll get them back," she promised. "Just wait right here."

That time she walked directly to the open door. By the light of the lamp she could see the single, large, open room that was all there was to the Reynolds house. As she expected, the ceiling of willow and dried grass was supported only by three branches propped on the single ridge pole.

"Mr. Reynolds," she called, not caring if it sounded rude and bossy.

He straightened from the corner where he was hacking away with a shovel. "Miss Findlay," he replied. "I thought you had left. Surely there can't be anything more you have to say."

"As a matter of fact, there is," she said hotly. "There's a good deal more. You accuse me of not liking you or your baby. What you are forgetting is people who are all puffed up with pride are not all that attractive. But I haven't got anything against your baby. If I did, I would just get on my horse, ride away, and never look back."

"Now I suppose you are telling me that I am not even capable of cleaning out a mud house."

"I suspect you would do it as well as you knew how," she told him. "But this is Kansas, not Chicago. This house has stayed empty, and now it's just plain dangerous."

He frowned, studying her. "Dangerous," he repeated doubtfully.

"Dangerous," she said again, holding out that great bunch of silvery snakeskins and waving them at him. "These are rattlesnake skins, Mr. Reynolds. They were shed in this house, and you shoveled them out with that trash, as if they were nut hulls. After Sanders left, the rats came in, and the snakes came in after the rats. If I were a betting woman, I'd bet you a team of matched oxen that you've got a big enough nest of rattlers in the roof of this room to wipe out the whole town and the men at the fort besides." With that, she whirled and walked away.

"Miss Findlay," he called after her, his voice suddenly higher, as if with shock. She heard the clatter of the shovel he had thrown aside.

"If you'll excuse me," she said, mimicking his own tone, "I need to get back to my work."

She was back on Dancie and digging her heels in the pony's side before Will Reynolds got out of the dugout.

"Jessica," Tad said, his arms tight around her waist as the pony bounced him along. "That man back there is running after you and trying to catch up."

"He's got a long way to go, Tad," she told him. "A very long way to go."

Chapter Eight

JESSICA, with her mind back at the Reynolds place, didn't notice the horse tied to the Findlay gate until Tad called her attention to it.

"That's Roy Blanding's chestnut mare," he told her. "Nobody but Roy has a saddle that fancy."

Jessica stifled a groan as she slid off Dancie.

"Wonder what he wants?" Tad went on, gathering his snakeskins into a careful bundle. "He's out of luck if he wants to see Dad. He's out on the range with his stock today."

It would be nice if Roy had come to see her father, Jessica thought. But not likely, not likely at all. She paused, staring after Dancie, who was walking to the watering trough. She herself was the one who was out of luck when it came to Roy. It had been hard to accept that she was partly to blame for Roy expecting her to marry him. If she didn't feel so guilty about him, it would be easy enough to answer right out with a speech that would settle everything. She had thought about that speech enough to recite it like scripture.

"Thank you, Roy," she would say. "You have paid me a great honor by asking me to be your wife. I'm sorry to have to tell you that I am not ready to marry anyone now, nor do I want to marry *you* ever."

She shuddered at how that last part came out. There had to be a kinder way to say that without it being so gentle that it led him on with false hope, as she had been doing all these years without meaning to.

She was startled to see Tad staring at her with concern. "You don't look happy," he told her.

She reached over to tousle his hair and then grinned at him. "Just thoughtful, Tad," she told him.

He grinned back and pushed his head hard against her hand. "If I didn't like what I was thinking about, I'd just change my head," he suggested.

Then, with one of those lightning changes of mood that were characteristic of him, he turned and ran toward the house. "Wait until Mom sees these snakeskins," he called back to her. "She won't even believe how many I got."

Jessica sighed and followed him, snapping Dancie's crop lightly against her leg. How had she let herself get into this bind with Roy? In truth, she didn't even remember when it all began. Sometime during her childhood, Roy had become her accepted "fellow." If she had ever had a real crush on someone else, as Agatha had done once every year since she was ten, or had fallen head-over-heels with one single fellow as Rachel had with Walt, she wouldn't have this problem now. It hadn't seemed important that whenever there was a house-raising or a sledding party, Roy had just naturally taken her. When the fiddler was tuned up at dances, Roy had always been there with his hand out, ready to lead her onto the floor. A lot of times she had gone with him only to wish later that she hadn't. If another boy as much as gave her a second glance, Roy went into one of those towering rages and talked about him forever after. More and more she had felt an uneasiness about refusing his invitations, as if he might turn on her with all that vicious rage. It seemed silly even to worry about that, since he was almost tongue-tied when they were together. But silly or not, he scared her a little. But in all that time, she hadn't had sense enough to ask herself where this would lead to in the end.

Tad reappeared at the door to shout, "Mom says come on in, you've got company."

Before she was even inside the door, Jessica realized why Melanie had sent Tad to call her instead of coming to the door herself. Melanie, with the screaming baby on her hip, was warming a little pan of water and milk on the stove.

With the barest nod at Roy, Jessica crossed the room and took the child from Melanie. Jimson was so furious that Jessica chuckled at the effort it took to hold him.

Roy was not amused. Looking huge in that small room, he stood with his hat in his hands, frowning.

"How did you get hung with that job?" he asked. "Is that the greenhorn's kid?"

"We're only helping out until his aunt gets here from Chicago." Then she glanced at Roy, feeling guilty. "Come on, sit down. I'm sorry I made you wait."

He glanced at Melanie and Tad before pulling the bench over a little nearer to her.

"What can we do for you?" she asked hopefully, certain that he would not launch into a proposal with quite that many people listening.

"Well," he began with hesitation. "I was just riding by on other business —"

He had not finished his sentence before a crisp rap sounded on the door.

Will Reynolds had washed the dust from his hands and arms and even brushed his trousers since Tad had seen him running behind Dancie. He nodded at Melanie, who stepped aside to let him enter. "Forgive me for bothering you," he began. Then his eyes fell on Jimson, and he crossed to look down at the child. Rude he might be, Jessica conceded, but he was certainly devoted to that baby.

Then, looking up, he saw Roy Blanding.

"I thought you might have met," Melanie said swiftly. "Will Reynolds, this is Roy Blanding."

"How do you do?" Will said, nodding genially.

Roy responded with a forced smile and a curt nod. "Maybe I should come back another time," he suggested in the brief, awkward silence that followed.

Reynolds frowned. "I hope I didn't interrupt anything by barging in like this. I just needed to talk to you, Mrs. Findlay."

Jessica looked at him with amazement. So he hadn't come to apologize. He hadn't even come to talk to her at all, even after that business there at the dugout. Clearly, he didn't know any more about apologies than he did about rattlesnakes. Jessica glared at him. Very well. If he had come to talk to Melanie, it would be Melanie he got.

Jessica turned to Roy. "It doesn't look as if I'm needed in here anymore. I'll walk out with you, Roy."

She wished Roy didn't feel as if he had to take her arm. She managed to get across her own kitchen floor without help several times a day. Maybe she imagined Will staring after them as Roy held the door open for her to go out.

Once outside, Jessica pulled free of Roy's arm. She must remember not to do anything to encourage him. Making it possible for him to be alone with her like that had been bad enough. Roy reached for her arm again. "Listen, Jessica," he began, "I've been trying to get this out for days. There's this piece of land south of here. Dad found it. It's still in long-grass country, and there's a little spring running through it. It can be had for a reasonable price, and I thought maybe. . . ."

His voice trailed off and he caught a new breath. "What I need to know, Jessica, is should I put a log house on it right away or would a sod house do to begin with? If we used the sod, we'd have a lot more money to spend building a herd and buying good plowing horses."

She realized it was rude to stare like that, but she was caught off guard. He wasn't going to ask her to marry him. He was going to presume it, just the way he had presumed on her always being ready to go where he wanted to go, dance or picnic, or whatever.

"I don't think I understand you," she said quietly. "Why are you asking me?"

He stared at her. "Why? Because I want everything to be just the way you want it, within reason, of course. If you wanted a frame house, I might have to consider a little."

Jessica found herself at a loss for words. If she pointed out to him that she had never said she would marry him, he would simply ask right there, and she would be back where she began. Yet if she didn't answer, she would be leading him on even worse than she had all these years.

When the clatter of hooves sounded behind them, Jessica felt her breath leave her lungs in a long, relieved sigh. She had never been so happy to see her father in all her life.

"Blanding," her father called, "get your horse and come along. Jessica, get those sacks out of the barn and load the water carriers. There's a fire coming across the prairie west of the Logan place. They'll need all the help they can get."

"The greenhorn's inside," Roy said. "Think he'd be any help?"

Without answering, Jessica's father dismounted, leaving the bay's reins trailing. By the time she had dragged the sacks from the barn and filled the second set of saddlebags, her father was out of the door with Will behind him. Within minutes, the three men galloped off to the west where a thin pillar of smoke wavered against the clear blue of the cloudless sky.

Melanie was at the door, studying the distant smoke with a frown. "What do you suppose started that?" she asked. "I didn't hear any summer lightning to set it off."

"As dry as the grass is this year, just any spark would do it," Jessica reminded her.

Instead of going back to her work, Melanie stood grinning at her. "Do you want to tell me about your conversation with Will earlier today?" she asked.

"I just talked. I was too mad to listen to myself," Jessica admitted.

Melanie laughed. "Whatever you said got his attention." She turned back to the cupboard and lifted the cloth from the bread dough rising in the wooden trough.

"He came to ask my help," she went on. "He wanted me to make a list of things he needed to do. Then he asked me how you get rid of snakes in a grass and willow ceiling."

When Jessica listened without comment, Melanie nodded briskly. "I realize that there's little love lost between the two of you. Jessica, did you realize that he can't even bring himself to speak your name but refers to you as 'your daughter' when he speaks to me? But you have to give him this, Jessica. The other night when your father was forced to speak his piece about having his wife's services there in that dugout, that young man listened. And whatever you said to him this morning, and no matter how tartly you said it, he was listening. He also said that he realizes that the baby would be better off here for a while, at least until he gets a well dug and the place fixed up. Now how is that for listening?"

"That's listening," Jessica conceded. Why did all this remind her of Roy? If Roy had only halfway listened to anything she had said to him in the past year, he sure wouldn't be jumping right past proposals and weddings to ask her what kind of house she wanted on a ranch she hadn't ever even seen.

* * *

The afternoon was half gone before her father and Will, smoke-stained and exhausted, rode into the yard. Melanie, who had been watching the window for three hours, set out a plate of sliced meat and cold vegetables dressed with some seasoned vinegar.

"At least you stopped that fire short of the Logan buildings," Melanie comforted her husband after listening to his report of the fire. "Grass grows back easier than houses. Did the wind switch to keep it from taking the house and stables?"

Will chuckled. "We plowed the fastest firebreak band of turned sod you ever saw."

"That was what saved the day, all right," Patrick Findlay agreed. "I would say you've done a little firefighting in your day, Will," he added, passing the plate of ham again.

Reynolds shrugged. "We've seen a little fire in Chicago."

Jessica's father looked up at him. "Ah, then you were there during the Great Fire, two years ago?"

"I was there," Will replied. Then, to Jessica's astonishment, he turned and caught her eye. For a moment there, she thought he was going to smile. She was remembering their earlier exchange about fighting fire with fire and was sure he recalled it, too. The moment passed, and he looked away again, without smiling. As Melanie had so delicately put it, there was little love lost between them.

"Silas Byfield from Ellis was in the bunch of folks that rallied to fight Logan's fire,"

Patrick Findlay told his wife. "He promised to come dowse for Will here in the next few days."

"If there's water anywhere on that land, he'll find it," Melanie said. "For heaven's sake, don't let our boys know when he's coming. They'd walk ten miles to watch a man dowse for water."

"I already heard," Tad said with a chuckle, catching his mother's grin.

On one of his trips back from town, Jessica's father stopped the wagon out in front of the house and gave Tad a letter for Jessica.

Jessica's old girl friend Agatha was the only person who ever wrote her. Because the only thing Agatha ever wrote about were the handsome young men in Victoria with whom she was madly in love, Jessica felt no haste to get her mail.

The first hint that the letter was different came from Tad himself. "Somebody sure writes strange," he told her, staring at the envelope.

As he passed Melanie, she leaned and looked over his shoulder. "Chicago," she cried. "Who do you know in Chicago, Jessica?"

"No one," Jessica said, almost cross with curiosity by then. "Let me see who I don't know that wrote me a letter."

"The address might give you an idea," Melanie suggested.

"That has to be from the famous Aunt

Floss from Chicago," Jessica agreed, tearing the envelope open. The letter was addressed in a straight, up-and-down handwriting unlike any that Jessica had ever seen. The envelope read: "To Miss Jessica on the nearest ranch to that of Will Reynolds, Late of Chicago."

Unlike Agatha, who began her letters with long, flowery expressions of good wishes about everyone's health, the writer, who signed herself "Florence Abney," went directly to what she had on her mind.

My dear Miss Jessica,

Along with the heartbreaking news of my cousin's wife and the blessed, safe birth of his son came word that you were caring for the child until I can get there to relieve you. Even though my gratitude to you is well beyond words, this letter comes to appeal for more help.

Every question I have asked in my attempt to find out what my nephew needs for the care of his child has gone unanswered. That isn't fair, really. He always answers the same way, that he thanks me but has everything he needs. That reply is not only typical of Will but obviously not true. Since Rosemary didn't know one end of a needle from the other, God rest her soul, I know that child needs things that I can bring with ease.

If you could send me a list of things

that the child needs, I will bring them when I come. I appeal to you because, in caring for the child, you must have the best sense of how conditions are.

I thank you in advance and look forward to thanking you more appropriately in person.

In complete sincerity,
Florence Abney

Melanie listened to the reading of the letter with a soft smile. "I think I am going to like Mr. Reynolds' Aunt Floss," she said. "And she certainly seems to be describing the young man we know."

Jessica nodded. "That isn't as easy a job as she thinks," she pointed out. "I haven't been into that place since the snakeskins were piled out in front. I haven't the smallest idea of what he has packed in that wagon."

Melanie nodded briskly. "Tomorrow, early, we'll ride over to see how the framing of the well is coming along. Once you are there, making a list for his aunt should be easy."

Jessica nodded but said nothing. The thought of going through Rosemary Reynolds' baby things filled her with horror. Why didn't this woman just come and take the baby off her hands? It was bad enough that she had lost her good teaching job without losing the whole autumn, too.

Of course, Tad couldn't keep a secret about anything. That evening when Will came by to see his son and talk awhile with Jessica's father, Tad told him that Jessica had received a letter from his aunt.

Will turned on the bench to look at Jessica. "Really?" he said, as if waiting for her to tell him what was in the letter.

"Really," she replied, looking away. "It was a very lovely gesture."

He laughed. "Floss never makes gestures. Everything she does is the real thing."

Melanie looked up from her sewing with a smile. "You sound very fond of her."

"I am," Will said. "She's all the family I have, but it's more than that. We grew up like brother and sister. Outside of this little boy here, she's the most important person in my world."

"That's unusual with a nephew and an aunt," Jessica's father observed.

"Floss is a most unusual aunt," he said, grinning to himself.

Jessica glanced at him, curious. He met her eyes with his brows lifted, as if to say that two could play at that game. If Jessica wouldn't tell him what was in the letter, he wouldn't tell her what was so unusual about his Aunt Floss. Jessica looked away, cross at herself for having been caught being curious about something she *really* didn't care a hoot about.

She just wanted the woman to come and give her her own time back to do with as she pleased.

Chapter Nine

IF Jessica had trouble getting along with Will Reynolds, she was the only member of the family with that problem. In the weeks that followed Rosemary Reynolds' death, Patrick and Melanie Findlay took the young widower and his son under their wings. Jessica's brothers had adored the baby from the first. When, on Sunday mornings, Will slid into the Findlay church pew beside Patrick, the boys vied for turns at holding Jimson. Even Jessica had to admit that Will's rich singing voice, blended with those of her father's and Melanie's, made the simplest hymn a glory to listen to.

It was natural enough for Will and the child to stop by for Sunday dinner with the family several times a month. But Will never came without some contribution to the meal, in spite of Melanie's protest.

"Let him be," Jessica's father told her. "He can't bear being in debt to anyone. It's just his way."

Jessica could never have whispered to anyone her own mean thoughts about this. Will, who could not accept a simple meal without profuse thanks and adding something of value to it, not only accepted the long hours she put in with his child without guilt or embarrassment but found it difficult even to be civil to her in her own home.

The baby was five weeks old when Jessica began to care for him in the Reynolds dugout. He wasn't exactly fat, but a wonderful dimple had come in his left cheek, and his arms and legs were rounded.

When school began, both boys had complained bitterly at being "hauled away to miss all the fun." Their chorus of complaint doubled when they realized that Jessica would not be riding with them daily, as she had all the years before.

"She is tied down here with Jimson," their father explained. "Until his aunt comes, your mother or I will get you there and home."

Melanie had taken Tad's worn baby clothes out of the hump-backed trunk to use on Jimson. When the dugout was ready, Jessica packed several baskets of fresh clothes to take along in the buggy when Jerry drove her over that first morning.

Already the coming of autumn was in the air. What bushes and trees had survived the long, dry summer were shedding red and gold leaves to blow through the dry grass. None of the cottonwoods had survived. In their naked branches, the abandoned nests of summer birds rattled forlornly. Never had Jessica seen so many tumbleweeds, nor such big ones. They rolled across the prairie end over end, huge, bleached balls of prickly lace so threatening that nervous horses reared at their approach.

The first killing frost, which often came on the tenth of October, was less than two weeks away. The rich smells of fall filled both the house and the cellar out back, where bundles of sage and mint had been hung to dry. Jessica was amazed that she and Melanie had managed to do the necessary September work. In spite of the many hours she had spent with Jimson, and the constant trips Melanie had made to the Reynolds dugout, the cabbage and pickles were into brine and the crocks of apple butter safely stored away. Because of the drought, wild nuts and fruit had been harder to find. But thanks to Tad and Jerry's intimate knowledge of every foot of the hundred-and-sixty-acre ranch, there would be some wild plum jam for winter bread and almost a quart of golden currants had been dried for Christmas cakes.

Jessica had not been to the Reynolds dugout since the day she had waggled the rattlesnake skins in Will Reynolds' face. Even from the outside, the change was visible. The pile of debris was gone from in front of the door. The wagon, stripped of its canvas top, was now behind the dugout, near the cellar that served for both food storage and protection from the tornadoes of spring.

Jessica had tried to get Melanie, who had spent long hours there helping Will, to tell her about the inside of the house. Melanie only smiled and said, "Wait," with a smile warming her mouth.

Even Jerry had to stoop a little to get through the door. Jessica, carrying Jimson, followed, only to stop inside the door with a gasp of amazement.

Instead of raw dirt, the walls were plastered with the fine clay that had been dug from the new well. On the wall facing the door, Will Reynolds had hung the canvas flaps that had covered the wagon. Pinned to that wall were two beautiful oil paintings framed in ornately carved frames, which were etched with gold. Between them, above a dressing table with delicate, carved legs, a huge mirror caught the light from the open door, reflecting the room and making it appear double its actual size.

Jessica had never seen a prettier rug than the one that covered the scraped dirt floor. The border, a swirled design in deep shades of red and blue, surrounded a pattern of interlaced leaves and flowers.

"Wow, would you look at this?" Jerry said. "A brand-new stove and everything."

Not quite everything, Jessica registered. She could see Melanie's fine hand in the dry goods boxes that were fastened along the wall to serve as cupboards for the dishes and pans. Indeed, the stove was brand-new. But instead of a table, another box had been set between nail kegs and a low trunk. The bed in the corner was covered with a rich, dark quilt. The carved cradle and the rocking chair that Jessica remembered had been placed nearby.

"It's wonderful," Jessica decided aloud.

"Then I can go back home now?" Jerry asked. Then, checking the covered bucket on a low stool, he added, "There's even fresh water drawn."

"I'll need a fire," she told him.

He made a face and then grinned. Jessica looked everywhere without finding anything he could gather buffalo chips in.

"Well, I'm not going to bring them back in my bare hands," he told her.

"How about using your hat?"

Even he had to laugh at that. Finally, she took a diaper and handed it to him. "Bring this back full. That should last the day. We'll remember a basket tomorrow."

Jessica stood in the doorway and watched him go. Once he thought himself out of sight, he began to run and swoop. She knew he would be shouting, taking threatening dives at any wild creature unlucky enough to cross his path. Gathering buffalo chips for the fire had been her job all those years before Jerry got big enough. She knew how boring it could be if you didn't make fun out of it for yourself.

While the baby slept, she went through the baby clothes stored in the trunk. She felt guilty and furtive, going through these things that Rosemary Reynolds had packed with such care. The scent of lavender rising from the open trunk brought tears to her eyes.

Maybe it was just as well that Will Reynolds' wife had kept herself hidden in the wagon the day that Jessica had come. From her appearance, like a cherished doll, and from the elegant possessions that furnished this room, Rosemary Reynolds had come from a different world than Jessica knew. It was no wonder that every time she spoke to Will, he closed the conversation by walking away.

She folded the baby clothes back into the trunk. What could she tell Will's aunt, except that the child needed everything? The long christening dress with the matching bonnet, the hand-embroidered lawn dresses, the delicate sweaters and caps were useless except for Sunday show. Aside from three flannel blankets and a dozen new diapers, there was nothing in that trunk that a frontier baby could use.

Jessica finished writing her letter to Miss Florence Abney before Jimson wakened. She hoped she had not been tactless. She told the woman that the baby was welcome to Tad's things as long as they fit. She suggested flannel gowns, heavy socks, and wool blankets against the coming winter.

She closed by saying that she was looking forward to meeting her. That wasn't exactly true, the way it read, but Jessica could honestly say she was really looking forward to having this "Aunt Floss" come and relieve her of her child-care duties.

Next to going through Rosemary Reynolds' things, Jessica had most dreaded riding home in the evening with Will. She found herself getting nervous about it halfway through that first afternoon. What if he grew tired of her, as he always did when they talked, and simply set her off and rode away? That was ridiculous. He wouldn't dare.

But what if he decided to ignore her, as he did almost all the time when he sat at her parents' table? She could imagine that three-mile ride in the chill of his withdrawn silence.

Twilight had just begun to fall when she heard the hooves of his horse outside. Terrified that he might come inside to get her, she scooped up the baby and was outside in a moment.

"How did your day go, Miss Findlay?" he asked very formally as he dismounted.

"Very nicely, thank you, Mr. Reynolds," she replied. "Your home is lovely."

He smiled at that. "Thank you," he said. She thought he was reaching for the baby. Instead, to her astonishment, he placed his hands around her waist and lifted her up to set her on his horse.

"What are you doing?" she yelled, hanging onto the baby and trying to wriggle free of him.

"Putting you on the horse, you little fool,"

he said crossly. "What did you think?"

"I can get onto a horse by myself," she said.

He shook his head and set her on the mare's back behind his saddle. "Show me your Wild West tricks sometime when you're not carrying my baby," he said.

Wild West tricks, indeed! She rode along grumpily, feeling like a perfect fool hanging on there behind him with the baby clinging to her.

Then, relaxed by the rhythm of the horse's easy gait, she began to think wistfully about the summer before, when she had practiced endlessly until she could leap from a ledge in the back pasture, land on Dancie bareback, and start off at a gallop. Without realizing it, she chuckled, remembering the day she had missed and rolled end over end until she was stopped by a tree.

"Did I miss a joke?" he asked, his voice sounding strangely intimate so near.

"Not really," she told him. "I was just thinking of something funny."

"I don't hear a lot of laughter in Kansas," he told her thoughtfully. "I think I miss it."

"You're not going to the right places," she told him. "I have heard Papa laugh until his tears ran down, after he has stopped in town and watched the court."

"The court?" he asked, turning to stare at her. "The law court?"

She nodded. "The justice in town is a real comedian, according to Papa. I've never seen him because he conducts his court in the saloon. You must ask Papa about Justice Schoenbrun and his verdict on the white calf."

"I will," he said. Then, with surprise, "I can't believe we're already here."

Jessica was surprised herself. How nice it had been to talk like that instead of forever fighting. But then, as Will Reynolds dismounted, he did it again. Instead of letting her slide from the mare's back with the child in her arms, he caught her around the waist and lifted her down to the ground.

"I can get *off* a horse, too," she told him angrily.

He looked at her and laughed. "If you think of something you can't do, be sure and tell me."

She would have stamped all the way inside, but she knew he was standing there watching and would laugh.

The next day he was the soul of propriety. He not only took the baby from her as she swung up in his stirrup, but he turned and gazed into the distance until she was settled on the mare's back. At the Findlay house, he reversed this process, lifting the baby from her arms and then turning away to let her drop from the mare's back onto the ground with a thud.

Even though Jessica chafed restlessly at long autumn days that she spent tied down with Will Reynilds' son, she was to remember that time like a gentle dream, so rich with simple pleasure that when the dream was past, the time seemed to be something she had imagined, that never could have happened at all.

For one thing, it took little work to keep the dugout neat, which gave her lots of free time during the day.

The evening rides home with Will were the most puzzling experiences. They would ride together in the most genial way possible for days at a time. They would talk about the crops, Preacher Allen's last sermon, the current cattle-rustling trial . . . whatever came to mind. Then, without warning, Will Reynolds would turn cold and aloof in that infuriating way. And never once in all that time did he ever call her by name. Melanie was Melanie, her father became Pat, but she was Miss Findlay. The other thing she noticed, and this was the most puzzling of all, was that no matter how well they got along as they jogged home on his horse together, the minute they faced each other, they would be at each other's throats.

Maybe we should wear masks like train robbers, Jessica told herself in frustration, *since apparently we can't stand the sight of each other.* But with every day, the arrival of Will's Aunt Floss grew nearer, and this was what Jessica counted on.

Jessica did feel guilty about the amount of time she wasted. She felt like apologizing to her father for letting him down in such a busy season. The words came to the tip of her tongue a dozen times, but she held them back. After all, he had been the one who put her in this situation. It was only fair that he suffer from it as much as she did, if that was possible.

But at least she managed to avoid any more of those sticky conversations with Roy Blanding. Melanie reported several times that Roy had ridden by and asked for her.

"Surely you told him where I was?" Jessica said.

"Did you want me to?" Melanie countered.

Jessica giggled. "Not at all. I just wondered how you got out of it."

Melanie shrugged. "Everyone in this county knows that you have been your father's right hand since you were big enough to trail after him. It's my part to tell people that you are not at home. It's the other person's part to figure out where you are."

Jessica saw Roy at church, of course. He sat in his pew glaring at Will all through the services. Then when he did catch Jessica to talk, it was always in a situation where he could only stammer out the most common talk, discussion of the continuing drought, and the health of the family. She found it remarkably easy to put him and his questions out of her mind through those delicious weeks.

She had several letters from Agatha, who was, of course, in love again. Agatha's letters also contained invitations for her to come and visit in Victoria. It seemed that her employer was so pleased with Agatha's work that she had grown concerned about her maid getting lonely away from "her own kind."

"I know that someone would want to hire you if you just came," Agatha urged. "You don't make a world of money, but it's all yours to save since there's no place here to spend it."

When Jessica wrote letters in return, she was deliberately vague about accepting these invitations. The care of little Jimson, which she had undertaken with such reluctance, had actually become a pleasure much of the time. He was friendly to everyone but claimed Jessica as his own, smiling at the sight of her and snuggling with delight in her arms. She was comfortable about caring for him until Will's aunt would arrive.

The most unsettling times were those days when Will grew morose and silent during their rides home. Sometimes it seemed to Jessica that he was so deep in his own troubles that he was not even conscious of either her or the child, who chirped and gurgled with pleasure as they rode. Then he would forget and lift her off the horse, as if she had never told him that she hated to be treated like that. His mind, she decided, was a million miles away. She wondered if he were grieving for his lost wife when he looked right at her and then looked away, as if the sight of her was painful to his eyes.

Rachel often came out after church on Sunday to visit with Jessica. She was still counting the days until she, too, would be sixteen. She was still bemoaning that while Walter Brannon seemed genuinely glad to see her when he came in the store, he treated her like a great friend, not the girl he wanted to spend his life with.

"Surely you wouldn't want a husband that you weren't good friends with," Jessica argued.

"Of course not," Rachel flared. "But neither do I want to see my good friend Walt up and marry someone else because he hasn't really noticed me."

At Rachel's suggestion, Jessica bought yarn and knitted bright woolen caps, which the Landers sold in their store. She was pleased with the profit since the caps, which sold for fifty cents, only required a quarter's worth of yarn. She began to think about nice surprises she could buy her family for Christmas. She spent long hours reading while the baby slept. When he was wakeful, she carried him out on the prairie. Sometimes she saw a distant wagon train trailing west, although there were fewer of these in autumn with the snowy mountains between the plains and the sea. Herds of ponies, being driven to market, came by in great, romping clouds of dust. Horsemen passed in the distance, swift silhouettes that seemed to swim through the bending dry grass. When the first geese honked by in a great triangle of beating wings, the child stared at them with a wonder like her own.

Then the peace of those October days was swept away in a single stormy afternoon.

Morning came that day, with high clouds borne swiftly on the wind. At breakfast, Jessica's father was as teasing and playful as a child who has been promised a treat. "Such a day could bring rain," he explained. "This country aches with thirst."

"Let it be a sweet rain, then," Melanie suggested. "Slow and steady, with the earth getting a chance to absorb it."

"Let it come any way it wants to," her husband corrected her. "I'm past being particular."

A little past noon, the rain began to fall from a curdled sky. In the beginning, it came just as Melanie had ordered it. It fell in widespread drops, pattering against the sod roof and chiming musically as it struck the fresh chimney pipe that Will had installed.

For a long time, Jessica sat inside the open doorway with Jimson on her lap just enjoying the lean lines of gray rain. The air was heavy with the smell of summer dust being turned to mud. From the slanting roof, a rivulet began to flow past the door, carrying twigs and dried leaves like boats on a wandering stream.

But with every hour, the force of the rain increased. Instead of slim, gray lines, the water poured in a thundering torrent from a dark sky. As Jessica dragged the chair back into the room and pushed the door shut, she saw the rain striking the earth with such force that it bounced back up in tiny umbrellas of spray.

Still she didn't worry. The raindrops found the open top of the chimney and pinged as they passed down the pipe to hiss on the hot coals of her fire. When the first trickle of water forced itself under the door, she moved the furniture around until she could roll up the precious rug to protect it from mud stains.

Her first real concern began when the trickle under the door turned into a stream. Its force was great enough to cut a channel there in the dirt where a threshold should have been set when the house was built.

It was impossible that the dugout could be flooded. She tried to remember all the stories she had heard of fall floods. She had never heard of anything like that happening. She told herself that the water would simply keep trying to come in until the rain stopped. Then the flood would recede and they would be dry again.

The threatening drumming of the rain affected her in strange ways. She had no idea how much time had passed since the first water had forced itself into the underground room. The water continued to rise from the ever-increasing stream. That filthy yellow current caught the empty nail keg and spun it dizzily around the room. She had set the cradle on the box that served as a table. Soon, even the box was bouncing and swaying with the force of the current. She couldn't think of a way to protect the canvas coverings on the walls. With Will's aunt expected within a week, she wished she could keep the muddy water from seeping up on the walls to leave dark stains.

"It can't get much worse," she told the baby, holding him against her as the water rose over her ankles and filled her boots. "Somebody will come for us and take us home. Rain stops. It doesn't just go on pouring down like this forever."

She tried singing, but even that didn't help, the hammering of the rain outside drowning out her voice.

The roiling water forced Jessica to face a difficult decision. At some point she must either dare the storm or submit to the rising water's dragging her and the child to their deaths. Her boots felt weighted with lead. The fabric of her long, full skirt and undergarments tugged her into the swirling current. Every object in the room had become her enemy. Floating wooden kegs, boxes, and benches, even Rosemary Reynolds' delicate dressing table, plunged about drunkenly in the rising yellow tide.

Although everything was sodden, she seized a bunch of Tad's diapers and bound them around the baby. Holding him high against her left shoulder, well above the waist-deep water, she twisted the handle of the door and threw her weight against it to force it open. The pressure of the water out-side braced the wooden door against her weight.

Only when her shoulder ached painfully from her repeated battering attempts to force the door, only when the thoroughly drenched baby began to scream in the sicken-ing rhythm of hysteria did she lose control and begin to scream, too. She knew, even as the sound of her voice filled the watery trap, that there was no one to hear.

She knew she must not even think of giving up. Sobbing with pain, she rammed herself against the blocked door again and again. The way the water was coming in, in surges, perhaps she might hit the door when the cur-rent was weak enough that she could force it open even a little way.

When the door finally gave, she lunged into the wall of water. Its sweeping force whirled her about and swept her back into the dugout as it poured through the open doorway. She felt Jimson being washed from her grip, and she clung to him desperately in that watery darkness. Even as she felt him being torn from her grasp, the pain struck above her left ear.

She felt herself spinning into a deeper darkness. She heard her own voice, as if it belonged to a stranger, still screaming, "Jim-son! Jimson!"

Chapter
Ten

JESSICA awakened to darkness and the muffled drumming of the rain. Her only other consciousness for those first few seconds was pain. Waves of dull pain snaked along her right shoulder. Her brain seemed to be thundering behind her eyes. Then memory came, bringing a different agony.

"Jimson," she whispered, feeling her heart tighten in her chest. "Oh, my God, Jimson."

"The child is fine," a voice said quietly out of the darkness. A very near voice, a voice as near as her own breath.

Her body tensed. Only after hearing the voice did she realize that someone was breathing beside her, a low, even breathing barely audible above the sound of the rain. But the voice was strange, a voice she was sure she had never heard before.

The accent was even strange. She was certain that a man had spoken because of the deep timbre of the voice. Yet his tone had been extraordinarily soft, very like the tone that Melanie used when she spoke to soothe her sons' fears.

Straining against the darkness she sought to make sense of where she was. This was a blacker darkness than she could ever remember. The air inside this darkness was close and warm even though the rain beat steadily on whatever sheltered them.

When she tried to move, she cried out with involuntary pain. And there was no room to stir around in, anyway. Whoever had spoken out of that darkness was pressed against her in a very tight space. That would explain the warmth of her body in spite of her drenched clothing.

"We must stay in this place until the rain is past," the voice counseled quietly. "No pony is surefooted enough to cross such streams carrying a burden."

"The baby?" she asked as a question. "You said he was fine?" It didn't matter where they were or how long they stayed as long as the child for whom she was responsible was all right.

"He is here," he said. "But look quickly." When he pulled back a fold of that enveloping darkness, the leaden light brought with it a swift rush of cold raindrops spattering against the face of the child he held in his arms. Jimson made a face and twisted away as he dropped the flap, again shutting away both the light and the rain.

She told herself swiftly that she had not seen what her eyes had registered. Against her in the darkness sat a young Indian cradling Jimson in his right arm with his left arm braced somewhere behind her.

"He sleeps?" she asked.

His chuckle was soft. "Very tired baby, very wet, too. He has strong voice. Not until he was dry and warm did he sleep."

Jessica tried to remember exactly what she had seen in that moment of dim light. Jimson had been wrapped in something dark, certainly not the pile of muslin diapers she had bundled him in.

And the Indian. His face had imprinted on her mind clearer than any picture. This was a handsome face, wide at the cheekbones and tapering in a smooth and graceful line to a squared jaw. His eyebrows, under a bright band of some kind, were shapely above warm, dark eyes. His eyes and his well-formed smiling mouth were clearest in her mind. Had she imagined that his face had shone with the hue of fine, polished wood in that dim light?

"Where are we?" she asked.

"On that high hill west of the house where I found you," he replied. "Only the high places are safe until the flooding from the sky is past."

On the high hill west. She frowned, remembering. A stand of bent native trees stood on that hill with a tangle of gooseberry bushes around their feet. Yet there was no habitation, not even a cave or a shed. She lifted her hand to feel the surface that shielded them from the rain. It was soft and supple like the finest of cloth. "Leather," she decided aloud with surprise.

"The skin of buffalo," he corrected her.

"I don't know you," she told him.

"I am called Wheeling Hawk," he replied, his voice even quieter than before. The stillness that followed his words was tense with waiting.

Jessica hoped that he had not heard her faint intake of breath. As close as they were huddled, he might even have felt it as she felt each deep breath he drew to speak. He was Indian, then. The air that had seemed so warm only minutes before held a sudden chill. Horror stories flooded into her mind like the stained rush of water that had boiled into the Reynolds dugout. She had been eleven the year of the massacre in Solomon River Valley. The grown-ups had repeated the story until the details had become the stuff of her nightmares. So many prayers had been said in the name of the dead that she felt them as near as kinsmen.

"My name is Jessica," she told him, hoping that fear had not altered her voice. "Jessica Findlay."

"Ah," he said. "The child of Patrick Findlay?"

"You know him?" she asked, surprised.

That soft chuckle again, as if the thought of his knowing Patrick Findlay were somehow amusing. "Only of him. He has the name of fairness among my people."

Jessica felt this as a reproach. Yet how could she be fair when she, like all her friends, had been raised in terror of just such men as this? How many nights had she awakened, weak with terror, from a dream that she had been kidnapped?

"My father is a fair man," she told him, reminding herself that she was her father's daughter, obliged to be as fair as Patrick Findlay himself. "And who are your people?" she asked.

She felt his body stiffen as if with pride as he replied, "Cheyenne," again in that soft tone.

"From around here?" she asked. She knew little more than the names of the tribes. She knew of the Cheyenne from the stories of the massacre. She had heard it said that the Arapaho and Sioux were even more warlike.

"Not too far," he replied vaguely. "Once we lived in a far place, but we have been moving, always moving these last years." His tone was not so much angry as sad.

He seemed to have withdrawn into his own thoughts as the rain pelted steadily against the buffalo hide covering them.

"Tell me what happened back there in the dugout," she finally said, breaking the silence. "I couldn't get the door to open for a long time, then suddenly. . . ." She shivered, remembering.

"A wall of water was pressing hard against

it," he explained. "I had seen you there with the child when I rode by. When I saw no smoke from your chimney, I thought you must be gone from there." He paused. "Then, after I passed, I rode back, just to be sure."

"Then it was you who pulled open the door. You saved our lives, Jimson's and mine."

"I had seen you there," he repeated. "Walking with your child."

"I can't thank you enough for saving us," she said swiftly. "I just don't know what to say."

As she spoke, the support beneath them suddenly changed position, as if the very earth had shifted. He caught her with a firm arm to brace her against falling.

"What was that?" she shrieked, her voice loud in that close space.

"My friend tires of his burden," he explained. Then he stirred and pulled back the buffalo robe again to look out. Only then did she realize that the three of them were huddled together under the buffalo skin on the back of a pony who stared back at her with a drenched face.

But the rain was slackening. He nodded approval at how the sky was clearing. "In a little while we can travel," he said. "That dugout will be flooded. There must be some safe, dry place you can go."

She studied him there in that half light. Although he was slender, he had the look of great strength. He was as handsome as she had thought in that first glance. And indeed, his skin was a delicious color. His eyes, so warmly intent on her face, were so dark that they had no color, only glinting lights that seemed to shine only for her. When he smiled, his even, white teeth caught that same light and tugged a smile from her in return. The only word she could choose for him was *magnificent*.

"My father's house," she told him hastily, embarrassed that she had made him wait for her answer while she stared at him. "If you would not mind taking us to my father's house?"

He nodded and turned his gaze back out onto the sodden prairie. His horse whinnied softly, and he patted its side.

"Why do you pass that dugout?" she asked, suddenly curious. She had heard talk of the Indians being confined to special places, reservations where they were kept to protect her people.

"My father was a peaceful man who tried all his days to work with your people. The agent here became his friend. Through that agent I found work to do." His teeth shone even and bright when he smiled like that.

"I have skill with horses," he told her simply. "When your people bring the pony bands north, I am the best to break them to gentleness under the harness. I pass here going to and from the Fairchild ranch."

Jessica slid her hand along her aching right shoulder and echoed his answer in her mind. She had heard the name Fairchild many times. Her father named Hamlin Fairchild as the best man with horse flesh in the state of Kansas. Why did she like the way Wheeling Hawk talked so much? It wasn't that faint accent that changed his words. It was his directness. He didn't put on any silly act of false modesty, nor did he brag or try to show off. "I have skill with horses," he had said in that nice, level way.

"I'm sure glad that you noticed Jimson and me," she told him. "If it hadn't been for you and your horse, we would have drowned in there like rats in a barrel."

How strange that she had never thought of an Indian laughing in that soft way. "Who could let a woman with hair like ripe grain drown like a rat?" he asked.

She smiled but said nothing. Had anyone ever said such a nice thing to her before? She couldn't remember anything ever bringing such a warm rush of pleasure to her mind. It was more than his gentle words, more than the rich symbolism of life-giving grain. The way he had asked the question in teasing laughter had lightened his flattery into something as delicate as the offer of a flower.

He smiled back at her, and they waited for a while in a comfortable silence. He sighed a little and then spoke.

"We have waited out the rain," he said quietly. "Perhaps I should take you to your father's house?"

"I would be forever grateful," she told him.

He was careful to keep the folds of the

buffalo robe closed around Jessica and the baby as he dismounted. The rain still fell in a lackluster way as he patted his horse and spoke to it. Then, turning, he reached behind Jessica and brought out the handful of sodden diapers she had wrapped around Jimson back in the dugout.

"We can use these to bind the child to your body," he said. "You may need your hands free for our ride. After such a storm, the way could be difficult."

His hands were graceful, with long, tapered fingers. His face was very near her own as he worked with the wet muslin, making a loose carrier to hold the baby in comfort. A glint of silver shone at his wrist now and then as he wove the pieces of fabric together. His eyelashes were like Melanie's, so thick and dark that they lay like shadows on his cheeks when he looked down. When he looked up at her, he always smiled, a slow, tender smile that made her want to reach out to him.

She thought suddenly of Will Reynolds, whose eyes could not rest even a moment on her face without sliding away in anger.

"You are a very nice person, Wheeling Hawk," she told him.

His eyes moved to hers as his hands stopped their work for a moment. Then he nodded. "Is it possible that you bring out the best in any person?" He obviously didn't expect an answer because he patted the baby and nodded again. "There, that should hold him."

Jessica was surprised that Jimson didn't protest the binding that Wheeling Hawk had made for him. Instead, the baby leaned against her, his head beneath her chin, and dozed off again without a whimper.

Jessica watched Wheeling Hawk untether the horse from the trunk of the dead cottonwood and stare east to where the Findlay ranch lay.

Following his gaze, Jessica gasped with astonishment. It was as if she looked on a strange country. Fields that had been cracked with deep clefts in the parched earth only the day before now flowed with swift, musical streams. This rush of water had seized everything in its path. Dead tree limbs, farm equipment left in low places, even the whitened skulls of bison slaughtered by the hide hunters lay in discarded piles here and there along the path of the rushing streams.

Having sat with Wheeling Hawk on his mount through the long storm, Jessica was startled when he did not mount again and ride with her and the baby. His horse, although small, clearly had strength enough to carry the three of them. Yet he had taken the reins in his hands to lead the animal down the hill going east.

"Wheeling Hawk," she called to him. "Come and ride with us. It is such a long way home, and your clothes are even wetter than ours are now."

When he paused and looked back at her, she

realized that he would not accept her invitation unless she insisted.

"Please, Wheeling Hawk," she called. "I want you to ride with us. I want that very much."

This time his hesitation ended with a smile and a shrug. When he mounted the horse in front of her, she draped the buffalo robe to cover him, too. When he turned to her, the expression on his face could only be called mischievous.

"The Cheyenne are a walking people," he told her. "But to walk in such flood is to make a boat of a moccasin."

She laughed, feeling the weight of her waterlogged boots pulling at her ankles. "To walk in this would make buckets out of my boots," she told him. In that brief moment when their eyes met in mutual laughter, Jessica felt an actual thump inside her chest, as if her heart had leaped the way she had read about in stories. That was ridiculous. Hearts leaped for love. There was no such thing as love between a white and an Indian. There couldn't be, not with the wars and the hatred and the bloodshed all these years. But there was no rule that one could not have an Indian for a friend. Let anyone tell her that Wheeling Hawk was not her friend, after what he had done for her and Jimson. And she was his friend, too, and always would be. Always.

It was indeed a long way home. The horse

picked a delicate path between raging streams that had come from nowhere. He slid on clay banks newly treacherous from the coursing water passing over naked earth. Jessica rested her hands on Wheeling Hawk's waist to brace herself, as she had when she rode behind her father all these years.

It was strange how much more natural it was for her to ride with Wheeling Hawk than with Will Reynolds. She felt no self-consciousness about holding to this man for support. With Will it was different. She always felt that she must hold herself stiffly aloof from him, lest he be offended by her touch. She and Wheeling Hawk, with the sleeping child between them, seemed like one single rider moving to the rhythm of their mount.

"That is a good child," he called back after a while.

"The best," she replied.

"You treat him well," he said. "I know you sing to him, but the wind carries the words too far for me to hear."

"You might be lucky," she told him. "I sing with more joy than skill."

Probably because the animal was so burdened, Wheeling Hawk kept his pony at a leisurely walk. When the path was even, they talked.

"I have seen you with a young boy," he told her.

"I have two brothers," she explained. "They are both younger than I."

He nodded. "It is the same with me. Have you no sisters?"

"None," Jessica told him. "Do you?"

"One only," he said. "She is called Spring Rain, and many young men come to see her, but she refuses them all."

"Maybe the right young man has not come yet," Jessica suggested.

He nodded. "My mother says the same. She says Spring Rain will choose to stand within the blanket of a brave man, as her mother did before her."

Jessica was glad he could not see her flush. Surely these long hours she had spent beneath the buffalo robe with him had no special meaning. She tried to hold herself stiffly apart from him, but after a moment it seemed silly to do that. Anyway, the slow pace of the horse conspired with her exhaustion. For a long time, she tried to stay awake. Finally, in defeat, she leaned her head against Wheeling Hawk's back, being careful not to crowd the sleeping baby. She dozed there against the warmth of his back, only being watchful that she kept a good grip on his waist so that she didn't fall from the horse.

Did she dream that after a while he began to hum a low, haunting melody that vibrated through his warm back? Dream or not, she only knew that some song, as soothing as a lullaby, as tender as a love song, filled that small world inside the buffalo robe with beauty as well as warmth.

"Forever," she thought dreamily. "I could ride forever like this."

Instead, she was startled awake by Wheeling Hawk's quiet voice. "We're almost there," he told her. "The house of Patrick Findlay lies just ahead."

She was astonished to see that twilight had fallen as she dozed and dreamed through that long ride home. She saw Jerry carrying a pair of swinging lanterns toward the barn lot, before she noticed the three men standing by the fence with saddled horses at their sides.

As Wheeling Hawk approached the yard, her father, Will, and Jerry hastened forward. She recognized the third man at once as Mr. Logan and wondered why he was there. Then, realizing what fear they must have had for the baby and herself, she threw back the buffalo robe so that they could see both her and the baby at once.

"Papa," she called. "We're here. We're safe."

Her father spoke first, crossing that few yards as if they didn't exist. "Jessica, thank God," he cried. "And the little boy?"

As if in reply, Jimson, startled by the blast of cold air, let out a howl of rage. Only Melanie, crossing the yard at a run, even seemed to notice Wheeling Hawk as he dropped from the horse and turned to lift Jessica down.

"Thank you," Melanie said to him swiftly, her eyes warm on his face. "Oh, thank you for bringing our children home."

Will Reynolds, his face white with strain, stared from Jessica to Wheeling Hawk with horror. "My son," he said, stepping forward. Jessica barely glanced at him before looking away. His eyes glittered on her with such furious anger that a knot of pain came in her stomach.

"He's fine. He's really fine," she insisted, trying to unbind the child who had begun to flail at her with angry fists.

Tad, dancing behind his father, was overcome with excitement. "A papoose," he said. "Jimson is a papoose now."

Jessica looked to Wheeling Hawk for the grin of amusement she had learned to expect. Only his eyes smiled. What was there about the presence of these men that shut his delightful humor away? It was silly even to ask herself that when, from the corner of her eye, she could see the stiffness in Mr. Logan's stance as he stared at the young man.

At that moment, she freed Jimson from his binding and handed him into Melanie's arms. Before Melanie even disappeared into the house with the baby, Jessica's father was firing questions at Jessica. "What happened, Jessica?" he asked. "Where were you? We searched everywhere, clear to Logan's place. . . ."

Jessica had never interrupted her father in her life. Usually she wouldn't have dared that Findlay temper with such rudeness. But this rudeness of *his* put all that out of her mind. How could these men, her father, their neighbor Logan, and Will Reynolds, ignore the man who had clearly saved both herself and the baby in that storm?

"Forgive me, Papa," she said swiftly. "This is Wheeling Hawk. He is the reason that Jimson and I are even alive. I was trapped in that dugout with water against the door too heavy to push out. He got us out and kept us dry and brought us back home."

Someday Jessica meant to ask if her father had ever shaken hands with an Indian before, but he didn't hesitate that time. Instead, he stepped forward swiftly and seized both of Wheeling Hawk's hands. "We are deeply in debt to you, Wheeling Hawk," he said. "Thank God you were there."

Wheeling Hawk nodded, a slow, dignified nod that somehow expressed his understanding of Patrick Findlay's sincerity.

"Come in," Jessica urged. "You must have a long way to travel. We have food, hot coffee."

Wheeling Hawk shook his head. Again, only in his eyes could she see that geniality. "I will ride on," he told her. "Night comes swiftly."

Jessica looked to the others for some help. They should be as quick as she was to offer hospitality and thanks to this man who had been so heroic to her and the baby. Instead, they stood like so many dead trees, staring at her and Wheeling Hawk. Angry that no one stepped forward to add their words to hers, she went on, trying to persuade Wheeling

Hawk to accept her hospitality. "At least let us refresh your horse," she insisted. "Would he like oats or water?"

"Oats would slow his passage," he told her. Then, standing as he was where the others could not see his face, he grinned. "Water he has seen more than enough of."

At that moment, knowing that he was about to leave, seeing him pass from her life so swiftly, she wanted to reach out to him, to hold him back, to keep him with her. But the men were watching, cold-eyed and ungracious.

"I can't thank you enough," she told him again, wishing for words as warm and intense as her feelings were. "I simply can't thank you enough. There must be something. . . ."

He swung onto the horse and looked down at her. "You live," he said, his voice so soft that the men, only a few feet away, could not possibly have made out his words. "Your life is reward enough for any man."

Jessica's father and the other men stood watching as Wheeling Hawk rode away. His body was as lithe as a willow as he bent to the horse's back and disappeared into the darkness at a rhythmic gallop.

The men were still standing there as Jessica flounced past them. Then, because her shoulder hurt and her clothes were wet and she was hungry and they were rude and horrible, she called back to them, "I'm going in to see how the little papoose is coming along."

Chapter Eleven

JESSICA wakened the morning after the flood to see brilliant sun streaming through the windows of the log cabin. Her shoulder was still bruised and sore from her efforts to force open the dugout door. She lay in her bed a long time, pressing her cool hand on that shoulder and thinking about Wheeling Hawk.

If she shut her eyes, she could see the smooth, glowing beauty of his face. If she blocked out all other sounds, she could bring back the softness of his laughter, the way his voice had sounded when he asked, "Who could let a woman with hair like ripe grain drown like a rat?"

Most of all she remembered the way her heart had leaped in her chest when they were together. It couldn't be love because he was an Indian and she was white. Yet, the thought that she might not see him again brought sudden tears.

When she finally got dressed, everyone else had eaten. She set the coffeepot over the heat and drank a cup of coffee in the quiet kitchen. From outside, she heard Major barking and Melanie laughing.

Jimson. Jessica leaped to her feet and ran to the door. In her dreaming about Wheeling Hawk, she had forgotten all about the baby. She was relieved to see Melanie holding him against her shoulder as she talked with her husband at the barnyard fence.

"There you are," Melanie called, seeing Jessica in the doorway. "We decided to let you sleep, and you did a job of it."

"But where are the boys?" Jessica asked.

Melanie laughed. "Off at school and Patrick back already. We'll keep Jimson here while poor Will gets that place cleaned out again. His aunt is coming Thursday, and he'll be lucky to have it done by them. What a mess!"

"It could have been a lot worse," Jessica's father said, smiling over at her. "A whale of a lot worse."

Jessica shivered at the suggestion. Without Wheeling Hawk's help, she would indeed have been drowned like a rat. But her father said nothing about her rescuer.

Within a few days, most of the signs of the rain and flood were gone. The dry earth had absorbed the water quickly, leaving only a muddy pool here and there.

Except for the flood damage done to dugouts like Will's, the storm had done more good than harm. Wells that had begun to run low were refilled with sweet water. Jerry spent his after-school hours on the prairie, gathering bundles of broken tree limbs that would make good firewood when winter came.

Even if Jessica had been able or wanted to forget her wonderful hours with Wheeling Hawk, she couldn't have done it. The story was everywhere at once, and everyone wanted to ask Jessica about it. Perhaps if only Jessica's family had been involved, she would have been saved all that talk. But Mr. Logan, having been there when she and Wheeling Hawk rode in, told the story in such dramatic detail that even Rachel dropped everything and rode out to see Jessica the minute Mr. Logan walked out of the Landers' store.

Rachel was so consumed by curiosity that her questions tumbled over each other.

"Weren't you terrified?" she asked Jessica. "How did you ever keep from going completely to pieces? What if that Indian had decided to —"

Jessica broke in, mimicking her friend's exaggerated tone. "What if that Indian had decided to ride on past and not see if anyone was trapped down there? Don't be like all the others, Rachel. Don't presume that every Indian is a savage. How would you like it if every man who worked with cattle was automatically assumed to be dirty and foul-mouthed?"

Rachel dropped her jaw in astonishment.

"That's awful. You know perfectly well that this very minute Walt Brannon is out on the range with his father branding last spring's calves."

"*That's* what I mean," Jessica pointed out. "Both this baby and I would be dead and buried if Wheeling Hawk hadn't noticed us there and stopped to see if we were all right when he saw that door half buried by water."

"It would scare me to think I was being watched by an Indian I had never seen. I hope you never have to go back to that dreadful place again."

"It's not a dreadful place at all," Jessica corrected her. "And as for going back, I probably won't need to with Will's aunt arriving this very week."

"Well, you're too late for the teaching job out by Pfeiffer. Mr. Reiner was in the store last week telling Papa that their school had a teacher now and was going fine. I hope that Mr. Reynolds and his aunt realize how much you gave up to take care of this baby."

Jessica's mind was wandering again. She wondered what would have happened if Wheeling Hawk had driven by and missed her there with the baby. She had seen many solitary horsemen while she was at the dugout, but they had always been too far away to recognize. Had she seen Wheeling Hawk and not known it? Certainly, he had seen her and heard her voice carried on the wind.

Later that same afternoon, Jessica had another caller. Roy Blanding, his face tight with concern, came by the house only a little while before Jessica's father and brothers were due in for the evening.

Melanie greeted Roy and invited him in. He took a seat on the kitchen bench near where Jessica sat knitting. "Mother and I just couldn't rest until I saw with my own eyes that you were all right, Jessica."

"I couldn't be finer," she told him. That wasn't quite the truth, but her shoulder was already feeling better and really wasn't worth talking about. Jimson watched Roy from his cradle, crowing for attention.

Roy glanced at the child with obvious distaste.

"I'll be glad when you are free of that greenhorn's kid. Look at the danger you've been exposed to, the flood, and then that savage Indian hauling you around on a horse." His tone turned plaintive. "Jessica, you must not have any idea what people are saying about you back in town —"

Even Melanie turned to stare at him with astonishment. "Roy," she interrupted. "I can't believe what I just heard you say. How dare anyone criticize Jessica for doing the neighborly service of caring for a helpless infant?"

"Well . . ." he hesitated. "After all, that greenhorn is young and healthy, without a woman. And Jessica stays there in his house all day with no chaperone."

"With Will off at work the whole time," Melanie reminded him firmly. "Please tell these people who have nothing better to do than gossip about our child that Will leaves in the morning when Jessica's father drops her off. And the minute he gets in from his work, Jessica comes directly home."

"But he rides her here every evening," he reminded her quickly, flushing at this reproach.

"Would it be more acceptable to those people if my father had to ride over to the Reynolds place every evening after his day's work to bring me home? Or my brother, maybe?" Jessica didn't care that her tone was caustic. If gossip like that was being whispered around town, Rachel would have been the first to tell her. Maybe it was mean of her to suspect that Roy and his mother were the "people" he was quoting.

Mean or not, that's what she thought. She was delighted to hear the scrape of her father's boot at the door and see Roy rise to leave. How silly and pompous Roy looked as he rose and spun that expensive hat between his hands. Maybe it was the lean, smooth gleam of Wheeling Hawk's face that made Roy look puffy and overfed.

Jessica couldn't remember a day as nerveracking as that Thursday when Will's aunt was scheduled to arrive. Will had finally given in to Melanie's insistence that his aunt would appreciate a chance to wash up after her journey more than anything he could offer. Since privacy was a constant problem in a one-room house like his, he agreed to bring his Aunt Floss directly from the train to the Findlays'.

"This will be a nice way for her to see little Jimson for the first time," Melanie added to Jessica. "And, by the time I set out a little lunch for our guest, it will be too late for Will to protest."

Although this was a hospitable idea and typical of Melanie's thoughtfulness, this arrangement added to Jessica's nervousness about meeting this Florence Abney. Jessica yearned to meet this stranger wearing her new birthday dress but knew that Jerry and Tad would tease her about "showing off." She and Melanie even had a hard time deciding how to dress Jimson. With his fine hair wisping in duck tails around his ears, he looked like a little girl in a dress. Yet even the smallest of Tad's old rompers was too large for him.

At the first mention of this aunt coming to care for the new mother and baby, Jessica had pictured someone like Mary Huffman, an older woman of great gentleness with gray hair pulled back from a face lined with experience. The handwriting in her letter and its no-nonsense style had confused Jessica's mental picture completely. The strong, up-and-down script had suggested that this Aunt Floss was a brisker, sturdier person than Jessica had imagined. At the same time, her name, Florence Abney, suggested someone citified and stylish. She wondered if she should have paid any attention at all to Will's remark about his aunt being very unusual. He had seemed to be teasing her when he said it.

When Melanie went to the door to welcome Will and his aunt, Jessica simply stood and stared. Never once had Jessica even thought about Will's aunt being a young person.

Yet the woman who stood in the doorway smiling at Jessica didn't look a day over twenty-five. She was about Jessica's height in her high-heeled boots. Her hair glistened black from under the brim of a pert scarlet bonnet, and her round cheeks had been whipped by the wind to almost the same brightness. Although she wasn't what Jessica would call slender, her jacket was nipped into a waist so small that Jessica wondered how she could draw a breath. Her high-heeled boots were fastened with tiny silver buttons as far as Jessica could see.

A white fur muff swung from a braided string as she stepped forward to seize Jessica's hands in her own gloved ones.

Trust Tad to break the ice for everyone. Before Florence Abney had a chance to speak, he was there in front of her, looking up with amazement. "I thought aunts were always old," he said. "You don't look old at all."

Even Will laughed. Floss herself knelt quickly and caught Tad's arms in her gloved hands. "I *am* a young aunt, and I love it. I would guess I was about your age when my sister, who was much older than I, brought

Will to show me. I was disappointed," she admitted with a grin at Will. "I had wanted a rocking horse. But I learned to like him in time."

"If Jessica were married and had a child, you would be *Uncle Tad*," Jerry pointed out. Tad's astonished face at this thought filled the room with laughter.

"And you have to be Jessica," Florence Abney said breathlessly. Before Jessica could respond, this fragrant woman pressed her cheek against Jessica's and hugged her hard. "You wonderful, wonderful person," she cried. "There's barely a soul in Chicago that I haven't told about you, and I didn't know to tell them you were also beautiful."

Over her shoulder, Jessica caught Melanie's startled eyes and her father's amused grin. Will, unsmiling but more genial than she had ever seen him, spoke up.

"Here, here, Floss, simmer down a little before you scare my son to death."

"Son," she said, seeming to freeze a moment there in Jessica's embrace. "Son."

Jessica had never seen Will pick up the child on his own before. She was surprised at how expertly he braced Jimson's small back as he held his child up for his aunt to see.

The baby was as fascinated as Jessica had been. He stared for only a moment into that bright face before his own widened in a delighted, toothless grin. He gurgled that throaty little sound that Jessica thought of as his own private chuckle.

Never had another woman's tears brought Jessica so close to weeping herself. The bright eyes filled with sudden tears, and a heartbroken sob escaped her lips. "Will," she said softly. "Oh, Will."

Without hesitation, Jessica reached for Jimson, leaving Will's arms free to catch his stricken aunt to his breast. He bent his head to touch the tip of that bright bonnet and held her silently until her sobbing subsided.

When she finally pulled away and turned back to them with an apology on her lips, Melanie shook her head. "You need not explain, my dear," she said softly. "Now go with Jessica and make yourself fresh. After a bite to eat, you'll want to hold Jimson yourself."

Florence Abney followed Jessica like a docile child. As she did on cold days in winter, Melanie had hung a cotton sheet to wall off a corner of the room where Jessica slept with her brothers. The steam from the pitcher of heated water had warmed that cubicle where fresh towels and Melanie's finest handmade soap had been laid out on the washstand.

All that vibrant strength seemed to have fled Florence Abney as she slumped on the edge of Jessica's bed. Jessica sat beside her, holding her as she had held Rachel so many times when her friend was overcome with despair.

"Rosemary," Floss whispered against Jessica's shoulder. "To have had so much and lost it all. And Will." Her tears began again.

Jessica waited silently for the storm to pass.

Finally, Jessica felt the woman's back stiffen. She took a handkerchief from her pocket and wiped her nose and eyes. "Forgive me," she said in a muffled voice. "I should have behaved better. I hope your family understands."

Jessica patted her shoulder. "If you had behaved any differently, we would never have understood you."

Floss raised her face to stare at Jessica, her lashes pasted together with tears and her nose as rosy as her cheeks. "You are a wonder, Jessica Findlay," she said quietly. "Remember to have me tell you what a wonder you are when I have time. But now I am keeping everyone waiting."

By the time their guest had washed the tear stains from her face and smoothed the mass of dark curls, she seemed to have her emotions under control. "You must call me Floss," she told Jessica with that wonderful smile. "The only time I ever hear the name Florence is when Will is cross at me."

By the time Will packed his aunt and his son into the buggy to take them home, Jessica felt as if she had known Floss Abney all her life. Jessica was fascinated to see a simple supper of cold meat and bread become a party by the grace of that lively woman. She even enchanted the boys with stories of Chicago — how the lake was so huge that you could see no land across its waters, and how the three-masted ships sailed up the river between tall buildings on either side.

Floss had questions of her own about Kansas. "Your home is lovely," she told Melanie. "And made of logs, isn't it?"

"You better be prepared for another kind of house," Will told her. "Ours is a dugout and like nothing you've ever seen."

As they talked, Jessica remembered Rosemary Reynolds' terror of that house, a terror so strong that she had borne her child in the wagon rather than seek shelter from the night and the wolves.

Floss, sensitive to all that went on at the table, caught Jessica's eye. "How thoughtful you seem, Jessica," she said. "You must be thinking of how much time you'll have once you are relieved of this little charge. You will be a free woman again." She smiled at the child sleeping by his father's side.

Jessica flushed at the truth in Floss's words but spoke quickly. "I was wondering if the change wouldn't be hard for you."

Floss giggled. "I shall make a hundred blunders in the first hour, but I shall learn fast."

"We certainly don't mean to abandon you or Jimson," Melanie said. "I thought one of us might ride over and see how you are doing sometime tomorrow."

'That really won't be necessary," Will spoke up. "We are so much in debt to you already."

"They didn't offer to come and pay a call on you," Floss reminded him with a teasing smile. "I am sure that by the time you get there I shall have a hundred questions."

The only unpleasantness in the whole evening came, of course, from Will. When Jessica stepped out to refill the water bucket to start fresh coffee, he followed her.

"I guess you don't know anything about those boxes of blankets and baby clothes that Floss brought with her, do you?" he asked, angrily winding the rope to bring up the water.

"She asked me what the baby needed and I told her," Jessica replied. "Would you have had me lie to her?"

"I would have had you mind your own business," he told her. "But that would be a great deal to ask, wouldn't it?"

Jessica, startled at the unfairness of his words, turned away to hide sudden tears. He caught her arm and spun her around. "If I thought it was Jimson you were worrying about, it might be different."

She stared at him, amazed. "Why else would I have written for warm things, if not for him?"

He sighed and turned away. "I don't know, Miss Findlay. I can't ever seem to deal with you. When you look at me with those cornflower blue eyes, I forget how dangerous you can be, always getting wound up in my life."

She stared at him. Wound up in his life?

What kind of a remark was that? If only she didn't have that quick fire of Findlay temper always ready to blaze.

"This is a joyful day, then, Mr. Reynolds. Now that your aunt is here, I will unwind and walk away and not have to be glared at and frowned at every time I raise my cornflower blue eyes."

She turned and stamped into the house, letting the door slam behind her right in his face.

That night Jessica slept fitfully, conscious that Jimson was gone from the cradle at her side. She heard the rustle of night creatures outside her window and thought of Wheeling Hawk. Only three days had passed since she had ridden home behind him through the darkness. Scarcely a waking hour had passed that she had not thought of him, remembered his voice and the wonderful way he had of holding her eyes with his own. Every time she promised herself that she would put him out of her mind, someone forced him back in. Roy Blanding with his narrowed eyes and tales of scandal. Will with his inability to say her name, much less look at her without turning away in disgust.

Rachel had told her that Jessica only minded growing up because she hadn't found the right person to love. What if the right person was wrong in every possible way? That was even worse than never having seen the right person at all.

Chapter Twelve

JESSICA had forgotten how it felt to wake up without a child to take care of. There had been that one morning after the flood that Melanie had taken Jimson away and let her sleep, but that was different. Now her right shoulder was barely stiff anymore, and she could move it any way she pleased.

What a luxury it was to dress without hurrying, and to stand before the mirror and brush her hair until it hung in a golden fall almost to her waist.

"Hair like ripe grain," Wheeling Hawk had called it.

She chose her hair ribbons carefully, instead of taking the first set that came to her hand. Then, remembering that she would get to call on Floss Abney that day, she plaited her hair with extra care before winding her braids in a great thick crown around her head.

Not until she was leaving her room did she notice that the window glass was white with overlapping circles of spidery frost. She looked at it and sighed. She had lost the entire autumn. Maybe winter, her least favorite season, would pass as quickly.

Her father grinned as she joined him at the breakfast table. "You only get rid of one job to have another one land on you," he warned her. "You'll have to ride the boys over to school for me and pick them up later. I need every hour I can get for a while, if we're going to be ready for winter here. The way it feels out there this morning, we could be in for some real cold within the week."

Jessica shivered at the thought. "I'm happy to take the boys and go get them," she told him, "but in all truth, I'm not ready for winter."

Her father laughed genially. "Neither am I. If I were, I wouldn't need the time," he reminded her. "But at least the cold will give us a chance to get the butchering done."

"And the soap made and the lard rendered and tallow candles poured," Melanie added, setting bowls of hot porridge in front of her sons.

"You will stop in on Floss Abney while you're out that way?" Melanie asked Jessica.

Jessica nodded. "I could leave a little early this afternoon and visit awhile before picking the boys up." She paused. "But surely Will won't leave her alone this first day."

Her father shook his head. "He doesn't have any choice. He took that one day off to meet her train, but he's helping Ben Smothers put up a cow shed."

The countryside looked like fairyland. Every twig and grass blade was thick with feathery white frost. Pale blue smoke curled above the Reynolds dugout as Jessica rode up. Dancie's breath looped around them like a cloudy wreath.

Floss was building up her fire to heat Jimson's milk when Jessica arrived. She had replaced her fancy traveling clothes with a deep-blue cotton dress trimmed with wide white ruffles. The ruffles at her cuffs were fastened back, and a white scarf covered her dark hair. She would have looked like a picture in a storybook if she had not also been wearing a pair of black kid gloves buttoned halfway to her elbows.

"Oh, these," she laughed, holding up her hands at Jessica's startled glance. "Will hooted at me about them, too. I defy anyone to find a persnickety bone in my body, but there are some things I simply don't intend to touch with my bare hands."

"Buffalo chips," Jessica guessed, stepping through that low doorway for the first time since the flood.

"Buffalo chips, indeed," Floss agreed. "I didn't believe Will when he told me what I had to build the fire with. I couldn't imagine that they would burn so well. I was absolutely positive that the smoke would smell dreadful, no matter what he said. Well, he was right about all that, but he was wrong when he said I would get used to handling them. I won't even try. A woman must draw the line somewhere."

Jimson came to Jessica with gurgles of delight and curled in her arms, staring up at her. Floss served tea in delicate china cups and set out a plate of delicious, crumbling white cookies that she unpacked from a decorated tin. "These come from Marshall Field's," she explained. "They are a real favorite of Will's."

Although she was full of questions about managing the little dugout, she acted as if each problem were a new challenge in a highly entertaining game.

Jessica was amazed at how easy Floss was to talk to. She was interested in everything, from the birds that sang around the door, to her nephew's plans for his ranch. She had a wonderful knack of poking fun at herself, laughing merrily at how ridiculous her Chicago clothes were for anyone coming to the frontier even for a visit. Jessica enjoyed herself so much that she overstayed her visit and had to gallop Dancie all the way to the schoolhouse to pick the boys up on time.

Jessica did not visit again over the weekend, but Will brought Floss and Jimson to join them in their pew at church. Jessica thought she had never seen so much craning of necks and peering from under bonnets as the congregation did that Sunday.

"For heaven's sake, tell me what I am doing wrong," Floss whispered to Jessica as they looked up the hymn number in the book they held between them.

"Don't worry about it," Jessica told her. "Those are the first leg-of-mutton sleeves they've seen in this cow town."

Jessica should have guessed what would happen. When Floss caught her little play on words and giggled, Will turned to glare at Jessica instead of his aunt.

Jessica had hoped to get a few more words with Floss, but Roy Blanding caught her coming out of church. By the time Jessica got away from him, her new friend was deep in conversation with the minister's wife, Mrs. Allen.

Each day of that next week, Jessica stopped by, if only for a few minutes. These had been such pleasant lighthearted visits that Jessica was unprepared for Floss's greeting on Wednesday.

That day Jessica felt something different in the air the minute she brought Dancie to a stop outside the dugout. Floss was waiting at the door for her with Jimson on her hip. "Come quickly," she told Jessica. "I have been bursting to see you. I had an adventure that I am dying to tell you about."

"An adventure?" Jessica asked, pulling off her bonnet and shawl to reach for the baby.

"Sit, sit," Floss said, practically bouncing with excitement. "The tea will be ready in minutes." Her eyes were shining and full on Jessica's face. "I had a caller late yesterday afternoon," she said in an important tone. "He really didn't come to see me, though. He was looking for you."

Jessica frowned thoughtfully and waited.

"Oh, come now, Jessica Findlay," Floss went on teasingly. "We both know that you have hair like spun light and eyes like the Kansas sky and the ripest mouth that ever warmed a face, but you can't have *that* many male admirers. Must I give hints? Must I remind you that he is dark of complexion and magnificently built for all that he is slender as a reed?"

Jessica felt the slow flush of color move into her face as her heart did that ridiculous thing again, that leap that left her a little breathless. Wheeling Hawk. Who could Floss be describing except Wheeling Hawk?

"Never mind," Floss said, rising and walking to the stove. "You don't have to tell me that you know who I mean. It's written all over your face."

Floss reached into the box that served as a cupboard and set out a cookie tin. She was careful to stay busy and not catch Jessica's eye as she chattered on. "The poor fellow, he's lucky that I didn't screech when he pushed open the door and walked in without even knocking."

"Indians always do that," Jessica explained swiftly. "I've always understood that it is because they don't think about owning land the way we do. They feel that all the land belongs to all the creatures, and each can go where he wishes. That habit of theirs has scared some people half to death."

Floss was frowning thoughtfully. "The minute I saw his face, I wasn't afraid. He looked at me with such a shocked expression that I actually felt sorry for him. He glanced at Jimson and then back at me almost as if he couldn't believe his eyes. Then he called your name urgently and said, 'She's all right, isn't she? Not sick or anything?'"

Floss paused, as if waiting for Jessica to explain. When Jessica could not find the words to begin, Floss spoke softly. "Jessica," she said, "never mind that we have known each other less than a week. We are friends. I had never spoken face-to-face like that with an Indian man. He is beautiful. Tell me about this man who calls himself Wheeling Hawk. Tell me why his face shadowed with such concern when he asked about you."

Jessica had trouble drawing a breath deep enough to answer. Floss must have sensed her difficulty. She rose again and turned away to pour the hot water on the tea leaves. She stood at the stove with her back to Jessica, waiting for the tea to steep.

"He saved my life," Jessica began. "Mine and Jimson's. There was a flood." She hadn't tried to tell anyone that whole story since the day it happened. She found herself shivering from the memory as she told Floss about those endless hours. Yet even as she spoke, she realized that she had replayed those hours over and over in her mind so many times that she remembered the tiniest little thing about Wheeling Hawk. She had to catch herself to keep from telling Floss more than she needed to, like the way she had felt so safe and so treasured dreaming against Hawk's back; how his song had come back to her over and over since that day.

Floss's eyes darkened, and she caught her lip between her teeth as if annoyed. "That Will Reynolds," she said crossly. "He hasn't always been that way, you know. When we were children, closer than brother and sister, he was the most wonderful, open person about everything. But since the fire. . . ." Her voice trailed off for a moment. When she began again, she spoke briskly. "But why didn't he tell me about that? You'd think he'd be so grateful that he would tell the whole entire world. Instead, he gives everyone a million chances to misunderstand him when a few words would make everything as clear as morning." She sighed and shook her head. "No wonder your friend was so concerned. No wonder he looked at Jimson bouncing on my hip with such relief."

She fell silent. When she spoke again, she seemed like a different woman. "Will and I are all there are, you know. My sister was the oldest child and I was the youngest. There was seventeen years' difference between us, which made it easy for Will to get an aunt near his own age."

She sighed and turned to the cupboard where the dishes were kept. "Your beautiful Indian friend left this for the baby," she told Jessica, handing her a wooden carving. "Along with his best wishes to you."

Jessica turned the toy in her hand. The wood had been carved by hand and polished until it felt like satin to her touch. A ball had been carved within a ball so that when she shook it, the inside ball rattled around. Jimson crowed and lunged for the trinket. Jessica released it into his hand with reluctance.

Looking up, Jessica realized that Floss, across from her, was slumped in that discouraged way she had been that first night in Jessica's room. Her bright eyes had darkened, as if with pain.

"Will really breaks my heart, Jessica. You can't imagine how close we've been since we were just kids. When Will lost his parents with cholera, as a baby, my parents took him to raise. Papa died the year I was sixteen. Will was only twelve. Mama simply gave up when everything was lost in the fire two years ago. Will and I are all the family that either of us has left. I want to help him more than anything in the world."

She paced the room restlessly a few minutes before taking the seat across from Jessica again. "I planned to come out and do what you have done, get the baby off to a good start while Rosemary got back on her feet. I can't stay, you know. I have a job I must go back to, if I don't want to lose it."

Her face flushed with sudden color. "I also have a friend I must go back to before he finds company he likes better than mine."

She was staring at her hands, twisting them together on the table in front of her. "You can't imagine how I have puzzled this problem of Will's in my mind. I feel so terribly responsible to see that everything goes right for him and the baby. Yet, even if I gave up my own life to come out here and help raise Will's child, it wouldn't be right for either of them. Will needs to marry again." She glanced up at Jessica as if pleading for understanding. "Will is a warm, loving man for all that stiff, shy way he acts. I have a confession to make, Jessica. When I heard about you, I hoped, really hoped, that maybe you and Will might learn to love each other. . . ."

She grinned at Jessica's startled look. "Don't worry, I knew better the first day we met. It was clear to me at once that you were a woman in love and that Will wasn't the lucky man. Being in love sets a sheen on a girl.

"Then when you went out for that water and Will followed you, I thought I would break up laughing right in the middle of the story your father was telling me. You practically caught him and the bucket in that door. I could tell he was mad enough to wring your neck."

She giggled. "In fact, I teased him about it. I asked him if he had been bold with you and gotten put down properly."

Jessica gasped. "You didn't."

"Of course I did," she replied in an airy way. "You mustn't tell him I told you this, but he just snorted and said he would just as soon put his hand into a bear trap."

"What an awful thing to say!" Jessica cried.

Floss stared at her. "Oh, you don't know Will well enough. From him that's a high compliment. Except for Rosemary, who was a very special case, Will really admires people who can take care of themselves."

She refilled Jessica's cup and then her own. "Knowing that you are a woman in love, I was still wondering when that beautiful young man came today. He was so bitterly disappointed not to see you here. And then, the very moment that you realized who I was talking about, your face told me that he is the lucky man."

Jessica felt a chill of shock at Floss's words. She needed to protest what Floss was saying. She needed to argue that a white woman and an Indian could not be in love. Not even to herself had she admitted how much her mind had dwelt on Wheeling Hawk since the day they met. She hadn't looked in a mirror without remembering his description of her hair, nor closed her eyes in sleep without recalling the warmth of that quiet ride, dozing against him as his horse picked its careful way home.

"Don't say anything, Jessica. If this is a secret, it is safe with me. But I need your help, as a friend, and as someone who loves little Jimson. Help me find someone who will come and keep this place and care for the child. Will will never let his son live away from him until he is grown, not even with me if I had a place. Yet he may never marry, either. He loved Rosemary as every woman dreams of being loved. Help me find someone that Will can hire, so he can go about the business of being a rancher and a father."

"I'll do everything I can," Jessica promised, hearing her own voice strange in her ears. Not even Floss must know how great a turmoil she had started in Jessica with her words about Wheeling Hawk. "Let me talk to Melanie and Papa. Surely there is some way we can help."

When she left that afternoon, Jessica turned and waved back at Floss and Jimson in the dugout doorway. Her body felt stiff in the saddle. Her neck hurt as if she had done a hard day's work and not had a chance to rest. How could she be in love and be so unhappy? Was this how it was to be in love, to be warmed and chilled at the same time, to flush with hope and ache with hopelessness in the same moment?

The washing that Jessica had helped Melanie hang out before she left to get the boys was whipping like ghosts on the rope line. After gathering it in, Jessica stood and folded it on the kitchen table as she told Melanie about Floss's problem.

Melanie nodded thoughtfully. "I wondered about her staying on out here when I saw how young she was, and how pretty."

"Surely there must be some woman out here who hasn't a family or all the work she needs," Jessica said. "Maybe someone who has lost a husband and is alone?"

Melanie frowned. "Usually such women go back East to live out their years with their families." Then she brightened. "Do you know who should know? Preacher Allen. He goes all over the countryside on his pastoral calls. And your good friend Rachel. Between the post office and that store, she knows everyone in the county."

She paused. "Maybe you should take your friend Floss on a little jaunt to town and introduce her to Rachel and her parents and tell them what is needed."

Jessica looked at Melanie thoughtfully. That was a good idea. And how much fun it would be to go into town with Floss. Then a sudden chill came as she recalled what Roy Blanding had said about "people talking." What if she really was the subject of gossip for staying with the baby in Will's dugout? What if people looked at her the way they looked at the dance-hall girls?

Floss was as excited as a child when Jessica proposed the trip to her.

"Now don't dress up," Jessica cautioned

her. "Anything you wear will be wonder enough to the people around here."

Floss giggled. "I have a very fancy hat with feathers that swoop. You don't recommend that?"

Jessica chuckled. "Not unless you want to fight off trail-weary cowboys with your shopping basket."

The townspeople guessed Floss's identity at once. She and Jessica were constantly stopped by neighbors and friends, wanting to be introduced to Floss Abney and to admire little James Reynolds, who responded to this attention with his father's unsmiling stare.

Roy Blanding, grinning from ear to ear, came striding toward them just outside Landers' store.

"Uh, oh," Jessica murmured under her breath.

"Trouble in a ten-gallon hat?" Floss whispered.

"We can always cross our fingers," Jessica told her, summoning a faint smile for Roy.

"I've driven by twice and missed you," Roy told Jessica when the introductions were over. His tone sounded like an accusation. "Would you ladies join me for a bit of refreshment?" He lifted his eyebrows archly at Floss. "You can't imagine how hard it is to catch up with this Jessica here."

"Oh, but I can," Floss assured him soberly. "If Jessica were in Chicago, the gentlemen would stand in line just to tell her good morning."

He looked at Floss doubtfully, then took Jessica's arm. "Well, let me tell you. If anybody tried something like that with my Jessica around here, he'd see the business end of a horsewhip mighty fast. You will join me?"

"I'm afraid not," Jessica told him, pulling her arm away. "We have lots to do before the baby gets worn out."

"But we need to talk about the house," he protested. "Mother says —"

They were saved by Rachel flying out the front door of the store. "Jessica," she cried, seizing her friend in a hug. "This has to be the famous Aunt Floss."

Lost in this exchange, Roy grumbled something and backed away as Rachel led them into the store.

Mrs. Landers listened to Floss's problem sympathetically. "Little ones are cherished out here," she told Floss. "We'll put the word out and see what we can do to help that young man. Nothing is forever, but if we could just find someone to see him through the winter, that would be a start."

While Jimson dozed on the sofa upstairs at the Landers', Rachel and Floss got acquainted over tea. When Floss began wrapping the baby to leave, Rachel rose to lead them out.

"I don't believe Mr. Reynolds has picked up his mail these past few days," she said as she showed them down the stairs. "I think there's even a letter there for you, Floss."

She emerged from her post room with two

envelopes. "Agatha again," she said, handing Jessica her letter. "And I was right, there is one for you," she told Floss.

Floss took the envelope eagerly, only to frown when she read the return address. Hastily, almost awkwardly, she thrust it into her muff. Her smile seemed forced as she thanked Rachel for her hospitality and her promise of help. The way the color had drained so suddenly from her face bothered Jessica through the quiet drive home.

At the dugout, Jessica helped Floss inside with the baby and her basket of purchases. "I hope the trip didn't wear you out," Jessica told her.

Floss shook her head. "It isn't that," she said. "I loved every minute of it. Thank you so very much, Jessica."

Floss's voice echoed in Jessica's head. She had never heard her voice sound so dispirited. She hardly could have been that discouraged by what Mrs. Landers had said.

Whatever it was, something had taken Floss Abney's mind a million miles away during that trip home and left her as unsmiling as her nephew, Will Reynolds.

Chapter Thirteen

THE winter that Jessica wasn't ready for frosted the fields with white as she delivered the boys to school that morning. By late afternoon the wind had switched and begun to whip in from the north. Daylight faded early under a curdled gray sky.

As Jessica was saddling Dancie to go after the boys, Melanie brought a lantern to the barn door. "You don't have to light this unless you need it," she told Jessica. "But there's no point in Dancie stumbling home in the dark."

Jessica rode through the dusk toward the schoolhouse buried in her own thoughts. She stopped at the Reynolds dugout only for a brief moment to tell Floss hello and explain that she feared that their daily visits were over.

"I understand," Floss told her. "Of course

I'll miss you, but Will is working here at home now, and I'll have him for second-best."

Jessica had ridden well past the Reynolds dugout when she heard a faint musical sound borne on the biting wind. She lowered the scarf from her face to look around for its source.

No bird made such a call. This was a tune, a plaintive melody rising and falling, seeming to come from everywhere and nowhere at the same time. She felt a sudden panic, unable to decide whether to try to light the lantern or brace her rifle against the saddle. As she groped in her apron pocket for matches, she realized that a shadow was separating itself from the grove of trees on the hill beyond.

Once clear of the shadows of the trees, the horseman remained stationary a moment until she could recognize him. Wheeling Hawk.

Why did her heart have to leap like that at the sight of him, slender and straight, smiling at her in the dusky light?

"Oh," she gasped with relief. "It's you."

He wheeled the pony to her side instantly. There beside her in that uncertain light, his smile was even more wonderful than she remembered.

"Greetings, Jessica," he said in that soft voice she recalled too well.

"Greetings yourself," she said, smiling back at him. "You know, you scared me."

"I hoped you would hear my flute and know I was there," he said. "Let me ride along with you. It is dark for you to be out alone."

"I'm only going to the schoolhouse and back," she told him, touched by this concern.

"I guessed," he said. "I have seen your father go and waited in the hope you might come." Then he spoke again into the silence with a question. "Why didn't you tell me the child was not your son?"

She brought Dancie to a skidding stop in astonishment. "It never occurred to me that anyone thought Jimson was mine."

He shrugged, his eyes warm on her face. "I saw you there caring for the child like any wife of a Wihio," he explained. "Then, at your father's house, the young father faced me with anger that we had ridden under the same blanket."

"But now you know," she reminded him. "Floss, the baby's aunt, must have told you."

He nodded. "Now she tends the child and you tend your brothers to the school and back. Such a maiden as you should have children of your own to tend."

Feeling the flush of color rise to her face, Jessica was grateful for the darkness. The things he said would have been rudely forward if anyone else said them. Yet, coming as they did, with such quiet directness, she felt no offense. And how safe she felt with him beside her.

But just ahead, light gleamed across the snow-patched fields from the windows of the sod schoolhouse where her brothers waited.

She changed the subject swiftly. "The flute," she said. "It sounded so beautiful back there."

He smiled and pulled it from his garment for her to see. "Such flutes sing songs of comfort and love for my people."

She turned the delicate wooden flute in her mittened hands. "It is beautiful." Then, handing it back to him, she smiled. "So is your name, but it is awfully long to say. Do your people have nicknames?"

"Nicknames," he repeated. "That word I don't know."

"It means a shortened name. For instance, my brother's real name is Thaddeus, but he is always called Tad. Hawk," she decided. "Can't I just call you Hawk? That's a beautiful short name."

"Whatever name you say is beautiful," he told her. Then he drew his pony to a stop. "From here you ride on alone, Jessica. It is better."

He didn't have to explain that the others wouldn't understand their friendship, that even the children would recoil in terror simply because his gleaming bronze skin and black braids identified him as Indian. They both knew, but this didn't keep the knowledge from flaring in her like anger. "I will see you again?" she asked, embarrassed at her own boldness but unable to hold the words back.

"I care for you," he said quietly. "We will ride together again if you are willing."

"I am willing," she whispered, suddenly fighting a rush of tears.

He smiled at her again. Then, wheeling on his mount, he was gone.

During those weeks that followed, Jessica felt that she lived in two separate worlds, moving invisibly from one to the other. The north wind continued to rage across the plains. It tore the last leaves from the sycamore trees and howled through the chinks of the log cabin. Each morning as Jessica set off with the boys, the sky seemed darker, as if even the sun dreaded to face the bitter days that came steadily, one after another.

Yet daily, Jessica, bundled completely to protect her skin against that freezing wind, rode forth into the dark afternoons with a light heart. She did not stop at the Reynolds dugout but cut a wide berth for fear that Will, seeing her pass, might also see Hawk come out of the trees to meet her.

Even knowing what significance it held for Hawk, Jessica did not protest when Hawk wrapped the buffalo robe around them both as they sat on their ponies. In that place of shared warmth, they talked with their fingers twined and their eyes seeking each other out in the dusky light. The time was always brief, yet Jessica never rode away from Hawk without pain. He sang to her. He told her stories from the lore of the Cheyenne. He told her that he loved her in a hundred subtle ways, until she even stopped trying to conceal her love for him.

And winter kept deepening. By the tenth of November, the light snows that fluttered in at night had begun to cling to the frozen earth.

Once the freeze was deep enough for butchering the hogs, the daylight hours were too short for the work that needed to be done. Jessica and Melanie rendered the lard for the winter cooking while tending the fires, curing the hams and side meat in the smokehouse out back.

After driving a row of heavy stakes into the earth the length of the house, Patrick Findlay laid boards against these supports, making an alley a couple of feet wide between this fence and the cabin's outside wall. Every moment that he was not busy at some other tasks, he wheeled barrows of earth and fallen leaves to fill this space and hold in what heat he could. He banked the sides of the barn the same way, filling those frames with stale hay and animal waste shoveled from the barnyard.

Although Jessica always saw Floss, Will, and the baby at church, and a few times Will accepted Melanie's invitation for Sunday lunch, Jessica had gone for weeks without a real visit with Floss. Not even Melanie asked Jessica about this. She thought she understood. Not only was Jessica needed for the work at home, but Floss was no longer alone in the dugout with Jimson. Now that Will had finished helping Mr. Smothers, he was putting up a barn on his own land.

Jessica let Melanie think what she would. She did indeed work hard at home, but she rode like the wind when she left to get the boys. Nothing must stand between her and those treasured moments with Hawk. How could she be a sensible guest when her heart was leaping ahead to the waiting figure in the grove beyond?

Once at church, Floss seized a private moment to ask Jessica a piercing question. "You aren't staying away because of Will, are you?" she asked. "For if you are, I promise I shall make him behave."

Jessica shook her head and laughed. It was an honest denial. Her time with Wheeling Hawk had pushed all other things so far from her mind that they might as well not have existed. Her conflicts with Will Reynolds seemed a thing of a far and distant past. In fact, as Jessica thought about it, she felt more kindly toward Will, because of things that Floss had said about him. Either that or she felt kindly toward him because she never saw him.

After the butchering was finished, the mincemeat was simmered to a thick, spicy stew, filling the house with its incredibly rich fragrance. Melanie packaged some of the fresh mincemeat and asked Jessica to go by early and take it to their friend.

Although she had passed the dugout all those weeks, she had not ridden near enough to see what changes had been made.

She was astonished to discover that Will had set a window into the sod wall by the door. Floss had taken advantage of this wide, sunlit windowsill and set her bread dough to rise there. The scent of the yeast perfumed the cozy dugout as Jessica entered. She was so surprised to realize that Will was building his stable of logs instead of sod that she mentioned it to Floss at once.

"The ground froze too fast for him," Floss explained. "Nobody can cut sod bricks from rock-solid earth." Jessica hid a grin at her friend's newly found knowledge of homesteading life.

"I wonder that he didn't wait for spring," Jessica said.

Floss's eyes flew wide. "My goodness. Then you haven't heard." She filled Jessica's cup carefully, holding the steaming teapot away from Jimson, who chortled and lunged at it from Jessica's lap. Only when Floss had filled her own cup and sat down did she explain.

"Preacher Allen found a woman named Jane Hogan, who has promised to stay the winter if she can go back to Ellis in time to help her daughter with a new baby she is expecting. She's widowed and alone and said right off that she couldn't sleep in the dugout with any man alive." A grin tugged at Floss's mouth as she spoke. At Jessica's confused expression, she laughed. "The woman is a hundred years old if she is a day."

"But Floss," Jessica protested. "If she's that old . . . how can she care for such an active baby as Jimson?"

"Oh, I only said she was a hundred," Floss laughed. "What I meant was that she's probably old enough to be Will's grandmother. Surely no one would gossip about them both being here."

"I wouldn't be so sure," Jessica said, thinking of Roy and his tale-bearing. "But then you'll be going back to Chicago!" Jessica realized aloud. "Oh, Floss, I really hate to see you leave."

"I'll miss you, too," Floss said earnestly. "And Jimson and Will. But it's time, Jessica. I will have been here over a month by the time they raise the roof on that shed of Will's. I need to be home."

That afternoon, Jessica sat silently by Hawk, not talking, just holding his hand and smiling at him.

"You grieve the loss of your friend," he said when she explained about Floss.

"It's not a loss like a death," Jessica admitted. "It is just that she is such a bright, lovely person. I hate to see her go."

"But it is right for her to go," he said.

Jessica nodded. "It is the only thing for her."

He leaned to her then and pressed his cheek against her forehead. "She may go," he told her. "But she will never leave you. She will live in your mind."

Jessica touched his face tenderly. Of course he was right. But there was more to the parting than Jessica had explained to him. Not only would she really miss Floss but she had never been able to shake off the sense of concern about her friend that had begun that day in town. She hoped that nothing had gone wrong for Floss back in Chicago, with her job or with her friend. But Rachel, telling tales out of school as usual, had reported that the letter Floss had received that day had been put back into the outgoing mail, marked "Addressee Unknown." What could be in an envelope that would depress Floss so much that she sent it back like that, unopened?

With Jane Hogan settled into the dugout to care for Jimson, Floss packed to leave for Chicago on Monday, November 16. After church, on the day before her departure, Melanie planned a surprise farewell party. The Findlay cabin, bright with baskets of pumpkin and squashes brought from the cellar, rang with Floss's infectious laughter when she arrived to find her friends there.

Rachel was radiant in a new sea-green dress that made her eyes seem the same marvelous color. She was singing at the piano with the others when Walter Brannon appeared in the kitchen where Jessica was cutting a fresh pan of warm gingerbread.

"Come in here and you'll be put to work," Jessica warned him.

"Funny that you'd say that," he told her. "I came in to ask a favor of you."

"Well?" she prodded him.

"It's Rachel," he said, dropping his voice to a hoarse whisper. "She's got a birthday coming up, you know."

"I do know," Jessica agreed. As if Rachel didn't count the days every time they spent ten minutes together.

"Well," he began again in that same hesitant way, "you know I worked cattle around the county for a lot of different people this year?" Since he asked this like a question, Jessica nodded, although she was totally befuddled as to what he was leading up to.

"Yes," Jessica said.

"So I had some extra money," he said breathlessly. "It was a lot for me, and I bought a horse and this. . . ." The jewelry box he pulled from his pocket bore the name of Cohen, the jeweler in town whose windows Jessica liked the best of any store. "Look at it," he ordered, opening the box.

Against the black velvet matting lay a brooch. It was real gold; she could tell from its rich tone. The gold had been worked into a lacy triangle with small but perfect emeralds set at the corners.

"It's beautiful, Walt," she breathed. "I've never seen anything so beautiful. Is it for Rachel?"

He nodded, beaming from her praise. "It made me think of her right off," he said. "So I want you to give it to her for her birthday."

Jessica stared at him, openmouthed. "You want *me* to give it to her? What's the matter with your doing it?"

He shook his head vigorously. "Oh, I wouldn't dare. I couldn't possibly. But I want her to have it, Jessica. It's hers, and you could give it to her for her birthday because you've always been such good friends."

"Now try to make a little sense, Walt Brannon. You saw this beautiful thing, and it made you think of one person in the world. You took a whole wad of money and bought it, and now you can't possibly give it to her? Remind me to buy you a new hat, Walter Brannon. You've clearly baked your brains away in the sun. Or maybe I'm stupid. Make me understand why you can't give it to her."

"It's not suitable," he said sullenly, obviously offended by her response. "This is something for a man to give to the girl he is going to marry or a best friend to another girl," he added hastily.

"Then may I suggest that you ask her to marry you? When she accepts your proposal, you give it to her and everything will be tidy."

"You don't have to get sarcastic with me, Jessica Findlay," he said hotly. "You know I can't propose to her, not an ordinary guy like me. She's different and special. I've never even heard of anyone like her before. She's so bright and lively, so beautiful, and a good businesswoman, too. Why, she's got more spunk than half the men in this town and any of the women. You can't ask a girl like that to marry a common rancher like me."

"I can't, but you can," Jessica corrected him, turning back to the gingerbread. Only at that moment did she realize that although Melanie was still playing the piano, with a chorus of voices following her song, Rachel's rich alto voice was not among them. Had she imagined that someone had been there in the doorway and fled at the moment she turned? Her eye had caught only the glimmer of sea green. Rachel.

Jessica heard Walt's words echo in her mind with horror. He hadn't once said Rachel's name during that long hymn of praise. For all Rachel knew, he could have been protesting his love for anyone.

She glared at Walt and flew into the next room with the gingerbread. A quick glance around proved her worst suspicion. Rachel was gone. Just that fast, she had gotten away, probably crying too hard even to see where she was going.

"Something wrong?" her father asked as he turned to her from his post behind Melanie's piano bench.

"Rachel?" she whispered.

"She stepped outside just a minute ago," he told her. Then he frowned. "I don't think she even took her coat. Maybe she left something out in the buggy."

"Buggy, my foot," Jessica thought angrily, whirling. Walt Brannon stood watching her from the kitchen door with a confused look.

"Now you've done it, Walt Brannon," she said angrily, tugging him back into the kitchen where the others couldn't hear. "Now my very best friend has gone pelting out there in the bitter cold with a broken heart because she heard you talking about being in love with someone."

"But, Jessica," he protested, turning to pull his sheepskin coat from the peg row inside the door. "I wasn't talking about someone, I was talking about her. It's just that I have no right."

"You have no right to be so blind," she told him, hastily scratching a match to set to the lantern wick. "Now take this light and go find her before she freezes. And while you're at it, let her decide if you're good enough for her."

When he glanced back at Jessica from the door frame, she felt a sudden surge of pity for him. What a nice guy to be so dense. "If she turns you down, I'll eat that lantern," she whispered after him. "Glass chimney and all."

The first few minutes weren't so bad. But as time passed and neither Walt nor Rachel returned, Jessica felt herself getting panicky. Finally, when Melanie's clock struck the quarter hour and they still weren't back, Jessica pulled Melanie's shawl around her shoulders and stepped from the darkened kitchen onto the back stoop.

The moon had risen in a sky as gray as schoolhouse slate. It silvered the snow patches in the yard and the drifts that had blown against the fenceposts. Far off, a coyote, whom Wheeling Hawk called the "little brother of the wolf," barked into the chill air. The wind ticked restlessly in the bare sycamore branches.

Then she saw them, two figures making a single shadow out by the well. Walt's head was bent over Rachel's as he sheltered her in his great wool-lined coat. The lantern, its light extinguished, sat on the ground beside Walt's boots. There was quite enough light from the moon for the two of them. In fact, Jessica thought, they probably didn't even need the moon at all. Jessica felt a painful sob rise in her throat as she stepped silently back into the house.

She stood inside the door a long time, holding her arms tightly against her chest, struggling to regain control of her emotions. Strangely, it was not Rachel and Walt that filled her mind but Wheeling Hawk. She felt that there was nothing in her life that she cherished more than those minutes of stolen time during their daily rides. Not only did she love being with him but everything he told her came back to her mind again and again. The voice of his flute, wavering with the gait of his pony, had become the music she loved best.

She had learned much from Hawk about his people, what they believed in, their words and phrases. But that night, there in the dark kitchen with the happy laughter of Floss's party sounding from the next room, she thought only of Hawk's phrase for courtship.

"Standing together in one blanket."

Like Walt and Rachel out there in the crisp darkness by the well. Like herself and Hawk. She shivered there in the doorway. She knew what lay ahead for Rachel and Walt. The future for herself and Hawk was something she didn't even dare think about.

Chapter
Fourteen

NEVER was there a worse-kept secret than Rachel and Walt's engagement. Yet, as Jessica and Melanie agreed, even if Rachel could have kept herself from whispering the exciting news to every "close friend" in town, her glowing happiness would have given it away, anyway.

"At least I got to write about it to Floss," Jessica told Melanie. "And goodness knows, there is little enough news to write to Chicago."

Melanie grinned at her. "Between your friend Floss and Agatha Williams, you get more mail than the rest of us combined. Did you write Agatha about Rachel and Walt?"

Jessica laughed. "Her mother had heard it and told her before I got a chance. Agatha has already made arrangements with her employers to come home for Rachel's birthday and engagement party."

"Nothing will be moving but sleighs by then, the way this winter is settling in," Melanie warned her.

Jessica's heart sank at Melanie's words. If the snow got much deeper, the boys' school would have to be closed. The thought of living from day to day without that quiet time with Hawk was unbearable. With every hour they spent together, their love had deepened. Although he talked very little about his own life, he was fascinated by everything that happened to her.

"They are in love then?" he asked her when she told him about Rachel and Walt. "In love as we are?"

She had taken a moment to think about that. "Very much in love," she finally told him, "but not as we are."

He had smiled and drawn her close. "I hoped you would say that. There has never been a love like ours before, Jessica."

She nodded, agreeing with him more than she wanted to. "Doesn't that scare you?" she asked.

He had pulled her away and looked intently into her face. Then he smiled that wonderfully tender smile that always melted her completely. "If I were afraid of new trails, I would not have followed this one."

New trails. Their trail to this point had been a hidden one, belonging only to themselves. What of the future?

Within a week of Floss's departure, the patches of snow had become a white blanket that stretched as far as the eye could see. On a sunlit day, the blaze of light was blinding, bringing tears to Jessica's eyes before she had ridden a mile.

"White winters are hungry winters," Hawk told her. "Only the strong will welcome spring."

The Sunday after Floss's farewell party, Roy Blanding approached Patrick Findlay at the close of the church service and asked his permission to drive Jessica home. "If Jessica wishes to join you," Jessica's father replied, his eyes on his daughter's face.

Without an excuse prepared, Jessica floundered miserably before finally agreeing to ride with him. Roy had glared so sullenly at Will Reynolds all through church that Jessica was sure she would have to listen to him rant on about "that greenhorn" all the way home.

Instead, to her surprise, Roy began at once to talk about Rachel and Walt. "I understand they plan a spring wedding," he said. "Why they want to wait so long I can't figure. Spring is every rancher's busy season." Without looking, she knew he was watching her face. "I'd thought about right after Christmas, maybe that second Sunday in January. Mother says —"

He must have seen her stir restlessly in her seat because he paused. "Something wrong, Jessica?"

"I guess not," she admitted. "But I do

wonder why you always quote your mother about everything."

"She makes very good sense," he replied. "She pointed out that the new house will be ready to use by then, and we'd have plenty of time to plan the garden and get trees in for that first summer."

Jessica tightened her lips together to keep her angry words back. So the house was ready. So there was a garden to plant and trees to set out, and that was how you got a wife. Not this one, she told herself angrily.

"You missed a nice party when Floss Abney left," she said, not caring how abruptly she was changing the subject.

"I was busy at my new place," he told her. "Anyway, I'm not much taken by any of those Reynolds greenhorns."

"Everybody was a greenhorn once," she reminded him. "At least this one is toughing it out."

"So far," he said. "There's talk around town that he's about out of money. He was already looking around to find hauling work for ready cash when he started building that log barn. What a fool's trick that was."

Since they had beaten the family home, Roy pulled the buggy in and settled back to smile at her. "You sure look pretty when the cold brings a little red to your face," he told her. "That Walt Brannon thinks he's got himself a prize bride. Wait until he takes a good look at mine."

Jessica drew her breath in slowly. Why

was she afraid to get this over with? Why couldn't she plunge right in like that first dip in a spring pond? Before she knew Hawk, Roy had only irritated and bored her. Now he sickened her. She couldn't look at his smug face without remembering the gentle eagerness of Hawk's expression. Roy's broad, strong body, which he dressed with such vain care, seemed lumbering and repulsive compared to the lean, smooth strength of Hawk's.

She looked at him thoughtfully. If she could only get over being afraid of what he might do. After all, what could he *really* do? Get mad? Yell at her? Tell people bad things about her? She needed to tell him that she wouldn't marry him, not in January, not ever. Instead, she pressed the backs of her mittens against her flaming cheeks.

"I do thank you for the ride, Roy, but I'd like to go inside. I'm thoroughly chilled out here." She paused. "You'll forgive my not inviting you in?"

"Your family should be along any minute," he said, peering toward the road hopefully.

"Then again, they might not," she warned him. "I heard Papa invite Will and his household over for dinner. They might stop by there on the way home."

She was half out of the buggy before Roy realized she was serious about going inside. As he came to help her down, he caught her by the waist and held her in midair for a minute like a helpless doll. He laughed heartily at her attempts to get free of his grasp.

"Put me down, Roy Blanding," she ordered hotly. "That's not funny and you know it."

"It's funny to me," he grinned, setting her on the frozen earth with a thud. "You've been a little feisty all your life. It's just lucky for you that I like you that way."

"Lucky for you, lucky for you," she mimicked him angrily after slamming into the house without looking back.

A single cup of coffee had been left in the pot on the back of the stove. She poured and drank it before starting a fresh pot for Melanie and her father. The hen Melanie had put in to roast had baked to a deep, glazed brown. The cornbread stuffing bursting out into the roaster smelled so richly of sage and onion that Jessica twisted off a crusty bite and popped it into her mouth. Just that one delicious taste was enough to raise her spirits and get her mind off Roy Blanding. By the time the buggy pulled into the yard, she had the table set and was singing so lustily that she didn't even hear the boys until they tumbled in the door. Will, holding his son, was right behind them along with his housekeeper, Jane Hogan.

"That's a happy sound," Mrs. Hogan said, smiling as she pulled off her shawl. "You must have had a joyful ride home."

"Roy Blanding brought her," Tad said. "He sure has a fancy buggy."

Jessica saw Will's eyes, thoughtful on her face in that brief minute before he turned

away. Something in his look made her flush.
Did he think she was singing like that because she had been squired home in somebody's fancy buggy?

"I was singing because I was so happy to
be home," Jessica told Tad.

"Anything special on Roy's mind?" Jessica's father asked.

Jessica hesitated, wishing she could talk to
him about her problem with Roy. That was
out of the question with their guests right
there in the room. She shrugged. "He wanted
to talk about that new ranch of his and the
house he has put up on it."

Her father nodded. "His mother has been
talking a lot about that place. She makes it
sound like a showplace."

"She has a real way with words," Jessica
said.

She was startled to have Will enter the
conversation. "Mrs. Blanding was talking to
Mrs. Landers about you when I was in the
store last week. She seems to think the world
of you."

Startled, Jessica looked up at him. He was
studying her in that disapproving way. She
looked away quickly, hoping he wouldn't see
her blush with embarrassment. It would be
just like Mrs. Blanding to pop off her mouth
about "dear Jessica and my Roy" in public
like that. Jessica would have given anything
to know what Will had heard, but she didn't
dare ask him. She only shrugged and turned
away.

With each new snowfall, Jessica saw her father's concern increase. The summer of drought just past had produced less hay than she could ever remember. He thinned his herd of cattle early, only to sell several more head when it was clear that they wouldn't be able to scrape a mouthful of grass from under the frozen layers of snow.

All of her life, Jessica had seen disaster coming and felt herself weaken with terror. Always when the danger had passed, the damage was less than she had dreaded.

A tornado had swept out of the southwest the April she was eight. She had felt the air pressing her body to the earth and seen the twisted black pillar sucking trees and barns and hay bales into the lowering sky. She had fled screaming to the darkness of the cellar. There she had clung to her father, crying helplessly, until the beating of the rain against the cellar door told them that the storm had passed. Although the roof had been lifted from their sod house, even her toy dishes were untouched, a cup half full of milk still in its saucer.

The year Tad was born, summer lightning had set off a prairie fire that blackened the sky as it crackled toward their cabin in scarlet waves. Even as her father had fought back the flames with carpets soaked in water, the wind had changed, turning the fury north onto the open prairie.

It was ridiculous, but the thought of not

seeing Hawk every day brought that same sense of panic. He was no longer just a part of her life. Instead, she sometimes felt that she was really only living when they were together. Maybe like the disasters of the past, their separation would not come about or, if it did, they would find some new place and time to be together. They had to. Even the thought of living without him more than a day or two at a time made her breath come short and tears rush to her eyes.

Thanksgiving weekend seemed to last forever. Will had come for dinner with his son and housekeeper. The meal had been lovely, but he had been so withdrawn during it that Jessica wanted to hurl something at him. When, after the dishes were done, she had fled the house with the excuse of getting some fresh air, he had followed her.

"I've never known anyone who thought stable fumes were fresh air," he said, coming up behind her as she patted Dancie in her stall.

"Every man to his own taste," she told him.

"Mrs. Landers invited me to her daughter's engagement party," he said after a minute.

"That was nice of her," Jessica said.

"I hope she understands why I can't come."

"You must have told her some reason."

"What do you mean, some reason?" he challenged her, suddenly angry. "And for someone who's such an expert on manners, didn't you ever hear of turning and looking at people when they talk to you?"

She turned obediently and looked at him, waiting.

It happened again. She almost couldn't believe it. One moment he was standing there, really close, talking to her, getting ready, she presumed, to tell her why he couldn't go to the engagement party. Then, as if the sight of her face was more than he could endure, he shook his head, muttered something, and stamped out of the barn.

She leaned against Dancie's steaming flesh and closed her eyes. Why was life so difficult? Will was so lonely without his Rosemary that he couldn't even be civil to another young person. Roy Blanding was so wrapped up in his own desires that he was going to have to be hit in the head with a two-by-four to understand that his dreams and hers were different. Only with Hawk could time be gentle and easy and warm with love.

On the Sunday after Thanksgiving, a fresh snow had come on such a driving wind that it had swept across the land like something swiftly running. That Monday morning, Jessica guided Dancie carefully between the drifts to get the grumbling boys to school on time. Back home, she went about her work so cheerfully that Melanie even commented on it.

"You are a happy one today," Melanie commented as Jessica let herself into the house after an errand to the barn. "Were you singing for Daisy and Brindle or just for joy?"

"Joy," Jessica told her. She ducked her

head as she unwound her scarf. How ugly it was to have secrets from people you loved. How lucky Rachel was to be able to go on about Walt to anyone who would listen. Even though she was almost bursting with joy at the hope of seeing Hawk that afternoon, she felt strained somehow that the cause of this happiness had to stay hidden.

Amazingly, Melanie did not even look as if she had a question. Instead, she sighed. "I wish that joy of yours were catching, like chicken pox or something. Your father went off to barter for some hay this morning with a face as long as a dry summer."

Jessica no longer carried a lantern on her saddle horn, even though nightfall came before she got the boys back home. Once the snow cover was complete, a sort of general glow shone everywhere so that one needed no artificial light to travel by.

Jessica tried to coax extra speed from Dancie without success. The pony stubbornly held her careful pace as they passed the Reynolds dugout.

Then, as always, Jessica looked to the grove of trees on the knoll to the west and felt her heart leap to know that Hawk was waiting there.

She was to remember the smallest detail of that meeting through the weeks to come. He rode his pony from the shadows and waited a moment, as always. There was no care in his pony's gait as he rode to her side, only eagerness.

"The days have been long without you," he said, reaching for her hand. His touch was brief, and her heavily knitted mitten should have kept her from feeling the warmth of his flesh, but it did not.

"I missed you, too," she told him, smiling at her own frankness with him. Hawk's natural openness had been "catching," as Melanie would say. As different as their lives and their ways were, together they were like one creature. Even when they didn't talk, Jessica felt his warmth, his reaching out to her, as strongly as if he had been shouting it.

"So there was great feasting," he said. "And music?"

Jessica nodded. "We always have music at our house on special days."

"Sing a song for me, and I will have the flute do it, too."

When she laughed, he cocked his head at her. "You have told me that your mother makes music on the piano to sing by. Why not a flute?"

He was right, of course. After a moment of indecision, she began to sing her father's favorite of the Christmas songs: "Angels from the realms of glory,/Wing your flight o'er all the earth." By the second line, Hawk had caught the melody, and the clear sweetness of the flute's tone almost stopped her voice in her throat.

She didn't want that song ever to end. She

wanted to go on like that forever, her voice blending with that other clear tone, spilling into the crystal air, accompanied only by the muffled rhythm of their ponies' hooves.

Instead, as the flute's voice fell silent, she felt Hawk's hand on her arm. She saw the sleigh the moment she glanced over. Her father's sleigh, loaded under canvas wrappings, had been passing on the way back from town. He had stopped the team and was staring at her and Hawk across the smooth drifts that lay between their path and the road.

"Papa," she whispered. Then she shouted it. It was too late. He had turned his face away and slapped the reins across the broad, steaming backs of his horses. They set off at a gallop, spraying fans of loose snow in their wake, as they moved east toward home.

The bells, she had heard no sleigh bells. The wind must have borne the sound away even as it had carried to her father the sound of her and Hawk's song.

"Jessica," Hawk said urgently, reaching for her hands.

She shook her head, fighting back tears. "It's not fair, Hawk. It's not fair, not right. It doesn't make any sense at all."

"Come," he said softly. "Come and be mine with my people."

When she could find no breath to answer, he nudged his mount back to motion. As they rode, he talked quietly, not facing her but speaking as if to himself, aloud.

"Around our campfires my people recite

tales about Wihio. Wihio is a spider, a trickster, a mischief maker, and a villain. In even the oldest tales, Wihio is brighter than the Cheyenne because he can fool us. Wihio, like all spiders, weaves nets to catch a man and drink the life from him."

He turned and looked strangely at Jessica. "The Cheyenne call the white man Wihio. His nets are woven of words, promises of land, of food, of safety and peace. But the web you have bound *me* in is love, and I cannot escape. I want you as my wife, Jessica. Yet I can promise you nothing better than your people have given us, endless wandering, nights of hunger, and guns leveled to kill."

Ahead in the growing darkness was the schoolhouse. Jessica could not hold back the rush of tears as she turned to Hawk. "I love you, Hawk. Oh, how dearly I love you."

He had brushed her lips with his before but never had he kissed her like this. He grasped her shoulders in those powerful hands and held her tightly before possessively pressing his mouth to hers. She clung to him, never wanting that embrace to stop. Then, before she caught her breath, he had released her, wheeled on his pony, and galloped away. She cried out in anguish, but her words, "No, Hawk, no," were whipped from her mouth by the bitter wind.

Chapter Fifteen

JESSICA barely remembered that long ride home with the boys. The moon was rising, angling paths of light across the crusted drifts of snow. Tad asked her something. Her answer must have satisfied him, but she could recall neither his question nor her own reply.

She felt as if she had been suddenly split into two separate beings. The physical Jessica held Dancie's reins and guided the pony between the drifts that lay between the schoolhouse and her home. The other Jessica was a spirit, hollowed by pain, off somewhere on a swift Indian pony, clinging to Wheeling Hawk.

"Come and be mine with my people," he had said.

She had only seen Indian villages in fuzzy photographs. She remembered clusters of tepees made of animal skin with crossed poles emerging at the top; campfires with women

and children around them. After the Indian
trouble five years before, the Indians had all
been moved onto reservations, and certainly
a reservation wasn't a place that anyone
would take a girl like herself. As she recalled
her mental picture of that Indian village, she
tried to imagine Wheeling Hawk there, moving among those campfires. It didn't work.
Her mind stopped short, refusing to picture
him in any world but her own, near her, his
eyes level and tender on her own.

She was not surprised to see her father
waiting at the gate of the barnyard. After
reining in at the back door to let the boys off,
she walked the pony to the barn.

She was prepared for her father's anger.
She was not prepared for the flinty coldness
of his eyes.

"You are never to see that Indian again,"
he told her.

She stared at him in disbelief. "Papa," she
protested, "won't you even hear me?"

"I heard enough this afternoon to make my
blood run cold," he said, loosening Dancie's
saddle with trembling hands. "I heard enough
and saw enough to realize that this was no
chance meeting. The way you rode together,
your song joined with his." His voice was
heavy with disgust. "Jessica, I swear to God
that only the memory of your mother keeps
me from taking a horsewhip to you, woman
though you may be."

"But Papa, we are friends, Hawk and I.
He saved my life."

"So now you will give back to him what he saved? Don't be a romantic fool. Did your mother bear you to squat among savages? Did your friend, as you call him, save you to become a root-grubbing squaw by a camp-fire? What can you have to say to a man like that, or he to you? What can you possibly have in common aside from both being young and foolish and romantic?"

"Much," she told him swiftly. "Hawk is *not* a savage as you say. There are differences of opinions among the Cheyenne even as there are among our people. He follows Dull Knife, one of the old chiefs who keeps trying to believe in our government's promises and trying to work effectively with the Indian agencies. That's how and why Hawk has learned to speak English so well, by working with the Indian agents in the hope that they may bring peace."

"And I suppose he is a young chief himself?" His tone so acid with sarcasm.

"Not a chief but a member of the warrior society. They serve like our police or militia. They're very important, even though they haven't a voice in the council."

"Dull Knife, warrior society, what kind of talk is this from a young lady? What need have you to know of the councils of the enemy? Jessica, I have seen white men dead because of these people, houses burned, and children stolen away never to be seen again."

"But, Papa," she wailed. Why wouldn't he understand? Hawk had talked of these raids without embarrassment. The Cheyenne had been a friendly people who had only turned warlike by necessity. Only after their own women and children had been massacred along with the warriors had the Cheyenne beaten war drums against the white men.

"I do not want this spoken of again," her father broke in. "And you are never to see that Indian again. Never."

He had turned away from her, his back stiff with fury. She stood a moment, staring after him. He had never used that tone with her before. Not in his worst tempers had she ever heard a coldness like this in his voice. She felt him lost to her in that moment, lost to her even as Wheeling Hawk was. She walked to the house, weighted by a grief too deep for tears.

On the first day they had met, the day of the flood, Wheeling Hawk had said that Patrick Findlay was known as a fair man. While Jessica felt that her father was brutally unfair not to let her explain about Wheeling Hawk, his fairness did extend to keeping the incident private between them.

How strange it was to go from his fury to Melanie's warm welcome in only a few steps. How difficult it was to turn her hands to their usual tasks with her mind and heart in such turmoil.

Only once that evening did she find herself perilously close to tears. As she knelt to check the coffee she was roasting, Melanie smiled down at her.

"How quiet you are this evening, Jessica," she said gently. "Where is the great joy with which you started this day?"

Jessica felt her father silently listening from across the room and forced a smile for Melanie. "Like the day," she said, "it has flown."

Usually Jessica loved the quiet evenings with her father and Melanie after the boys yawned off to bed. Often she and her father took turns reading to Melanie, who knitted or sewed until sleep overtook her. That night Jessica escaped to her bed early, only to lie staring into the darkness, numb with grief. Melanie must have sensed her husband's need for comfort. A little after nine, Jessica heard the scrape of the piano bench as Melanie sat down to play for him, softly so as not to waken the children.

The wind rose during the night, howling around the cabin like a band of wolves. Whimpering that he was freezing even under his comforter, Tad crawled in to nestle spoon-fashion against Jessica.

When morning came, a sun dog wreathed the sky like a giant rainbow. "It has to be twenty below to do that," Patrick Findlay said, lining stones along the back of the stove to heat for the animals' water troughs.

"Then I guess we won't have to go to school?" Jerry asked hopefully.

"I'll take you myself in the sleigh," his father replied, avoiding Jessica's eyes.

This, then, was how it would be, Jessica

195

thought. She had been a loving daughter and an obedient one, tending that child all that time without so much as a thank-you. All of that was swept away, forgotten. She would be a prisoner.

As short as the sunlit hours were, that day seemed to last forever. A few minutes outside, even with her face covered and her mittens drawn high under her sleeves, were enough to bring a painful bite of frost to Jessica's skin. The chickens huddled together on their roost, too miserable even to cluck their complaint. Only the barn gave a sense of warmth, clouded with the breath of the horses and the rich, moist scent of their flesh. Although Melanie stoked the range steadily all day, the rooms stayed chilly.

"We'll never get yeast to rise in this air," Melanie said, laughing. "Thank goodness for the buckwheat we laid in last fall."

In midafternoon, Jessica's father harnessed the horses and left to get the boys without comment. By the time the sleigh bells sounded again in the yard, an iron skillet of sausage patties had sizzled brown on the back of the stove, and Melanie was piling the buckwheat cakes on a warm platter in the oven.

Jessica was there, but not there, in a strange way. With some mumbled excuse, she escaped to the bedroom to stare at herself in the primping mirror on the shelf beside her bed. She was amazed that she looked the same. How could she hurt so much and not have it show? As she turned away, her eyes fell on the cornstalk doll Tad had made for her birthday. She lifted the tiny figure from the shelf and cradled it in her hand, tilting her palm to make the doll stand straight up.

How long ago that birthday seemed. Yet only a little more than three months had passed. But so many things had happened. Rosemary Reynolds had died. She had cared for Jimson all those weeks. The rainstorm had come with the flood and her miraculous rescue by Wheeling Hawk. Her friendship with Floss Abney was an experience Jessica couldn't have dreamed of. But Wheeling Hawk. Wheeling Hawk had been the changing force in a life that now seemed without flavor or hope. Jessica drew a deep breath and shut her eyes a long moment before replacing the doll on the shelf.

But those were all events, things that could be put into words and told about. The saddest and greatest change could not be expressed in words at all. It could only be carried like a hollow place down in her chest. Back then, under that blazing August sun, she had felt so warmly close to all the people in this house. She had been a part of everything that happened within these walls. Suddenly, she felt like a stranger to each of them, separated from her father by his anger and fear, from the others by the secret that had bled the joy from this day.

By the end of that week, Jessica feared for her own sanity. School had been dismissed on Wednesday because of the severity of the cold. The boys, restless and confined, went from one mischief to another in boredom. They whined and fought with each other, teasing poor Major until he sought refuge in the barn with the stock. Jessica would have been tempted to follow him there if she hadn't been afraid of frostbite. She and Melanie had both read themselves hoarse trying to amuse Tad. Jessica felt that if she had to play one more game with Jerry, she would throw the checkers into the fire, board and all.

After almost being lost in a blizzard between his own back door and the barn a few years before, Jessica's father had installed a line of large metal eye bolts from the back door along the fence to the barn and chicken yard. At the coming of winter, he threaded heavy rope through those rings. Even in the most blinding snowfall you could find your way if you never let that rope out of your hands. This was the first year that the icy wind was so strong that her father gripped that rope line to hold his balance when he went out to his stock.

By Friday, Jessica realized that in spite of her most valiant efforts, Melanie had figured out that something was amiss. Jessica had trouble reading. She would open a book and begin, only to have the memory of Hawk or her father's fury come between her and the print on the page. She caught Melanie's concerned eyes as she stared numbly into space.

"You are sure you feel all right, Jessica?" she would ask.

"Positive," Jessica would reply, trying again to act as if nothing had changed. Inside, she felt a rising desperation. Her sense of shock and pain couldn't last much longer; it simply couldn't.

Although the cold tempered enough by the weekend for her father to drive the sleigh to town for supplies, it was still dangerous to be outside uncovered for more than a few minutes. Even then, Jessica's breath froze into ice crystals on the scarf she pulled over her face when she went to draw water or to bring in fresh buffalo chips for the fire.

The boys pleaded to be taken along to town, but Patrick Findlay shook his head. "It's no warmer there than here," he reminded them. "This kind of cold means danger. Church tomorrow is more than soon enough to get you out into it."

Usually Jessica knew what errands took her father to town. Usually she and Melanie went over the list together, deciding more on what they could do without than what they needed to buy. This time Melanie only asked if Jessica wanted her father to bring more yarn for the caps she was knitting. Jessica shook her head. She was too listless to keep the needles flying as she had all fall. And she hated to ask any favors of her father, knowing how changed he was toward her.

Melanie began to watch for her husband's return as soon as darkness fell. Although nothing was said, Jerry walked by the window, peering out every few minutes. When the jingle of sleigh bells sounded from outside, Melanie flew to the door with the boys tumbling after her. Jessica, awkwardly alone by the stove, watched the jubilant greeting as her father stamped the ice from his boots at the door. Tears pressed hot behind her eyes.

None of the news her father told at dinner was good. Some of their neighbors had lost stock that had strayed and been frozen without shelter. One of the soldiers from the fort had been caught that night of deepest chill and suffered terrible frostbite. He would live, they said, but one of his legs had been amputated at the knee.

Suddenly, her father's eyes were on Jessica. "I made some plans for you, Jessica. I was visiting in the store and it all just fell together. You are to take your things to church, and one of those English families will deliver you over to Victoria for a visit with Agatha."

Even as she stared at him, speechless with surprise, Melanie spoke up swiftly. "I might have started that whole thing, Jessica," she said quietly. "I have been worrying to your father about your being so shut in here. You've looked so peaked lately that I've been concerned. I thought maybe a change of scene. . . ." Her voice trailed off doubtfully, her tone pleading for understanding.

"It's all right," Jessica said. "It's really all right. I just didn't expect it."

His voice became more buoyant, as if he were relieved by her words. "The timing is perfect. Agatha's planning to come up for

Rachel's party next Saturday. You could come back home with her and still have had a week away."

"Even if it turns warmer, there still won't be much to do around here," Melanie added. "Jerry will be happy to take over your chores."

"He doesn't look so happy," Tad said, watching his brother's face.

The laughter that followed cleared the air a little. Jessica rose and brought the iron skillet of cornbread to the table to pass fresh wedges around. Jerry cut his and laid a slice of pale butter inside. "If I have to do the work of two, I guess I'll have to eat for two," he said in a resigned tone.

"That's fine with me, as long as Jessica isn't the one you're eating for," Melanie said, passing him the dish of honey to spread on his hot bread. "If she gets any skinnier, she's going to fly in the wind like a tumbleweed."

Jessica insisted on doing the dishes alone over Melanie's protest. "I need to think," Jessica protested. "I have to decide what to take, and nothing clears my head like hot, soapy dishwater."

Washing the dishes didn't clear her head, it only confused her. Melanie was innocent of any suspicious motives; Jessica knew that. But Melanie had always been too quick-eyed to fool. She had been openly concerned about Jessica's listless manner and how loosely her clothes had begun to hang.

But what about her father? Had he set this

visit up to keep her from sneaking off to see Wheeling Hawk? Surely he trusted her more than that. And yet, he hadn't let her out of the house alone since the day it happened. She didn't dare ask herself what she would do if she had a chance. She knew what the answer to that was.

As for going to see Agatha, Jessica sighed at the thought. She liked Agatha, always had since they were little. And except when she got off on the subject of some young man, she was bright, amusing company. But Jessica felt mysteriously old, as if her grief over her father's feelings and her loneliness for Hawk had lost her youth for her.

Melanie was more interested in her packing than Jessica herself was. Melanie insisted on sending with her the fine camel's hair shawl that had been a gift to Melanie from an aunt in the East.

"I wish you had a pair of shoes to wear while you are there," Melanie said. "Those people dress awfully fancy from what I hear. I'm afraid you will be uncomfortable in your boots."

Jessica smiled and shook her head. She wished she cared even that much about the impression she would make. But it didn't matter. Nothing much seemed to matter a great deal anymore. Except Wheeling Hawk, who looked past appearances to the heart that beat within.

Chapter Sixteen

ONLY that Sunday morning as Jessica wound her thick fair braids around her head did it really dawn on her that she would be away from home for almost a whole week. It wasn't unusual for her father to be away, often for a month or more on a cattle drive. Sometimes during roundup time, Jerry spent a night or two with a friend from school. But except for those infrequent times that Jessica had spent Saturday afternoon and night with Rachel, she had never slept in any bed but her own.

She would be among strangers except for Agatha, whom she had only seen briefly after church since Agatha had started work in Victoria in the summer.

Her instinct was to fly into the kitchen and tell her father and Melanie that she had changed her mind. She stared at the mirror with unseeing eyes. "I'm tired of new experiences," she told herself silently. "I'm sick of being tugged this way and that every time I turn around."

It was almost laughable to remember how she had dreaded her sixteenth birthday. She had been so afraid of having to take her life into her own hands. Instead, she had been caught in one helpless situation after another. Not that she regretted taking care of Jimson. She couldn't love him any better if he were her own.

And she certainly didn't regret her meetings with Hawk. If anyone had told her three months before that the joy of loving was worth the pain it brought, she would have scoffed at the words.

Hawk's voice echoed in her mind, as they had over and over since that day. "Come and be mine with my people."

Melanie was calling that breakfast was ready. The heavy scent of smoked meat in the stale air of the closed-up cabin made her feel a little nauseated. Maybe she was going to be sick, she thought hopefully, then she wouldn't have to go off among strangers in Victoria.

"Nonsense," her father announced when she explained why she didn't want to eat. "Everybody gets a jump under the belt when he tries something new. You just tough it through. You'll laugh about it tomorrow. See if you don't."

"Why are they coming to our church, anyway?" Jessica asked. "They have a church of their own in Victoria. Agatha says it is really different. She calls it the queen's church."

Jessica's father nodded. "It seems that one of the gentlemen has a younger brother here for an early Christmas visit. Rachel said he was very excited about local life, so they are bringing him over to see our church."

Jessica stared at him. Why did this make her angry? Who did these people think they were that they had any right to come and gawk at her own church, as if it were a freak show?

"I wonder what else is on his list," she said, not bothering to hide her distaste for the idea.

Her father's eyes met hers in a cool, level glance. "Probably buffalo, a cattle drive, and an Indian village," he said, as if challenging her.

She dropped her eyes and fell silent.

Rachel's mother introduced Jessica to Mr. Montgomery and his brother just as church was about to begin.

"So you are Agatha's dear friend," the elder Mr. Montgomery said, offering her his hand. "You cannot imagine how delighted we are that you are finally going to pay us a visit."

Jessica, who had ridden all the way from home with growing dread, could not honestly return this compliment. Yet she was amazed to feel her stiff-backed resentment melting away at the warmth of his greeting. She thought the man handsome, for what he was of course, which was a completely different kind of man than she had ever met before. The flesh of his face was remarkably pink beneath a carefully trimmed gray mustache. His eyes, as blue as Jimson's, glistened with pleasure as he turned to present his brother.

Never had she seen two brothers less alike. Young Mr. Geoffrey was as slender as his older brother was portly. His eyes, of the same remarkable blue, were hidden behind spectacles, giving his long, unbearded face a solemn aspect.

Yet, when he bowed over Jessica's hand, she would have sworn that he winked at her.

Church would have been vastly more enjoyable if Roy and his mother had not taken every opportunity to crane their necks to stare at Mr. Montgomery and his brother there in the Findlay pew. Will Reynolds seemed even colder and stiffer than usual, sitting very quietly and staring stolidly straight ahead.

That was one nice thing about her father's plans for her, Jessica decided. She would miss one Sunday dinner with Will ignoring her while Melanie chattered away with Mrs. Hogan.

Jessica was relieved that her hosts did not dawdle after church but whisked her into their sleigh as soon as she had kissed Melanie good-bye.

She knew it was mean, but Jessica almost giggled at the expression on Roy's face as the matched gray horses sped the sleigh away with the liveried driver up in front and herself with the two men bundled under furs in the compartment in back.

The twelve-mile ride to Victoria passed at record speed. By the time they arrived in the little town, Jessica had learned that Geoffrey was at the university in Oxford and had ambitions to become a scholar himself. His accent was no stranger than his brother's, but he had a sly way of jesting that caught Jessica off guard. She would be puzzling about what he had said, only to realize that his eyes were twinkling merrily at her from behind those heavy glasses.

Agatha embraced her, tearful with joy. Mrs. Montgomery, a genial blonde woman as generously built as her husband, was as cordial in welcome as he had been. Jessica caught only a glimpse of the magnificent furnishings before Agatha whisked her off to her own quarters.

"You talk like them," Jessica cried in amazement as Agatha hung Jessica's spare dress away. "And that outfit is darling."

"It's not an outfit," Agatha corrected her. "It's my uniform. But isn't it wonderful?"

Jessica had to agree. The black of the trim dress set off Agatha's auburn hair beautifully, a tiny cap poised on her generous pompadour like a captive butterfly.

"You can't go out in that hat," Jessica said, horrified.

Agatha giggled. "Oh, heavens no. I have a bonnet, but they like to have everything here in the house to appear to be just as much like 'back home' as possible.

Then, turning, she clasped both hands and tightened her shoulders. "What did you think of him? Of Mister Geoffrey? Isn't he adorable? Did you ever see a man wear such elegant clothing?"

"No," Jessica told her after a moment's thought. "In fact, I wondered that his legs didn't freeze in those pipe-stem pants with nothing more than a layer of that fine woolen flannel to cover them. Mine certainly would."

"Jessica, you are such a one. He's not just another skinny young man, you know. He comes from real aristocracy. His father is called sir, you know. Isn't that the most romantic thing ever? If a girl was to catch that man, she might get to meet the queen, Victoria herself."

Jessica looked at Agatha in astonishment. What kind of crazy idea did Agatha have about herself and Geoffrey?

Why did Agatha's mind work like that? "The most romantic thing," Agatha had said. Her words recalled Jessica's father asking her, in that sarcastic tone, "And I suppose he is a young chief himself?" Had her father considered her feeling for Hawk as ridiculous as she found Agatha's giddy excitement about an English title? The thought made her blush with shame.

"Jessica," Agatha was saying, "are you all right?"

"I'm fine," Jessica assured her, dragging

her mind back to her friend. "Still catching my breath from that drive."

Jessica realized that Agatha's job had many parts. She served as a lady's maid when Mrs. Montgomery was dressing or readying for bed. She helped with the housecleaning, as well as serving the family meals prepared by Boney, as Agatha called the dour cook who controlled the kitchen. Boney's husband was Ned, the houseman and groom, who had driven them home from church at such a marvelous clip.

"Boney and Ned have a little sod house in back by the stable," Agatha explained. "In the spring, the master plans to build them a proper house, as well as add several rooms to this one."

"This is already a big house," Jessica commented.

"Nothing like what they have back home," Agatha said proudly. "Wait until you see the pictures. It's like a castle."

Jessica listened thoughtfully as Agatha chattered on. Agatha was different here among these people. Not only had she acquired that faint British accent, but her manner was changed. Jessica wasn't sure that she liked these changes very much. There was something snobbish about the way Agatha dwelt on the titles in the family, the value of the gold candlesticks on the mantel above the hearth, and the crystal and porcelain that adorned the table.

She was relieved when Agatha finally quit

209

bragging about money and position and mentioned her mistress.

"You can't imagine how pleased Mrs. Montgomery was when the master said your father had approached him about this visit. We've both been so eager for you to come. I just hope that you will like it well enough to come back to work here. You and I would share this room and have lots of good times. The work is really not hard, nothing like what you have to do at home."

Jessica studied her friend thoughtfully, startled by Agatha's words. "We'll see," she said vaguely. "How did you say that my father and Mr. Montgomery connected to make these plans?"

"Well, I wasn't there, of course," Agatha said. "But as I understand it, Rachel's mother told your father that the master was my boss. Then your father just walked up and talked to him."

"I see," Jessica said.

"What do you see?" Agatha asked, frowning at her friend's tone.

"Just I see." Jessica shrugged.

Agatha had not exaggerated about the beauty and value of the furnishings in the Montgomery home. Neither had she exaggerated about the ease of her job. These people seemed to play at life. Guests, bundled to the eyebrows in fine furs, came by daily to laugh and talk by the fire over sandwiches and cakes. When they were not entertaining at home, Mr. and Mrs. Montgomery went off to visit friends, quite often taking Agatha along with them. Agatha said that many of these parties did not end until the early hours of the morning.

The contrast between their lives and that of her parents overwhelmed Jessica. She felt guilty to be so warm and snug by this roaring fire when she knew that Melanie was heating bricks to warm the children's beds and measuring every cup of meal in an effort to make the food stored in the cellar last until spring. Amazingly, Agatha, who had been raised in a sod house on a barren ranch, was as wasteful of time and fuel and food as her employers were.

The other thing that Agatha had not exaggerated about was the attractiveness of young Geoffrey Montgomery. And strangely enough, Jessica's enjoyment of his company began with a fight.

Geoffrey hung around her in a way that got on her nerves. Whenever Agatha was busy or away with her employers, so that Jessica could possibly get an hour to herself, he appeared out of nowhere and sat grinning at her. Then he asked questions that she considered insulting.

"Did you go to school?" he asked when he found her sitting and staring into the fire.

She stared at him. "Of course I did. Why?"

"I was just curious," he said. "Do you like to read?"

"Very much," she told him.

He was barely smiling but clearly amused

when he asked, "And whose work do you like to read?"

"Dickens," she told him. "Thackeray, and Hawthorne sometimes."

"Well," he said, nodding as if with grudging approval. "And can your friend Agatha read?"

"What do you really think of us out here?" she asked, her voice rising a little. Of course, Agatha could read. She had had the same chance to learn that Jessica and Rachel had. But Agatha had never been very fond of school, now that Jessica thought of it. Still, Jessica didn't like this young man asking in such a patronizing way.

Instead of answering, he slid down the side of the fireplace from where he had been standing to sit cross-legged on the hearth rug. Suddenly, he looked as boyish as Jerry. The firelight reflected in his glasses as he plucked at the braid of the rug thoughtfully.

"I don't know what to think," he said finally. "I'm really interested, you know. I hoped to learn a lot about life out here, but instead, my brother and his wife have simply made a little corner of England here at the end of the world. And it's much too cold and too far from place to place to explore on my own."

"I'm really sorry," she said. "I thought you were making fun of us. Ask me. I'll tell you anything I can."

Sometime during that conversation, she must have forgotten that he wasn't Jerry.

When the Montgomerys returned, with Agatha in tow, she and Geoffrey were both sitting on the hearth rug, staring into the fire and talking a mile a minute.

Geoffrey jumped up without embarrassment to greet his brother excitedly. "Wait until I tell you what Jessica —" only then did he pause and blush as he corrected himself — "Miss Findlay has been teaching me."

That night, when both girls got upstairs, Agatha turned on Jessica in an absolute fury.

"What kind of a friend are you?" she challenged Jessica. "You have a lot of nerve coming over here to visit me and then flirting in that outrageous way with Mr. Geoffrey."

"Flirting!" Jessica cried. "I was only being polite!"

"Polite," Agatha growled, throwing herself into her bed. "You aren't fooling anybody with that blue-eyed innocence of yours."

Jessica stared at the lump in the bed for a long moment. Then she shrugged and began to undress herself. It was a good thing they were scheduled to leave the next day. Never had she seen a better example of what Melanie called "wearing out your welcome."

Agatha didn't speak to her as they dressed that next morning. Jessica, not knowing what else to do, packed her things and went down for breakfast as usual.

The cold weather had eased. While it was anything but warm, the sun blazed clear and brilliant when Geoffrey invited Jessica to walk in the garden with him.

"The garden?" she asked in disbelief.

"All right, so you can't find the garden for the snow," he admitted. "But I want to talk to you. Alone," he added when she looked at him askance.

"What would you say about my immigrating here the way my brother has?" he asked. "There's still land to buy, and I could build a house."

Jessica turned and studied him, realizing that during those days she had grown fond of him in a peculiar way. He was a gentle, teasing, sometimes arrogant young man whose quick mind she had thoroughly enjoyed. It hadn't been easy for her to find a single word for such a complex man. The word she would choose for his mind was *brilliant*; other than that, she kept thinking *helpless*.

But the way he was looking at her presented a problem. She certainly didn't want to be like Agatha, thinking that every man who looked at her twice was in love with her. Yet there was the situation she had gotten into with Roy Blanding. She could have nipped that in the bud before it grew out of hand as it had. She would just have to admit to herself that either this young man thought he was terribly attracted to her or he was one of England's finer actors.

"Geoffrey," she said finally, "you are one of the nicest people I have ever met. I have had such a wonderful time with you, but I don't think you belong in Kansas."

He looked so crestfallen that her heart went out to him. "Listen, Geoffrey," she said earnestly. "The best you could do is what your brother has done — leave home only to take his home with him."

"If you came to England, would you bring Kansas with you?" he asked.

She shook her head, smiling. "Me in England? Impossible. I would have nothing in common with anyone there."

"Jessica," he thundered, interrupting her. "Here I am, trying to tell you how much I care for you. I want you to come home with me to England, Jessica. If you won't do that, then I'll come out here to be with you. I don't care where we end up, Jessica, as long as we're together. What I am saying is the most important thing I have ever said in my life. We could make things in common, Jessica."

Why did her father's words haunt her so? "What have you in common beside being young and foolish and romantic?" he had asked about herself and Hawk.

"I like you very much, too, Geoffrey," she said, taking his arm to soften the blow. "But people can't *make* things in common, they have to be there in the first place. Agatha is different here in your world, and I am sure I am, too, even though I can't tell. how. You would have trouble understanding, much less fitting into mine. And that's all right. The real trick is to find someone you are so comfortable with that your worlds are the same."

"But, Jessica," he insisted, "I love you so much. I enjoy you so much. I want to be with you always."

Wheeling Hawk's voice echoed in her mind. "The web you have bound me in is love, and I cannot escape."

"And what would we talk about after I had told you all my stories?" she asked him, forcing her mind back to this pleasant young man staring hopefully into her face.

He grinned at her, almost admitting with that smile that he knew she was right. "Dickens?" he asked, "Thackeray, and sometimes Hawthorne?"

She was glad that by the time they went back inside, they were both laughing.

Agatha's parents brought their sleigh to take Jessica and Agatha back home. Over all those miles, Agatha ignored Jessica, chatting with her mother about Rachel's engagement-birthday party and the news her mother had to tell her of home.

When the sleigh stopped at the Findlay house, Jessica thanked Agatha again for the lovely visit.

"It's nice that you and young master Montgomery enjoyed yourself so much," Agatha said. Her voice was genial enough for her mother to overhear. The coldness in her eyes was for Jessica alone, and unmistakable. "And I wouldn't count on getting that job over there, either, if I were you."

Chapter Seventeen

AT the start, the party Mr. and Mrs. Landers were giving to celebrate Rachel's birthday and to announce her engagement to Walter Brannon promised to be just like all the parties Jessica had ever gone to.

The first difference came when Mrs. Landers arrived at the Findlay farm with a basket of fine groceries under her arm.

Melanie stared at them in disbelief. "What in the world is all this about?" she asked.

Mrs. Landers flushed. "I came to ask you a big favor, Melanie. I'd appreciate your baking Rachel's birthday cake more than I can say. Then we could surprise her. And that's not even to mention that you make a better cake with your hands tied than I do sweating."

Melanie laughed merrily. "Of course I'll bake Rachel's cake, but all this is unnecessary."

"I won't have it any other way," Mrs. Landers said firmly, sinking with a sigh into the chair Melanie offered. "I've been so upset about losing that girl that I'm not half myself."

"Consider the cake done," Melanie said, setting a cup of coffee before her guest. "Now what else can I do to help?"

Mrs. Landers shook her head. "On my way home, I mean to stop and urge Will Reynolds to come to Rachel's party. He needs to get out and mingle with the other young folks."

Melanie nodded. "I agree, but you won't find him home. He is doing some hauling for a rancher over by Ellis and won't be home until after dark."

"I'll leave a message with Mrs. Hogan. Losing Rachel makes me think of other lonely people like him." Suddenly, she began to cry. "I just can't imagine not having that Rachel around, chattering until my head spins and minding everybody's business but her own."

Jessica let herself out of the kitchen quietly, leaving Melanie to comfort Mrs. Landers in privacy.

She walked toward the corral, tapping her mittened hand on the frozen guide rope. As always when she was alone, Hawk's voice sounded in her mind: "Come and be mine with my people."

How strange for Mrs. Landers to go to pieces like that. Rachel's engagement shouldn't have been any surprise to her. Walt Brannon had always hung around the Landers house. They treated him like a son already, and Rachel would live nearby for the rest of her life. Yet her mother grieved.

Given a break in the weather, Jessica's father had sent the boys to the far pasture to gather wood. Dancie nickered as Jessica stepped inside the barn.

Wheeling Hawk had seldom left Jessica's mind during her time in Victoria. Now that she was home, she thought of little else. She was overwhelmed by such a sudden painful desire to see him that she leaned against Dancie, clinging to the pony's warm neck. "Never," her father had said. "Never see him again."

She heard her father's sleigh bells and was coming out of the stable when he reined the the horses in.

"What's the matter?" he asked, his voice gruff. "What were you doing out there?" Then, glancing at the Landers' rig and horse, his tone softened as he asked, "Who's inside with Melanie?"

The suspicion in his voice made her a little sick. He would never trust her again. Yet, remembering her thoughts of a few moments before, she knew his suspicion was well grounded.

"Rachel's mother is in there crying on Melanie's shoulder," she explained. "I thought it was more polite to leave them alone."

Jessica's father grinned weakly. "Nothing's gone wrong between the young folks, has it?"

Jessica shook her head. "She's crying at losing the last chick from her nest."

He nodded, then brightened. "Wait'll the boys tell your mother the news. Come look in the sled."

She wasn't prepared for the dead antelope lying in the sleigh. Its head, with staring eyes, was bent over the bullet wound in its chest. Its legs were crossed at the ankles the way a lady would sit at a party.

She felt her head swim. She must think of that animal as meat for the rest of winter. Half of the hams and most of the sausage had been eaten already. They had to keep the rooster and the rest of the hens alive or there would be no eggs to hatch into baby chickens in the spring.

"Good news," she echoed falsely, her stomach churning.

Once with Hawk, she had seen a herd of antelope pass a few hundred yards away. Hawk had wheeled in to watch them, his eyes tender. Something had startled them into flight. They had flowed like water borne on air, smooth, leaping arcs of buff and white with their necks all curved at the same angle.

Hawk had turned to her, smiling. "If you flattened your hand on the earth," he said, "you could feel them pass. They don't make a thunder in the ground like buffalo do. They go like a drum, swiftly beating."

Her father reached into the sleigh. "Give me a hand getting this carcass over to the shed, then send Jerry out with the knives."

Melanie was letting Mrs. Landers out as Jessica went back to the house.

"Bring your skates, dear," she said. "We hope to have a skating party." That was to be the second big difference between Rachel's party and all the ones that had gone before.

Rachel was the star of the party, as she should have been. Melanie's cake was the success it deserved to be but Mrs. Landers had failed to persuade Will Reynolds to come.

About four o'clock, Patrick Findlay gathered up his family to go back home. When Jessica reached for her shawl, he shook his head. "It's all arranged. You young people are going skating over at Baber's pond. He's got the lanterns hung and the fire lit already."

"But I want to go home with you," she told him.

"It's all arranged," her father said. "Roy says it's no bother to come home by our way."

"Please," she begged, but he shook his head and left.

Jessica was surprised at how many of the skaters she didn't know. Rachel had invited several young people whom Jessica had seen only in church.

Agatha passed swiftly, smiling up at a young man whom Jessica knew only as Eddie. Walt and Rachel, like Roy and herself, had skated together so much that they moved through figure after figure without having to think about it.

After about an hour, Mr. Baber started, in

apparent innocence, the game that was to end so badly.

"Hear, hear," he shouted from the side of the pond. "Let's make a circle and skate in couples. When the missus here bangs on the cider pot with her spoon, all the girls skate forward to join the man just ahead. We'll keep moving up until you girls get back your original partners."

"Maybe I don't want all those fellows skating with my wife-to-be," Walt called in a good-natured way, grinning down at Rachel.

Roy grumbled as Jessica skated ahead at the signal. The game turned out to be a lot of fun. You never knew whether a turn would be short or long. Sometimes Jessica barely caught her new partner's rhythm before having to skate on. She and Eddie, Agatha's friend, circled the pond twice before Mrs. Baber swung her spoon at the pot.

As Jessica joined Eddie, she asked if he was new in town.

He nodded. "My father was transferred to the fort, and I am out here looking around."

"What do you think of it?" she asked.

"Not much until just now," he said gallantly. "Why haven't I seen you before?"

"We live on a ranch, and I don't come in town a lot," she explained. "How did you meet Agatha? She's gone so much of the time, off in Victoria."

He replied, "We just met today at Rachel's party. That's a real fine girl, isn't it?"

"Agatha?" Jessica asked.

He looked at her and shrugged. "I guess so, but I meant Rachel. Walt's a lucky guy. But then, so is Blanding. He tells me that you and he are the next to be married."

Jessica almost stumbled at his words. "He didn't!" she challenged him.

He laughed. "Maybe I jumped to a conclusion. I figured that was what he meant by telling me in no uncertain terms that you were spoken for."

The clang of the iron pot almost drowned out his last words. Jessica called a swift thank you, and skated on, flaming with anger.

The spoon clanged, and Jessica realized that the skater ahead was Roy. She swerved away and skated to the crowd of adults beside the bonfire, leaving him to glide on alone.

At the end of the game, everyone but Roy rushed for the hot mulled cider. He skated straight to Jessica, frowning angrily.

"Are you trying to make a fool of me?" he asked.

"I was cold," she said, trying to turn away.

Seizing her arm, he shoved her back to where she had been standing. "If you're so cold, stay by the fire," he ordered her. "You need to make up your mind about what you want and stick to it once in a while."

Jessica, painfully conscious of the listening crowd, lowered her voice to coax him. "Listen, Roy," she said quietly.

"I've listened to you too long," he said angrily. "But I've been listening to other folks, too, don't think I haven't. Not just my mother, either, for your information."

"Roy *is* a bumbling fool," Jessica told Rachel later. "And even though I don't know why, I'm afraid of him."

Rachel shrugged. "You wonder how people like that get along. I bet he was the only person who paid any attention to that silly talk of Agatha Williams'."

"Agatha?" Jessica asked, her heart suddenly plunging. "What talk?"

"Typical Agatha prattle," Rachel said. "How you went down to Victoria and flirted so outrageously with this young British nobleman that you even put her job in danger."

Jessica breathed. "What in the world?"

Rachel grinned at her. "How can you care what the gossips in this town say about you?" she asked. "You're a stronger person than that. The truth always comes out in the end, other gossips see to that."

"I hope you're right, Rachel. I really hope you're right."

"What really happened in Victoria," Rachel asked, "between you and this young Mr. Geoffrey?"

"Nothing," Jessica told her, trying to keep the anger from her voice. "We became friends. He's very bright and well educated. The last day I was there he asked me if I thought he should move out here, and I told him I didn't think it was a good idea."

"That was all?" Rachel pressed. "No playing around on the rug in front of the fireplace with him, no walking in frozen gardens, none of that?"

"None," Jessica said firmly, "but people are going to believe exactly what they want to."

"Just one thing," Rachel said. "Why did you tell that man not to settle in Kansas?"

"Those people are playing at being settlers, Rachel," Jessica told her. "Kansas is real. A lot of them are going to suffer when the game's over."

"But this is a country of greenhorns," Rachel protested. "Look at Will Reynolds. He seems to be making it."

"But Will is tough and willing to work and as stubborn as a Missouri mule," Jessica told her. "Geoffrey isn't made of that kind of stuff."

Rachel laughed. "I never thought I'd hear you say a good word for Will Reynolds. This is a turnaround."

"It's not a turnaround at all," Jessica told her. "I can't spend five minutes with that man without ending up shouting at him. But that doesn't keep me from knowing a lace handkerchief from a steel file. And believe me, Geoffrey Montgomery is no steel file."

Jessica heard piano music as she let herself in the back door. The song stopped at once, and Melanie came to the door with Jessica's father following.

"It's early," Melanie said. "Didn't Roy want to come in and warm up before going home?"

Jessica was tempted simply to say no and let the truth come out in time. But that was how she had gotten herself into this predicament in the first place.

"Roy left without me," she said. "Walt and Rachel brought me home."

"All right," he said furiously. "What did you do now?"

Melanie turned to stare at him in disbelief. His challenge hung there, like a single blinding beam of light, revealing his anger at Jessica to Melanie for the first time.

"Patrick," Melanie breathed.

"She knows what I mean," he said heavily, his eyes cold on Jessica.

Jessica drew a deep breath and pulled off her mittens. "I know what Papa means," she told Melanie, "but you both need to know that I got fed up with that bumbling fool. And he got fed up with the lies that people tell about me."

That last sentence had been an appeal for her father's understanding. He didn't even hear it.

"You've seen fit to put up with him for a long time," he said angrily.

"I'm older now," she told him. "And wiser."

She knew that only Melanie's restraining hand on his arm made it possible for her to pass them and go into her room.

Chapter
Eighteen

JESSICA lay in bed, staring into darkness. In her haste to get away from her parents, she had not brought the wrapped brick from the stove to keep her bed warm. Across the room, Jerry breathed evenly as Tad stirred in his dreams, rustling his cornhusk mattress.

She had heard the sound of the fire being banked and Melanie closing up the house. Even though her parents had gone to bed, she heard, for a long time, the muffled rumble of her father's voice and Melanie's soft tones in answer. She shivered, knowing they were talking about her. Now even Melanie would turn against her, watch her suspiciously, look at her with cold eyes.

At last the voices were replaced by the sounds of a winter night. The wind howled around the cabin, and a rustling from the kitchen informed her that the prairie rats that Melanie had fought all winter had found another way in to warmth.

Finally, unable to bear the cold, she rose and went into the kitchen. The flame of the buffalo-fat candle in the window wavered from the flow of air through the glass. She stood behind it for a moment, looking at the shaft of light it sent onto the curved drift of snow beyond the sill.

More than once, when winter storms battered the plains, her family had been wakened by the pounding of strangers led to warmth and safety by such a single candle as this. Beyond that beam stretched the endless night of the prairie. In that starless sky, the moon was a vague circle of haze. She knew what wild hunters stalked in that darkness, wolves and coyotes, their eyes green in the night. And off somewhere to the west, Wheeling Hawk's village was whipped by the same wind, lit by the same wan moon.

Where was the candle that promised warmth and safety for her? She didn't dare count the people she had turned against her in these months past.

Fighting tears from a sense of hopeless loss, she took the warmed brick from the back of the stove and carried it back to her icy bed.

That next morning, she wouldn't meet Melanie's eyes. When her father took the boys off to school, Jessica put on her wraps to do the outside chores.

"The chickens can wait," Melanie told her. "Come and sit with me. I want to talk to you."

Just those words were enough to bring tears to Jessica's eyes.

Melanie poured two cups of coffee and set one before Jessica before sitting down across from her.

"You know your father talked to me last night," she began quietly. "I'm sorry he chose to keep the trouble between you a secret for so long. I knew that something was amiss but had no idea what until last night. I have wept bitter tears for the distance I saw growing between you."

"He wouldn't listen," Jessica said swiftly. "He wouldn't let me tell him how it was. We did nothing wrong, Hawk and I."

"You don't have to tell me that," Melanie said softly. "I know you, Jessica, and I feel that I know your friend Wheeling Hawk from seeing him the day he brought you back to us, you and little Jimson. His eyes were those of a gentle man."

Jessica groaned. "Why doesn't Papa see that?"

Melanie shook her head. "For the same reason that you can't see your father's coldness for what it is. Fear makes all who love blind. Your father loves you so much that he can't see your friend Hawk as a person. He sees him as a threat, a danger that could separate you from this family, from your own people, to plunge you into a hopeless life as a lonely, persecuted member of a group where you wouldn't even be welcome except to Hawk himself."

"But Melanie," Jessica began.

"Let me finish," Melanie insisted quietly. "Then you can talk. Because, Jessica, the same fear that has changed your father has blinded your own eyes. You see your father not as the loving man you know him to be, but as a threat, a danger to your desire to be with this man."

"I love Wheeling Hawk," Jessica said.

There, she had said it out into the air and seen the words turn Melanie's face pale and unsteady her hand so that she set her cup down with a thud.

"I have no doubt that you do," she said quietly.

"And he loves me," Jessica went on defensively.

"That, too, I accept."

This was a child's game, around and around and back to where they had begun. Her father was cold toward her from fear of losing her. She was cold to him because she feared he would lose Hawk to her. Nothing solved, nothing changed. Only that sick sense of loss, heavy on her heart.

"I think I should go melt water for the chickens," Jessica said, rising.

"I think you should try to see your father as a man facing an enemy he doesn't know how to fight."

"And how should I try to see myself?" Jessica asked, pricked by these words to resentment.

Melanie's calm eyes studied her. "That's a question I haven't asked myself," she admitted. "I have only loved one man in my life, your father. Because it never occurred to me that he would love me, I never imagined my life with him." There, for a moment, she seemed to forget Jessica. A soft smile warmed her mouth. "I have heard Rachel dreaming aloud of how wonderful it will be to be Walt's wife. I never did that. I really can't answer your question."

Outside, Jessica moved about her work, her head wreathed in clouds of her own breath. Melanie's words had struck a painful chord. Over and over she had tried to imagine herself as Hawk's wife, how she would spend her hours, where she would live. It didn't work. No pictures came to her mind. She could only see herself with Hawk as they had been together, in a secret place that lay between their worlds and was a part of neither one.

Never ever had the two weeks between Rachel's birthday and Christmas passed so swiftly. School was dismissed, and the boys came home giggling with excitement. Still wearing snowy boots, they scurried to the bedroom to hide things, making terrible threats to anyone who "poked around."

Roy Blanding had come only a day or so after Rachel's party. He arrived midafternoon when only Jessica and Melanie were there. Melanie would have excused herself and gone to clatter in the kitchen to give them privacy, but Jessica asked her to join them.

Roy, forced to apologize to Jessica before her mother, sweated visibly in spite of the chill in the room. "I was hasty that night of Rachel's party," he told her. "I should have checked out Agatha's story before I talked to you like that."

Not even Melanie's perfect manners could betray her growing curiosity.

"And how did you manage to check out this story, whatever it was, that Agatha told you?" she asked.

"My mother." He glanced at Jessica and flushed. "She happened to be in Landers' store when the gentleman from Victoria was there purchasing supplies."

"And she asked him about that vicious slander that you believed from Agatha?" Jessica asked, incredulous.

"Well, not exactly asked," he admitted. "She overheard the gentleman visiting with Rachel. He was telling Rachel how they had never had a lovelier guest in their home than your daughter here." He nodded to Melanie. "And that they were forever indebted to her for counseling a young member of the family who wanted to make a bad decision. I realized at once that I had made a terrible mistake, and I'm asking you to forgive me for my rudeness."

Jessica felt wonderfully grateful to have Melanie there beside her. Her fear of Roy had only deepened since the night of the party, but she had to settle this business between herself and Roy sometime. She might never get this good a chance again.

"You did make a terrible mistake," she agreed quietly. "But it's over now."

He didn't even let her finish but broke right in, grinning from ear to ear, his voice rising with relief.

"I knew you'd be a sport about it," he exulted. "Now you just watch and see if I don't make it up to you."

"I'm not through," Jessica said firmly. "As I said, it was a terrible mistake, but I'm glad you made it. It made me realize that you don't trust me enough for us to have any relationship."

"But, Jessica," he wailed. "You can't mean that. You can't mean that you're breaking off our engagement over a misunderstanding like that."

"Engagement?" Melanie asked quietly. "Have you asked Mr. Findlay for permission to propose marriage to our daughter? Is there some understanding between the two of you that Jessica's own parents don't know about?"

"Yes," he said swiftly, even as Jessica said no with equal force. Melanie looked from one to the other soberly.

"Well," Melanie said briskly. "It appears that you two have a misunderstanding all the way around."

She rose. Smiling graciously, she asked, "Roy, will you join Jessica and me in a cup of coffee, or do you have other errands this afternoon?"

Melanie's standing had forced Roy to rise also. His look of shock changed swiftly to anger as he looked from one of them to the other. "Jessica," he began, in that threatening tone of barely controlled fury.

"Would you care for coffee, Mr. Blanding?" Melanie interrupted smoothly.

He looked at her and flushed. "No," he said. "No thank you, ma'am. Yes, I do have other errands." At the door he turned to glare at Jessica. "I'll see *you* again," he said, his tone threatening.

Melanie closed the door behind Roy, leaned her back against it, and let her breath out in a long, slow whistle. "Well," she said. "I hope I was getting your signals right."

Jessica ran to her, folded her in her arms, and began to dance her around. "Oh, I have wanted to do that for months, years maybe. I can't believe it's finally over."

"Let me go, you little crazy," Melanie said, laughing and pulling herself free. "I am going to make us a cup of coffee and not from that toasted carrot stuff we've been drinking, either. Mrs. Landers insisted on making me the gift of some real coffee, in return for baking that cake. I was saving it for a celebration. That's clearly what this day deserves."

Only with the steaming cups before them, with the rich fragrance perfuming the room, did Melanie turn thoughtful. "He may be a bumbling fool, Jessica, as you suggested the other night, but I don't think you've seen the last of him."

"I hope you're wrong," Jessica told her.

"I hope so, too," Melanie agreed, "but I wouldn't put up anything I valued against that man being very unpleasant about this before this is all over."

The arrival of another bitterly cold spell of weather cut down the number of parties that were usually held during the holiday season. Jessica was relieved. Inevitably, the town tongues would fly about her not turning up everywhere with Roy. The longer that could be put off, the better, as far as she was concerned.

Jessica wondered whether Will Reynolds kept coming for Sunday dinner because he enjoyed being there or because Mrs. Hogan enjoyed getting away from the dugout so much. Whatever his reason, he was a wonderful guest. He played checkers with Jerry and argued politics with his host. He never arrived empty-handed but always brought some treat that Floss had sent from Chicago, or a brace of dressed rabbits for Melanie to add to the meal.

In all those months, Jessica and Will had never exchanged cross words publicly. At the same time, they had never been alone together five minutes without her ending up furious at his bullheadedness. In Melanie's company, he played the perfect gentleman. With Jessica he was a rude, arrogant bore. He literally changed personalities the minute they were alone. "Like a lizard," she told herself angrily, smarting from some rebuff she hadn't expected. "He changes color according to where he lands."

Sometimes she wondered what he had been like back in Chicago. Even though he now wore the boots and heavy work clothes of the frontier, she could imagine him dressed in that city way again, using those company manners that he saved for everybody but her.

The last Sunday before Christmas, he was sitting with Jessica's father when she reached for her shawl to refill the fuel basket. He leaped to his feet to follow her.

"Here, let me help," he said.

She stared at him, amazed. She had gone in and out of that door a hundred times while he sat there visiting. It had never occurred to him before that she needed help drawing water or carrying fuel. She clung to the basket. "Thanks, anyway," she said. "I'm fine."

"I'm going to help you," he insisted, taking the basket from her forcibly.

She stamped out the door. Now what was he up to? Whatever it was, she didn't appreciate his making her father laugh at her like that while she struggled to hold on to her basket in the blast of wind from the open door.

With the way things were between herself and her father, every little thing mattered. Whatever Melanie had said to him that night behind their closed door had changed him. Although the old warmth had never come back, she often noticed him making a special effort to include her in jokes and conversation. But she was self-conscious about him. He had never mentioned Roy Blanding, even though she was sure that Melanie had related that scene to him. The gulf between them didn't need any laughter at her expense.

"Now what was all that about?" she challenged Will the moment the door was shut behind her.

"I was trying to get a word with you without starting a scene," he said. "I should have known better than to try."

"Well, you got a bargain," she told him. "You got both the scene and a chance to get your word in." She pulled the basket back and began filling it with dried buffalo chips.

He sighed, shook his head, and helped her fill the basket. "I wanted to talk about Christmas," he said. "Floss sent a box of things for your family. She has some romantic idea of playing Santa Claus to the boys and surprising your parents without any warning. She thought maybe you wouldn't mind helping."

Jessica paused and looked up at him thoughtfully. This was really a little strange. Floss wrote regularly. In fact, Jessica had received a letter from her within the week. Why hadn't Floss come right out and asked her?

"I'm sorry I made that fuss," she told him. "She doesn't have to do that, you know."

A sudden grin lit his face. "I know that," he said. "Don't you remember? You were the one who told me that Kansans don't do things because they have to but because they want to. Maybe she stayed in that dugout long enough to be part Kansan. Anyway, I have the packages and need your help."

"You and Jimson are coming for dinner that day, aren't you?" she asked. "Along with Mrs. Hogan, of course."

"Mrs. Hogan is spending the day with some friends from church," he replied. "But Jimson and I will be here. But that seems too late. Doesn't Santa come in the night here, like he does in Chicago?"

She nodded thoughtfully.

"Maybe if I brought the gifts over to you after dark that Christmas Eve, you could hide them until morning."

A shaft of light fell across the snow as the back door opened. "You need help out there?" Jessica's father called.

"We're coming," Will called back. "I'm still fighting this girl of yours for the basket."

As her father's laughter echoed over the snow, Jessica glared at him. "You had to say that, didn't you?"

"I had to say something," he reminded her. "The truth seemed as good as anything going." At that, he wrested the basket from her arms and started briskly toward the house.

She glared after him. On that glaze of ice, it wouldn't take much of a shove to send him and the buffalo chips sliding halfway to the road. She shrugged and followed him, her hands beginning to tingle from the cold. As unpredictable as he was, she might have to go pick up the chips and carry them in herself. It wasn't worth that chance.

Christmas Eve dawned cold and clear. The wind that had howled for a solid week eased up. For the first time since Rachel's party, the temperature was high enough for the boys to sled on the slope behind the burying ground without their cheeks turning blue. The excitement of secrets crackled in the air as Melanie and Jessica made taffy for the boys' stockings.

Jessica was to meet Will in the barn at seven o'clock to get the gifts hidden. By that time, the chores would be done. They agreed on the bobsled box as the safest hiding place.

Once supper was cleared away and the dishes washed, Melanie fixed her hair and went to her piano. Jessica watched the hands of the clock pass six-thirty and move toward seven as the four of them sang their way through all the carols they knew. Tad was as jumpy as a cat. He kept hearing things, sleigh bells outside, scratching sounds on the roof, somebody singing. Melanie laughed at him so merrily that she stopped in the middle of a song.

Amazingly, the music didn't stop. Tad stared at her and flew to the window.

"A sleigh," he shouted. "Santa's out there."

"Santa, indeed!" Walt Brannon laughed as

they threw the door open. "We sang ourselves hoarse out here trying to get your attention."

"Carolers," Melanie cried, clapping her hands. "That makes Christmas Eve complete. Come in, both of you. The gingerbread is still warm from supper, and we'll mull some cider."

The room echoed with laughter as Rachel and Walt told of their adventures caroling the neighborhood. As the hands of the clock reached seven, Jessica slipped out the back door with a dark shawl over her head to wait for Will. She had no more than shut the door behind herself than she heard a delicate melody rising and falling on the crisp air.

The clear, soft voice of Hawk's flute, wistful and searching, called to her from somewhere in that darkness.

With both hands pressed tight against her thundering heart, she ran toward the sound, only to have it die as she stood, anguished, in the middle of the barnyard.

"Hawk," she cried softly. "Hawk, where are you?"

The voice that answered was Will's. "Miss Findlay," he said, his tone imperative. "Are you all right? Speak up, are you all right?"

She wasn't all right. She struggled for balance in the deep snow, wanting Will gone from there, wanting Hawk to speak to her again in that tender, plaintive song.

But Will was there. He seized her by both shoulders, holding her very tight. She could feel the warmth of his breath there in the darkness as she clung to him for balance. When he spoke, his voice was rough with concern.

"My God, Miss Findlay. When I saw that Indian ride away, I was scared to death. I thought he might have harmed you. How could I live with myself if I had lured you into your death out here in this darkness?"

She had never heard his voice so altered by emotion. There was fear and a tenderness that sounded like caring. But that couldn't be, not from him.

"It's all right," she said hastily, stepping back a little to be free of his grasp. She was annoyed at herself at being touched with tenderness by his concern. "I just lost my balance," she assured him. "What Indian? I saw no one."

"He was here," he said roughly. "I saw his silhouette and heard a wailing of some kind. I must have startled him away."

A wailing. Jessica felt a shiver of sorrow tremble along her body. If she had only come out a little sooner. If only Will had been a little slower in coming. But he was watching her, still standing very close, his eyes intense on her face. Will was a dangerous man, she decided. It was a good thing that she knew him as well as she did. A girl who didn't know him would be stirred by what seemed to be a tenderness in those eyes. She had almost been trapped into that herself, in the pain of having missed Hawk.

She had to get away from him before he

tricked her into believing his concern. "Let's move the things before they miss me inside," she said, not caring how rude it sounded.

Only when he tried to set the box of gifts into the bed of the sleigh did he discover it already half filled. "My God," he said, "There must be fifty pounds of fresh buffalo meat in here. Did your father go hunting today?"

"My father didn't go hunting," she told him dully. "I think that must be a gift from a friend."

"A friend?" he asked, his voice suddenly cold. "That Indian, you mean?"

"A friend," she repeated firmly. "Your friend as well as mine if you were man enough to admit it."

He muttered something angrily before turning to mount his horse and ride off.

"Where were you?" her father asked as she let herself in the door.

"I heard a sound out there," she said, truthfully enough.

"Santa," Tad decided, jumping to his feet and running to the window.

In the laughter and teasing that followed, Jessica dipped a cup of the hot, spiced cider and warmed her face in its fragrance. As she turned back to the room, she saw Melanie studying her with puzzled eyes.

Chapter Nineteen

MAYBE she would not have gone to sleep, anyway, who knows? But after Walt and Rachel jingled off in their sleigh and the boys were finally settled down for the night, Jessica lay sleepless in her bed.

The sound of Hawk's lonely flute echoed in her head. "For songs of love and comfort," he had told her. Who would believe that the coming of love would also bring such need for comfort? She had no more than lifted the burden of Roy Blanding from her consciousness than she had this new crisis dumped on her. With morning, she would bring in the gifts for the boys and the others. As soon as Will came, the news of Hawk's visit would be out in the open. Even if Will said nothing, which was certainly unlikely, how could anyone explain away fifty pounds of fresh buffalo meat?

Fifty pounds of fresh buffalo meat!

She sat up in horror. The wolves would catch the scent of that meat before morning, if they had not already done so. That meat had been a gift, a touching gift, since Hawk's people must be fighting hunger this white winter. That such a gift be thrown, literally to the wolves, because of her fear of facing her father, was unthinkable.

The offense against her father's will had already been done through no fault of her own. To let that meat go to waste while men were hungry would be an offense against God.

She tugged on her boots, wrapped a shawl around her night dress, and rapped at her parents' closed door.

"Who is it?" Her father's voice, thick with sleep.

"Jessica," she whispered. "I need to talk to you."

The cabin was dark except for the fluttering light of the buffalo candle in the front window. He seemed immense, standing over her in the doorway, frowning like that.

"I have a problem," Jessica said, struggling for the words. "I can't handle it myself."

"Surely it can wait until morning," her father said.

"No, it can't," she told him, unable to meet his eyes.

"Give us a minute," Melanie suggested. "We'll be right out."

"You need to dress for the out of doors," Jessica whispered, still not knowing how she could tell him without triggering that sudden and terrifying temper of his.

She was in her own warm clothes, sitting at the table and staring at her folded hands when they joined her.

"Now what's all this about?" her father demanded.

"Sit down, Patrick, please." Melanie said, sliding onto the bench and taking Jessica's hands. "Now, Jessica, what happened tonight while Walt and Rachel were here?"

Trust Melanie to make it easy. Without raising her eyes from her hands, Jessica tried to tell the story as it happened. "Will had some gifts from Floss that he wanted the boys to have first thing in the morning, as if they came from Santa Claus." Even without looking up, she could feel her father's impatience building. "When I went out to take them and hide them, someone else had been there."

"Someone else? What is that supposed to mean?" her father asked roughly.

"A friend of mine had come and left a gift there. Will saw him leave."

"No," Patrick Findlay said angrily, staring at Jessica's face. "He couldn't have, he didn't dare. Believe me, Jessica, there are laws about Indians." His voice had risen.

"A gift," Melanie prodded her.

"Buffalo meat," Jessica told her. "Will guessed there was fifty pounds of it there."

"Good Lord, Jessica," Patrick Findlay cried. He rose to his feet and began to pace the room angrily. "You accept no gift from that man, nor any Indian. What is the matter with you?"

"This is not a question of accepting a gift, Patrick," Melanie reminded him. "Jessica went out there and found it. Is that why you woke us up, dear?" she asked.

It was harder even than Jessica had feared to face her father's anger like this. She nodded, so close to tears that her voice sounded watery and small to her own ears. "I thought it would be sinful to let the wolves come for it tonight with so many people hungry."

Her father stared at her dumbly for a long minute. Finally, he repeated, "Sinful," in a careful, teasing tone. Then he sighed, turned, and started for the door. "The child is right," he said in a tone of defeat. "Come, show us where you found it."

Major was barking wildly from the chicken house as they let themselves out. From the darkness beyond the barn shone the glinting yellow eyes of crouched beasts.

"The dog and that candle are the only things holding them back even now," Jessica's father said as he stared toward the barn. "Where did you find it?"

"In the bobsled," she told him, and then had to run a little to keep pace with him the moment the words were out.

Melanie carried the gaily wrapped presents to the house while Jessica and her father stored the great slabs of buffalo meat in the safety of the cellar.

Back in the kitchen, Patrick Findlay slumped tiredly on the bench by the table. "Thank you, Jessica. It must have been hard to make yourself come in there and wake us."

She nodded, lacking spirit to speak.

He frowned, as if trying to find words for something more he wanted to say. Apparently, the words couldn't be found. Then he sighed and rose. As he passed Jessica, he laid his broad hand awkwardly on her shoulder.

"Jessica, Jessica," he said. "You have dug yourself a hole that I don't see any good way out of. Merry Christmas, my child." He turned and followed Melanie back into their room.

All Christmas mornings were special, but Jessica was sure that the boys would never forget this one. When Jerry unwrapped his small box from Floss, he was struck dumb. Tad, wildly curious, leaned over to cry out, "A knife. Jerry has a knife of his own."

Clearly, this was more than a knife to Jerry. The handle was of richly toned horn, and more blades leaped from its center than Jessica could even have found a use for.

The strange click from inside Tad's box made sense once he emptied the leather bag inside. Marbles of every color of the rainbow spilled across the floor, sending him scrambling after them in delight.

Floss had chosen no gift lightly. Melanie's robe was of sheer cotton and the same shade of blue as her eyes. The heavy leather gloves, lined with sheep's wool, fitted Patrick's hands as if they had been made to order.

Jessica's was the largest box and the heaviest. She wanted to keep it unopened as long as possible, but everyone was eager to see what treasure Floss had found for her.

The box was marked "Fields and Leiter." The dark packing paper unfolded to reveal a pair of soft black leather shoes, very low-cut with a dainty little curved heel.

"Put them on," Tad shouted. "Come on, Jessica, put them on."

They almost didn't fit over her knitted stockings. "That only means they'll be perfect with real hose," Melanie assured her. As Jessica stepped this way and that to show them off, she felt her cheeks flame with some confused mixture of embarrassment and delight.

"Will you look at that?" Patrick Findlay's voice boomed with pride. "Our daughter has ankles."

"Those are shoes to get married in," Jerry said, flipping the catch on his knife again to watch the blades spring out.

It was Christmas all over again when Will came in with Jimson, carrying a carved horse. There were kisses all around for the baby, and Will turned a glowing scarlet when Melanie stood on tiptoe to kiss his cheek.

Only then did Will look Jessica's way. "The

joy of the season to you, Miss Findlay," he said. A steel trap.

Melanie's bread was even lighter and more fragrant than usual, and the meal was wondrously festive. Only as Jessica and Melanie were clearing the table to serve dessert did Will bring up the event of the night before.

"I guess your daughter told you about the visitor at your barn last night."

Jessica, from the corner of her eye, saw her father's nod. "In fact, she helped me store that meat away before the wolves could get to it," he told Will.

A wave of something like weakness moved down Jessica's body. That was over. For once she had done something right. Maybe her luck had finally turned.

Later that same day, she wondered about her luck when she and Will got into one of those impossible exchanges that always left her so frustrated.

"I don't know how I can ever thank Floss for those beautiful shoes," she said quite honestly.

"Floss doesn't want to be thanked," he said bluntly. "In fact, I think she might be offended if you even wrote anything to her about them."

"Why, that's ridiculous," Jessica told him. "Of course I'll write and thank her."

"I wish you wouldn't," he said quite earnestly. She stared at him, something she usually avoided doing. She forgot when he was around so much with her father and with

that reminded her of a story Hawk had told her, a Cheyenne story full of magic, with humans and animals changing places and understanding each other's language.

Rachel and Walt were priceless to her during those empty weeks. When they rode out together for an evening, they often stopped by to take Jessica along or just to visit awhile in the Findlay house. Rachel never came without news of one kind or another. Sometimes it was pure gossip, like the word that Agatha had been fired from her job in Victoria and was back home, going very steady with a young soldier from the fort.

Rachel not only brought Jessica her mail but talked about the mail that other people got and sent. "That job is going to be too big for one person one of these days," he told Jessica one evening in early February.

"Two people are doing it now," Walt pointed out, explaining that he had stayed up all night helping Rachel sort a late mail train that had been stalled in the snow to the east and arrived with the regular mail train coupled to it.

"Would you believe that by the time we got that mail straightened out, Will Reynolds had three of those letters?"

Jessica looked at her, puzzled. "Three of what letters?"

"Oh, you remember the day Floss was there and I gave her that letter that turned her white as a sheet?"

Jessica nodded. Indeed she did remember.

"That envelope had three names all printed together in the corner with a Chicago return. She sent that letter back unopened, but Will Reynolds has gotten letters from that same place every week or so since then. I see them going back in the mail, all marked that the addressee is unknown. It's very mysterious altogether. If I had just a little more spunk, I'd ask him if he wanted me to write that on them and pop them right back and save him the delivery."

"Well," Walt grinned at Jessica. "We're relieved to find out where your spunk stops. We weren't real sure it had an ending, were we, Jessica?"

"She's not listening to you," Rachel pointed out. "She's buried in all the news from the big city. *Aren't you, Jessica?*" she shouted, sending Jessica flying out of her chair.

"Excuse me," Jessica said, laughing at herself. "That was rude of me, but I hadn't heard from Floss since the letter I wrote her after Christmas."

"It got caught on that snowed-in train," Rachel explained. "What did she write?"

Jessica shrugged and folded her letter. "Just about Christmas. She liked the things I sent, and her friend gave her a beautiful garnet ring."

At Rachel's squeal, Jessica shook her head. "There's no date set. She hasn't even accepted him for sure. She wants him to meet Will first."

"And I thought it was tough to get past a

mother and father," Walt teased.

"That was really tough, wasn't it?" Rachel smiled, rising to leave. "You should come into town and spend some time with me," she told Jessica. "We're wearing out this road coming out here."

"Wait until spring breaks," Jessica told her. "You never know what will happen this time of year."

With Rachel gone, Jessica curled up in the sun by the window and reread Floss's letter carefully. It wasn't the handwriting but the strange way that Floss had expressed things that made the letter confusing.

There was the part about the ring:

. I wish you could see the beautiful ring that my friend gave me for Christmas (along with his heart, or so he says). The stone is garnet for my birthday, and it is looped all around with wonderful coils of gold that seem to float above my finger. He wants a promise, but I can't give that until he meets Will. Oh, what a problem. I do wish Will felt safe coming back here. There's no proper way we can travel out there together, even if train tickets were free. When do people make garden in Kansas?

"When do people make garden in Kansas?" Jessica repeated aloud, trying to figure out what that had to do with anything.

Melanie, across the room, answered quietly.

"When spring breaks, of course."

"But why would Floss ask me that?"

Melanie held her tongue between her teeth thoughtfully for a moment before nodding brightly. "I remember," she said proudly. "When Mrs. Hogan came to care for Jimson, she planned to stay until her daughter's baby came. At the same time, she mentioned that it would be time then to plant the garden back home. Could that be it?"

"That could be it," Jessica agreed. "But that is also when the men go south to get cattle. Isn't Will riding the cattle drive with Papa this year?"

Melanie nodded. "So I understand."

With that settled and unsettled at the same time, Jessica turned back to the letter. The part about Christmas was just as strange, although in fewer words.

How dear of you to be so flattering about my taste. I'm just so happy that everything was right. It was so important to Will. I think he was even nervous about leaving the shopping to me. I hope I see you in those little slippers some day. For all I know, you have no ankles at all, dear, beautiful Jessica.

She couldn't mean what it sounded like. Will couldn't possibly have bought all those handsome gifts and passed them off to her as coming from Floss. Or could he? And if he could, why would he?

Chapter
Twenty

FEBRUARY was always a seesaw month. As if to tease the exhausted settlers, the weather went from promises of spring to blasting reminders that winter was still firmly in the saddle. Some days came clear and pleasant. Even though the air was icy if any wind at all was stirring, the sun was strong enough to start rills of melted snow water running from under the drifts. Then overnight, the temperature would drop, freezing those little streams into ribbons of solid ice and setting a new glaze on the warmed drifts.

The one flat rule about February was that Melanie's birthday, February 28th, always brought a storm. The family laughed about "Melanie's Birthday Storms," but some of them hadn't been very funny while they were going on.

It seemed to Jessica that each week seemed to last forever. Sundays were the only days she really looked forward to. It was almost worth having Will and his family there every Sunday to hear his deep, clear voice raised in song.

Roy Blanding and his mother stared straight ahead during church those days. Jessica smothered a giggle, maybe a nervous one but a giggle anyway.

Jessica hated to admit it, but Sundays were also special because Will always brought his little household over after church. Now that she didn't have the care of Jimson, Jessica really enjoyed having him around. He was the terror of the floor after he learned to crawl. He chased poor Major until the dog even begged to be let out into the cold. A sturdy, laughing child, he played and wrestled with Tad and Jerry.

As Melanie pointed out, having Will to talk politics and ranching with seemed to take Patrick's mind off his troubles. They talked endlessly about the money panic in the East, which was sending a new surge of settlers westward, and whether President Grant could turn the economy around after losing so much confidence from the scandals of his administration.

Jane Hogan never came without something to add to the meal, a pot of smothered prairie hens with dumplings or a loaf of her hickory-nut and currant bread, which was better than any common cake. The way she and Melanie chatted away in the kitchen like magpies led Jessica to wonder how much Melanie was going to miss this genial woman when spring broke and she went back home.

The middle of February passed with the house cluttered with the Valentines that Tad drew for Melanie on every piece of paper he could find. The nights were almost as bright as day that week Hawk had called the moon of February, "the Hunger Moon," because it came after all the food was eaten and no new grass was springing up for the animals to eat. By the end of the month, there had been enough of those bright days that the very top branches of the tallest peach trees had broken through the snow drifts that had covered them since November. On Melanie's birthday, Patrick Findlay left early in the morning to check the cattle in the far pasture and visit with a neighbor over there. He kidded Melanie at breakfast that for once she would have to settle for a birthday without a storm.

Although the days seemed be be lengthening, the waning half moon was already rising as Jessica came out of the barn after her evening milking. She stopped at the gate, startled by the ribbons of black clouds that had begun to scud across the moon's face during that brief time she had been in the barn.

Twilight always depressed her. At about this time of day, Hawk would be riding, his slender body as straight as a wand, from his work back to his village. After so long, he sometimes seemed like someone she had dreamed. Only the memory of his voice kept him alive in her mind. No one ever reminded her of him in any regard.

Had she imagined his remarkable gentleness? Had she, as her father suggested, been silly and romantic to think that the two of them had anything in common aside from "youth and foolishness"?

The very question terrified her. She would never know until she was with him again, and that had been forbidden.

Suddenly, she frowned. The ribbons of clouds had become a churning blackness from which the moon's light only briefly glinted now and then. Turning, she ran to the house as fast as she could with the half-full buckets swinging at her sides.

"I think we have a high wind coming," she told Melanie as she set the milk inside the kitchen.

"Enough to batten things down?" Melanie asked. "Your father won't be home till late."

"Go and see," Jessica urged her. "Maybe I just imagined how ugly it looked."

"You didn't imagine anything," Melanie said, forcing the door against the wind to get it closed behind her. "Come on, let's fasten down the barn and see what can be done about the chicken house."

With Jerry helping, they cleared the snow away so they could close the big wooden doors that would shield the animals from the rising wind. The roof of the chicken house was a problem. It had buckled along the edge, giving the wind a hold that could lift it like a kite.

"Snow," Melanie suggested. "Sod would be better, but may be the weight of snow will hold it down."

Jessica climbed up on the roof and took the buckets of snow that Melanie and Jerry handed up to her. By the time she had piled heavy mounds all along the line of the roof, she was fighting to hold her balance in that gale.

The wind was howling now, bending the sycamore trees toward the earth like willow switches. With both apron pockets heavy with candles, Jessica dragged a full bucket of water toward the cellar. Behind her, Jerry jerked Major along, whining with complaint. Melanie, with Tad clinging heavily to her side, slid on the icy glaze and went to her knees twice before getting her frantic child to the door of the cellar. With the door shut behind them at last, the sudden quiet after the screaming wind was almost a physical shock. Even Major flopped to the earthen floor, panting with relief.

"Mama," Jerry said with mock reproach. "I hope you know that we're all getting pretty tired of these storms of yours."

The laughter helped everyone but Tad, who had always been terrified of storms. He shamelessly cried himself to sleep on Melanie's lap while Jessica got Jerry to start singing along with her.

A dullness settled over Jessica with the passage of that unmeasured time. Jerry found a pile of withered apples back under a storage shelf. By peeling away the dried parts with his Christmas knife, he was able to feed Tad enough tough bites of stale apple to soothe his hunger when he woke up.

When the air grew dense from the smoke of the candle, they blew it out and sat in darkness. After much shoving each other around, the boys settled with their heads on Major's dense, warm coat. Only when their deep, even breathing assured their mother that they were both asleep did she speak to Jessica in a careful whisper.

"Your father wouldn't try to come home in this, would he?" she asked.

Jessica groped for her hand in the dark and squeezed it hard. "Not likely," she said. "Not likely." There in that smoky darkness she had been asking her own heart's version of that question: *What would happen to the frail leather tepees of the Cheyenne on such a night with such a wind?*

Jessica must have dozed there against the cold smoothness of the pickle crock. She started awake, blinded by a sudden light.

"Hey, there," her father called. "Come out and let's count heads."

As they climbed out, cramped and chilled, they found the storm had abated, and Patrick Findlay was safe.

Chapter
Twenty-one

WITH March came teasing promises of spring. The patches of snow dwindled, exposing green roots of grass. The sun melted snow, sending rills of water chiming from under the lacy shelves of the drifts. Early every morning, Jessica's father drove to the far pastures where the cattle had wintered. The young calves were being born, usually at night. He took the buckboard in case a mother cow had failed to survive the birthing and left a newborn calf that must be raised by hand back at the ranch.

Mrs. Hogan brought disturbing news that second Sunday of March. Before she even took off her bonnet, she set a carrot-and-raisin cake down and turned to Melanie.

"I heard from my daughter in Ellis," she said. "She thinks her baby might come early. What would happen if I had to leave before

Will got home from the cattle drive?"

Jessica's father frowned. "When is that child due?" he asked.

Mrs. Hogan sighed. "They said the middle of April. Remember? I figured to be there to plant garden."

"Could we leave earlier than we planned on that cattle drive?" Will asked Patrick. "If we left right away and were gone three weeks, we would be back in early April."

Patrick nodded. "Spring does look on the way," he agreed. "Every nice day cuts our chances of another storm."

Jessica, making gravy, shut her mind to their words. Every nice day only made her restless. How could people talk about cattle drives when she lived with a war inside her heart?

Wheeling Hawk.

Maybe it was spring that made her think constantly of love. It didn't help that Rachel's wedding was drawing near. Jessica had been both delighted and terrified when Rachel insisted that she sing at the wedding. Standing by Melanie's piano, singing the tender songs that Rachel had chosen, brought tears to Jessica's eyes. The same sadness came when she sat embroidering the fancy lace-trimmed petticoat she was making for Rachel's wedding outfit. Whatever the cause, thoughts of love were painful because she missed Hawk so very much.

Sometimes she felt that she would give anything, even her life, to be with him for an hour. Then she would shiver at the thought of falling even farther from her father's graces.

Already the days were lengthening. Jessica tried to be outside when Hawk might be riding home. Every afternoon she searched the horizon with her eyes, watching for that solitary horseman. Hawk *knew* where she was. Not knowing where he was made her feel lost and desolate.

She didn't know how many times Melanie called her name before touching her arm.

"You were off in your dreams," Melanie said. "Will asked you a question."

They were all watching as she turned, her father frowning and Will Reynolds giving her that cold, measuring stare. She flushed. "I'm sorry," she said swiftly. "My mind was a million miles away. What did you ask, Mr. Reynolds?"

"Will," Jerry corrected her. "All of us call him Will."

After a quick smile at Jerry, Will looked back to her, his voice losing the easy warmth it had when he talked to the others. "I realize from church that you are widely acquainted in the area. I wondered if you knew anyone who might fill in for Mrs. Hogan if she's called away while I am gone on the cattle drive."

Jessica pulled the iron skillet from the fire and stared at it thoughtfully. Most of the girls who had finished school with her were either already married or had jobs somewhere, teaching or clerking in town.

"The only girl I know without a job is Agatha Williams."

"Would you mind asking her about it?" Will asked.

Jessica looked at him, startled. She would die rather than ask Agatha anything. The girl hadn't spoken to her since the night before Rachel's birthday party.

"I think it would be better if you did that," Jessica told him.

"Jessica," her father said, clearly astonished. "That's a very small thing for Will to ask."

His tone of voice was like a slap. Jessica burned with shame and anger. She forgot that her father hadn't heard about Agatha's gossip, which caused the rupture with Roy.

Melanie, knowing the whole story, opened her mouth to speak. She didn't get the chance. Jessica's anger flared too swiftly.

"If it is such a small thing to do, I don't see why he can't do it for himself."

Her father sat in stunned silence a moment before roaring, "Jessica!"

Jessica wondered that she didn't actually tremble as she looked back at him. In that silence, she could hear the faint chiming of water down the drainpipe outside the window. Jerry stared at her in horror as Tad's eyes sought his mother's face for reassurance.

Will broke the silence with words that flowed as soothingly as cream. "Please, Patrick," he said quietly. "Miss Findlay is absolutely right. I should do that job myself.

I couldn't put Jimson in the care of someone I hadn't met, anyway."

Mrs. Hogan scrubbed her hands together nervously. "We'll just pray that it won't come to that," she suggested.

With the meal on the table, Jessica slid in beside Jerry. The knot in her stomach was the size of her father's fist. The thought of putting food down there made her ill. Yet, with her father watching, she had to eat, lest she trigger his anger again. She just wanted to be away. Far away, she decided, as far as a horse could carry her, as many miles as lay between her and Hawk.

If they would only change the subject. But her father was not a man to leave a problem unsolved. At any moment, Jessica expected him to offer her services again as he had in the fall. Instead, Melanie spoke.

"I don't see any problem," she said. "Jimson isn't a newborn baby needing constant care. He may be a little mischief box, but I've had lots of experience with those." She raised her eyebrows at her sons, sending them into the giggles.

"The boys adore him and can help when they are not in school. Other than that, he can play around and watch me garden as the others have. If my friend here" — she smiled at Mrs. Hogan — "is called away, Jimson will stay with me until the men get back."

They hadn't even mentioned Jessica. She felt that she had become as invisible to her parents as she was to Will, except, of course, when they were having one of their arguments.

Eager to escape, Jessica rose to slice Mrs. Hogan's cake. She was glad her back was to the room as Will went on about his emergency arrangements.

"I need to leave a horse for you, Mrs. Hogan," he went on. "That will give you freedom of movement if anything happens."

Mrs. Hogan shook her head. "That's not necessary," she insisted. "If Jessica just ran by every few days, I'd feel secure."

"Jessica will not be coming by," Patrick Findlay said firmly. Then to Will, "I would offer our pony Dancie, but we'll need her. Jerry here can get himself and his brother back and forth to school on her." He paused, frowning. "Logan has an old mare who's past pulling a plow but broken to ride. He'd probably be glad to get her out of his lot if you fed her."

Somehow Jessica lasted through dessert. She even lasted through the dishwashing. With Melanie and Mrs. Hogan still chatting as they polished plates, she let herself out the back door.

The outside air smelled sweet after the steamy kitchen. A songbird, not a native because Jessica didn't recognize the song, swayed on a branch of the sycamore, repeating the same lyrical question over and over. With her arms crossed over her shawl, she walked past the chicken house to stand staring at her mother's grave.

There had been times during her childhood when her loneliness had best been soothed by coming here and humming aloud to herself the tune she remembered as her mother's. She didn't know the words, had never known the words, but the tune came wistfully to her throat.

She heard the back door close but didn't look around. That would be her father performing his task as jailer. Had she ever believed that he would forgive and relent? If so, she had been wrong. He had not offered her services to Jimson, not because he valued her time, but because he didn't want her away where she couldn't be watched. "Jessica won't be coming by," meant he didn't trust her even to drop in on Mrs. Hogan now and then. He preferred the risk of Jerry and Tad traveling so far alone to having her move freely away from these acres.

She waited to hear the door bang again to know that her father had gone back in. Instead, Will's voice spoke very near her.

"Miss Findlay?"

He stood by the fence to the burying ground, his hand on the post, his eyes watchful.

"I'm sorry to disturb you," he said in that formal voice he saved for her. "I am sorry I put you into that embarrassing situation in there. I wasn't thinking, or I wouldn't have asked that favor."

"It's all right," she said, turning away. So he did know how to apologize. Then, remorseful because his question had been innocent enough, she explained, "My father doesn't realize that Agatha and I are no longer friends."

After an awkward silence, she asked, "Is that all you came out here to say?"

He sighed. "I also wanted to talk to you about Floss. Has she said anything?"

"About what?" Jessica asked.

He shrugged. "About anything important."

How frustrating he was! "Everything Floss writes to me seems important because I like her so much," Jessica told him.

"She isn't talking about coming out here again, is she?"

"Yes and no," Jessica told him, trying to remember exactly how Floss had phrased it.

She could see his mouth tighten with annoyance. When he spoke, his voice had turned angry. "She didn't tell you any reason why she couldn't come out, did she?"

He had been so civil that Jessica had forgotten how rude he could be.

"If she had, I would be obliged to keep her confidence," she told him, not caring that her tone was haughty.

She couldn't remember when he had touched her before. Now he stepped forward and seized her arm. He held it hard, before shaking his head with a sigh. "You are a trial, that's what you are, young lady, a trial. I try to find out something very important to me, and you give me yet another lesson in manners. This isn't any childish game I'm playing, Miss Findlay. Keep what you know to yourself, but do just that. If you are obliged to hold my aunt's confidences from me, for God's sake, keep them from everyone else, too."

He turned and walked away in swift, angry strides, without looking back. Jessica touched her arm where he had gripped it. He had muscles of iron to have left her flesh tingling like that. She wanted to call him back, to tell him what Floss had said, to assure him that she knew nothing important enough to justify such a display of fury. But the door had closed behind him and he was gone.

That Sunday night, Patrick Findlay completed his plans to leave on the cattle drive early with Will.

"You'll have to see to the spring calves," he told Jessica. "You know the far pasture where they are being held. Take just enough hay every day to keep them going. Go as early as the light will let you. That will give you a fighting chance to save any new calf whose mother might have died. Take Major along in case of wolves."

Jessica nodded, not meeting his eyes.

Wednesday morning at dawn the men rode off. They would be joined by two neighboring ranchers before they left the county. The night had been cold. The steam from Patrick Findlay's horse rose around him in a cloud, making him seem ghostly and unreal as he turned that last time to wave.

"Early out is early back," Melanie said wistfully. "With any luck at all, they'll be home in three weeks."

"To dance at Rachel's wedding," Jessica said, trying to cheer her up.

"To dance at Rachel's wedding," Melanie repeated joylessly.

Jessica lifted the buckets from inside the door to start the milking. In her father's absence, she was responsible for the outside work. This time, for a change, she approached this labor without pride.

She patted Daisy's smooth, twitching hide and began to tug the warm streams of milk into the bucket. Her father had told her goodbye with an awkward pat on the shoulder instead of a hug like the old times. "Behave yourself," he had said, a vastly different farewell from his old "Be a good girl."

Will had called her a trial. How much more trying she was to herself than she possibly could be to anyone else. Here she sat, mooning by a cow's belly, feeling bleak and lonely and unloved.

If she was unloved, it was her own stupid fault. Rachel had managed to fall in love with someone proper to marry. Certainly, her father and Melanie had a love that fit in with things. But she had to be bored and fearful of Roy Blanding, and feel too old and wise to be more than a friend to Geoffrey Montgomery.

"My father hasn't made a prisoner of me," she admitted to herself. "I built my own prison by falling in love with Hawk." At the thought of him, she leaned her head against the cow's warm side and wept.

Jerry appeared at the stall door behind her with Major wagging at his side. He called her name softly. "He'll be all right, Jessica," he told her. "Papa will get home all right, just wait and see."

She turned and smiled at him. "Thank you, Jerry," she said gently. "Here, get a pan and we'll give Major some of this warm milk."

It was strange on Sunday to have the Findlay pew not filled. Jessica and Melanie sang extra loud to make up for the voices of Patrick and Will being gone. Jimson made Tad giggle and have to be glared at. Not until Jerry punched Jessica in the side and waggled his head did she notice that Roy had a girl beside him in their family pew.

Jessica couldn't stare, of course, but by the end of the service, she had seen enough to judge the girl as pretty and well dressed. Her hair was blond like Jessica's, but she had a stronger jaw and her eyes, under a rose-colored bonnet, looked dark and shiny.

Jessica didn't feel jealous, only mean. She hoped for the girl's sake that she was too stupid to be bored by Roy's conversation. Suddenly, she had an even better idea. Maybe that strong jaw meant the girl would be stubborn, maybe even stubborn enough to put Roy's mother in her place.

Chapter
Twenty-two

JESSICA dreaded those early-morning rides to the far pasture. Just the thought of launching herself into that cold darkness made her shudder. That first morning, she literally had to force herself from her warm bed. She dressed without even a candle for fear she'd disturb the boys and start Melanie's day too early.

Outside in the stable, the bay horse stood dreaming, both eyes shut and one hoof cocked like a dancer while the steam of his breath swirled around his head. Once free of the barnyard, the wagon rattled along between the drifts, startling hares from their burrows to leap in great zigzagging arcs across the snow. Major, beside Jessica on the seat, whimpered and trembled to be off in chase, but she held him back with her voice.

Although the moon was gone, clusters of

bright stars silvered the trees. Barren of leaves, they stood boldly on the high ground only to swim waist-deep in mist as the wagon careened down through the hollows. Shadows moved in that mist, low to the ground and furtive, the hunters of the night still seeking their prey.

Dawn had flooded the countryside with richly colored light by the time she found the cattle, still at rest in a grove of trees. They rose awkwardly, shoving each other aside as they gathered around the wagon for the hay. One of the last to come was a heifer cow with a fresh calf at her side. The little creature wavered on his new legs, staring at Jessica from his dish of a face.

She had pitched the last of the hay onto the ground when Major began to growl. With a cautioning hand on his back, she followed his gaze. Standing in the wagon bed, she felt taller than the trees he was staring at. The hair along his back was a stiff brush under her hand.

She had leaned to bring her rifle into the crook of her arm when the song of the flute began.

Tears. Never had tears sprung so quickly to her eyes. She scrambled down and ran wildly toward the sound, blinded by her own tears. Just short of the grove she stopped, halted in her tracks by the memory of her father's thundering voice: *"You are never to see that Indian again."*

As she stood there in anguish, Hawk

walked alone from the shadows of the trees, leaving his pony standing. He was smiling, and without a word, he walked to her, opened his blanket, and folded it around them both, holding her close.

"Moons," he whispered into her hair. "How many moons have I dreamed of this time?"

"My father," she whispered without moving from his embrace.

He shook his head. "Don't talk of him now," he told her. "This is our time."

"How did you know to find me here?"

He laughed softly. "By the friendship of stars. Each morning your father rode forth in the darkness as I passed to my work. Each morning I watched him go, since that was the closest I could come to you." He paused and smiled down at her. "This morning he looked changed. I asked myself if Patrick Findlay had been shrunken of his height by some spell. I asked myself why his walk had turned from a heavy stride to a light, skipping dance." He chuckled. "I followed. I was only sure that it was you when you began to sing . . . you and your friend." He nodded toward Major, stiff and wary at her side, his throat still rumbling with suspicion.

"But your work," she thought aloud. "What will they say when you do not come?"

The flesh of his face was as smooth as she remembered, smooth and a burnished gold in this light. His hair leaped in a shining fall from under the band that crossed his forehead.

"I will go," he told her. "When I come late, they will ask me where I have been. I will tell them that I was on my mother's business."

At her doubtful look, he laughed and drew her close again. "I will tell no lie. Men may be chiefs, but the power of a tribe passes through its women. I *want* my love for you to be my mother's business. I cannot face such hungry moons again, swelling and shrinking one after another while I dream of you."

"Oh, Hawk," she cried, feeling his heart beating against her own. "What can we do? I don't know what we can do."

"Decide," he said. Drawing back, he took her hand. "Come." He led her to the wagon and lifted her up, then leaped up beside her, taking her hand in his. "Each time you step from your tepee, you decide. Do I go left where the snake may be coiled? Or do I go right where the wolves crouch? There is no safety, only chance. Each step carries a man toward death somewhere. But even as every wild creature chooses what mate walks to death beside him, so can we."

Her tears had begun again, hot and hateful, streaming down her face. As she shook her head, he flattened his hand softly against her cheek. Then he leaned and touched his lips to hers.

"No more grief," he ordered. "Let us trade songs."

When she hesitated, still fighting tears, which were half joy and half pain, he took out his flute and began to play.

Listening, Jessica could not imagine that melody written down. It was not so much a song as an enchantment. Surely such a song had drawn the sailors of Ulysses to drive their ships against the rocks.

In exchange, she sang a song from Rachel's wedding music. Accustomed to piano accompaniment, her voice stumbled at first. Then, encouraged by his eyes, she sang.

> Amazing grace!
> How sweet the sound,
> That saved a wretch like me.
> I once was lost but now am found,
> Was blind but now I see.

When her voice stilled, he held her close. "Is this the day, Jessica? Is this the day you come and be one with my people?"

When she shivered in his arms, he dropped them to his side. As he moved away, she reached for him, unable to face parting. He smiled and touched her cheek.

"Other days will come. One will be the right one. You will come back tomorrow?"

When she nodded, he leaned and pressed his lips to hers. "We will be waiting for you, the morning and I."

Jessica watched until horse and rider became one moving shadow, then nothing. She gave the bay his head going home as she sobbed with her face in her hands. This was even worse than she had thought all those months. With him she felt breathlessly alive, without him the color of life faded to gray.

"I will think more clearly by tomorrow," Jessica promised herself. And Hawk would be there. She began to sing again, in that bold, loud way while she still could.

True to his word, that next morning Hawk was waiting. Jessica, having walked as if in a dream, ran into his arms and raised her lips to his at once.

"I am brazen," she said as they pulled apart to smile at each other.

He stared at her, frowning. "Made of brass?" he asked.

"Your speech is so good that I am always amazed when you don't know a word," she told him. "That word means a woman without pride who is bold with men."

"Are you bold with men?" he asked soberly.

"Heavens, no," she told him. "Only with you."

He relaxed. "That's different," he told her. "It is different when two will walk together."

Some days they sang. Some days they only talked, sitting on the edge of the wagon, swinging their legs like children on a fence.

He tried to teach her to play his flute, but she could only produce a plaintive squeak.

He taught her to carve a flute from a sapling branch. She didn't dare take it home for fear Jerry would find it and ask hard questions.

He told her stories of brave men and

beautiful women who were turned by magic spells into wild creatures to lead new and beautiful lives.

Each day with Hawk was different from the last. Each joy she had with him was a different joy. And although his questions differed from day to day, all these questions asked the same thing: *Was this the day that Jessica would come with him and be one with his people?* And always when he greeted her, he held her tight inside the warmth of his blanket, their hearts beating close together.

Jessica's father had been gone a week when a bitter wind forced the temperatures down again, glazing the prairie with sheets of ice. That night, as Melanie banked the fire against going to bed, she turned to Jessica.

"Wait until light to go to the cattle," she urged. "The minute the sun is up, the air starts to warm."

Jessica shook her head. "I love watching the dawn come." That was the truth. "I wrap up extra warm." That also was the truth. She did not add the third truth that brought her from a warm bed into the chill with a glad heart. There was no cold intense enough to keep her from that precious hour with Wheeling Hawk. She had even begun to load the hay for the cattle onto the wagon the night before so she could be with Hawk without delay.

That morning, the hay was crisply frozen, and the bay horse skidded on platelets of ice where water had overflowed the trough. Jessica hugged herself for warmth by the time the horse crested the last hillock. She leaped to her feet in the wagon. Something was wrong in the field ahead. Instead of dozing among the trees, the cattle were swift shadows, running in wild abandon. Even with the wind blowing the other way, she heard the bawling of a cow, plaintive in the darkness. She slapped the reins across the bay's back and pulled down her rifle as she raced toward the field.

Hawk ran toward her over the frozen grass. "Quick, Jessica," he said. "With speed we can save her."

It was obvious what had happened. A young cow, trying to defend her calf from wolves, had been savagely torn about the legs and flanks. Weak from bleeding, she now lay on the ground, her calf nudging her and bawling. A few yards away, two coyotes lay frozen where Hawk's rifle had caught them.

Hawk seized the pitchfork and tossed the hay off the wagon. "You must get this creature to help, or kill her."

"Not kill her," Jessica whispered, fighting to keep her eyes from the anguished calf.

"Then help me," he said urgently.

"But she weighs several hundred pounds," Jessica told him. "What can we do?"

"Go to the woods," he ordered. "Find two strong dead trees as thick as your arm. When you've found them, call me."

One tree was longer than the other, but both were as tall as herself. Together they dragged them to the back of the wagon where

Hawk bound them with ropes of bent saplings. Then, with the two tree trunks laid at an angle like a *V*, he made a bed between them of shorter branches strapped together.

"We call this a travois," he told her. "The Cheyenne carry all things with such. Now help me."

Together they worked the anguished animal onto this frame. When the cow pulled away from Jessica's tugging, Hawk worked the framework farther beneath her until most of her body weight rested in the travois. Then he bound her there. Her eyes were wide, even as her voice failed from loss of blood. With the calf's legs bound to keep it in the wagon, Hawk nodded approval.

"Now drive as fast as you can."

As he spoke, he frowned. "Oh, Jessica," he said. "We have lost a day." Stepping forward, he pulled her inside his blanket, murmuring something in his own language softly against her hair. Then he pulled away, saying, "Go for the life of that creature."

Jessica caught his face between her hands and raised her lips to his. "Thank you, Hawk," she whispered. "I love you."

The cow was silent by that last hill. By the time Jessica dragged the travois past the chicken yard, the mother cow stared blindly as her calf bawled hoarsely from the bed of the wagon.

Melanie was out of the house and running alongside the wagon before Jessica reached the barn lot.

"Oh, my God," she cried, her hands against her mouth.

"Coyotes. We did everything we could to save her," Jessica said. Then, looking up, she saw the astonishment in Melanie's eyes. What a fool she had been. How had she thought she would explain making this Indian carrier, lifting the full-grown cow onto it?

Melanie looked away.

"Help me with the calf," she said. "The little thing needs milk."

When Jerry returned from school, Melanie sent him on Dancie to make Mr. Logan an offer.

"Tell him one of our heifers was killed by wolves and that I will share the meat if he will butcher her for me."

Mr. Logan, astonished by this windfall, didn't ask questions until the hide was on the pegs and the meat hanging to freeze.

"Then the wolves came right into the lot?"

Melanie didn't lie but neither did she answer his question. "They are as hungry as we are this winter," she reminded him. "Hunger makes all creatures bold."

After Mr. Logan had gone with his bounty of fresh beef and the boys were settled for the night, Melanie went to her piano and played softly for a long time. She didn't finish songs but drifted from one to another in a thoughtful medley. With her fingers still on the keys, she looked over to where Jessica was making a bouquet of French knots on Rachel's petticoat.

"Being a stepmother is a delicate thing," she said slowly, as if feeling one at a time for the next word. "My loyalties are too easily split when my daughter is also my friend. At a time like this, what do I do? Do I take my husband's laws as my own and try to stand where I think he would stand? Or do I stand apart with you and risk the charge of being a bad wife?"

"I don't know where you stand," Jessica reminded her.

Melanie sighed. "I see your young Indian friend in swift scenes and few of these set by you. His rescue of you and Jimson during the flood could not have been of your making. That he met and rode with you those days in the fall when you were going for the boys is something you share. If you had not wanted his company, I cannot imagine his being there. The buffalo meat at Christmas was another time that he reached out and you had no control. I don't understand this business today. That was a Cheyenne travois and clearly you could not have loaded that cow and calf alone. I can only think that he met you there and when you needed help, he gave it.

"Men do not walk this far out of their paths for friendship alone. Women do not mourn as you did after your father talked to you from loss of friendship alone. If you love this man, I grieve for your problem. But my grief will no more heal your love than your father's anger will. I will stand apart from this, Jessica. However it works out must be your own decision. Only know that I grieve for your pain, and love you whatever happens."

Jessica thrust the linen away and flew to Melanie's arms. Perhaps Melanie's tears were from grief. Jessica's were from the relief of being understood and loved.

From that day forward, Melanie neither asked about Hawk, nor did Jessica mention him. Altogether Hawk and Jessica were to have nearly two weeks of stolen dawns before Patrick Findlay's careful plans ran into trouble.

Melanie had already begun watching for her sons to return from school when the strange buggy rattled into the yard. Mrs. Hogan, with Jimson in her arms, was on the ground and to the door in record time. "Dwayne is bringing in Jimson's things," she told Melanie "I'm needed in Ellis. The baby could get there before I do."

Melanie sent her off with fresh beef and fervent prayers.

"Your father and Will should be home soon," Melanie reminded her family. "Won't they be surprised to find two babies here? Jimson and Bridie?"

At this last, Melanie smiled at Jessica. Tad, having adopted the orphan calf, had named her Bridie after his teacher at school.

"Bridie's bigger," Tad bragged.

"Teach her to clap her hands like Jimson does and I'll be impressed," Jerry told him.

Chapter
Twenty-three

THE Landers family, as Jessica's father put it, "spared no horses" for their youngest daughter's wedding. As maid of honor, Jessica had a special dress. It was the same shade of blue as her eyes, and the waist was tucked in almost past breathing. The very tiniest fan of a pleated bustle perked it out in back, and the sleeves puffed out above the elbow like a dress from an Eastern fashion magazine. It had even been made by a dressmaker instead of at home.

As she tried the dress on at home, Melanie sighed. "How beautiful you are, Jessica. Oh, and you can wear those wonderful slippers that Floss sent with it."

"Oh, no, she can't," Jerry protested. "Those are wedding slippers."

"This is a wedding," his mother reminded him.

He shook his head stubbornly. "Those are

for her own wedding," he explained. "Jessica's wedding, not Rachel's."

"What if I never marry?" she asked him.

Tad looked at her, astonished at this idea. "I'll marry you, Jessica," he said.

In the laughter that followed, no more was said about the slippers. As she dressed for the wedding, Jessica tried them on. They were perfect with her dress, no doubt about that. Then she put them back into their tissue and pulled on her freshly cleaned boots. Was it because she knew they were really a present from Will instead of Floss that she couldn't wear them? In any case, this wasn't the right day to wear them.

From where she stood by the organ during the ceremony, Jessica could see the Findlay pew clearly. Only someone who knew Melanie well would be able to read the concern in that beautiful face. Patrick and Will were already a week overdue. Melanie said nothing about her fears, but Jessica heard her in the night, prowling through the dark rooms, checking the candle that guttered in the front window.

Just as Preacher Allen asked if Rachel would "love, honor, and obey" Walt, Jimson let out a shriek and began to wail so loudly that Melanie had to take him out of the church.

Afterward, at the reception, Melanie apologized over and over for his interruption of the service.

"Not another word," Mrs. Landers beamed.

"I never heard a prettier sound. Didn't you know that the cry of a baby during a wedding is an omen of a full cradle for the new couple?"

"Mother," Rachel whispered fiercely, turning as red as Jessica had ever seen her.

"Never you mind, Mrs. Brannon," Rachel's mother said, laughing at her daughter's embarrassment. "I'm only letting go of you in the hope of getting grandchildren back."

Jessica was proud of Rachel's mother. What a brave show she made of "letting go." She teased about the work Rachel was dumping on her at the store and the post office. But Jessica remembered too well her anguished tears at the thought of Rachel gone from the nest.

"Is this the day that you come and be one with my people?" How strange to have Hawk's voice echoing in her head in this room filled with friends and neighbors. They were two worlds farther apart than scattered stars. She didn't realize that tears had sprung to her eyes until Mrs. Landers pressed her hand. Jessica smiled back through waves of guilt. How could Mrs. Landers know that Jessica wept not for Rachel but for herself?

Hawk sensed her mood the morning after Rachel's wedding. "She has always been my best friend," she explained.

He studied her, his dark eyes thoughtful. Then he smiled. "See how little I know? I don't know whose tepee she will make her

286

home in now, her own mother's or that of her husband."

"A new one," she told him. "Her own and Walt's."

He nodded, thoughtful. "I have seen many marriages between the Wihio and my people. Sometimes, when women are taken in raids, they later marry a man of my people. Sometimes they only marry to get better treatment."

"How do you know this?" she asked.

"If they get a chance to run away, they abandon their husbands and children. Many Wihio have seized our women and treated them as wives only to abandon them when they grow tired. Long Hair did that, you know, the soldier Custer. He took a girl of our people and used her as a wife. He tired of her and the son she bore." He smiled. "He is a nice child, named Yellow Sparrow because his hair is as fine and golden as his father's."

He turned and took her shoulders between his hands. "I have not pressed you, Jessica, because of love. I would not take you any way but in love. But, Jessica, the time grows short. Now that the buffalo are slain, the Wihio in wagons want even the land that grows our corn. The blue coats press our chiefs, and the agents have no power with your President Grant. That is why I always ask you if this is the day. If the tribe votes to move on, I must go, too. As a warrior, I must guard my people, go where they go, and stand against their enemies."

When she didn't answer but only laid her head against his chest and clung to him, he sighed and rose. "There will be a day."

Before Jessica and Major reached the barn with the wagon, the snow had begun to fall. By the time she had finished the milking, it spun almost knee-deep in the barn lot. When she let herself into the kitchen with the milk, she found Melanie crying. "I know it's silly," Melanie sniffled when Jessica took her in her arms. "I know a dozen things can slow a drive without harming the men. I only want to see your father's face and know him safe. And now look at that snow. A late storm of any size could delay them another week."

"It's April," Jessica reminded her. "How can we have much of a snow this late?"

"I remember," Melanie said bitterly. "More than one I remember."

When Major began to whine at the door a little after noon, Jessica let him out and saw Jerry and Tad turning in on Dancie. The air seemed soft, almost warm, after the bitter days of the week before. But the snow was already to the ledges of the window, and the sky was thick with it still coming. Jessica thought the boys' teacher had wisely dismissed the children early because of the snow.

Seeing Jessica at the door, Jerry called urgently, "Come get Tad. He's really sick."

"Sick?" Jessica asked, reaching for her shawl. Before she could pull it from the peg, Melanie had sped out the door to her son's side.

Only then did Jessica realize that instead of clinging to Jerry's back, as he usually did, Tad was in Jerry's arms, with his head against his brother's shoulder.

"Miss Bridie sent me home with him," Jerry explained, bracing his brother as Melanie reached up for him. "He's talked funny all the way home, making no sense at all."

It was like Jerry to respond to fear by being cross. Jessica could measure the extent of his concern by the tightness of his frown.

"Jump down," Jessica told him. "Go warm up. I'll take care of Dancie."

Instead, he dropped to the ground beside her and stared after his mother, carrying Tad limply into the house.

"What's diphtheria?" he asked.

Jessica, with her hand on Dancie's bridle, felt her knees turn weak. She braced herself against the pony's side, trying to keep her panic from showing with Jerry's eyes so watchful on her face.

"Why do you ask?"

"That Ruthie girl with the red hair has been out of school all week. Today her uncle came for her things. He told the teacher it was diphtheria."

"Did Miss Bridie say anything to you kids?"

He shook his head. "She went around and felt everybody's head and sent Tad and me home. And she kept sniffling like she wanted to bawl."

"But Tad hadn't been sick before that?"

"He acted funny last night, bouncing around in bed. He said his head hurt this morning, but you know how he makes stuff up when he doesn't want to go to school. Then he got hot-looking at school, but we were all hot because that's really a good stove there." He paused. "Jessica?"

"Listen, Jerry," she said. "Diphtheria is a really bad sickness that people catch. You put Dancie away and give her some hay. I'll go talk to Melanie and be right back."

"Tad's not going to die," he said, almost shouting, his tone angry like his father's.

She turned and touched his cheek and smiled. "Not if we can stop it, Jerry Findlay. Right?"

He ducked his head and grinned a little. "Right," he echoed softly, taking Dancie's bridle from her and turning toward the barn.

Melanie, with Tad in her arms, was trying to set the teakettle over the heat. Her anguished eyes turned to Jessica. "He's burning with fever, Jessica. What will I do?"

Jessica took the teakettle and led Melanie to her rocking chair. "I'll make the tea," she said. "Then Jerry and I will go for Mary Huffman."

Melanie stared at her.

"Just in case," Jessica told her. "There's diphtheria at school."

"Oh, my God," Melanie breathed. Then, her eyes wide, "Jimson."

The two women stared at each other.

"Babies under a year almost never get it," Jessica quoted without knowing from where.

"Babies on their mothers' milk," Melanie corrected her. "What can we do, Jessica?"

"Wait," Jessica said. "There's a way. I'll take Jimson and Jerry over to the Reynolds place. No, I'll take them both with me to Logan's. There are people there, and horses, so someone can go get Mary Huffman. You will be all right here alone?"

Melanie nodded. "But don't bring the children back here. Take food and fuel and stay at Will's place."

As she spoke, Tad moaned and began to cough, a thick cough that racked his little body. At the sound, Jimson startled awake and began to howl from the next room.

Melanie shook her head urgently. "He'll just have to cry. Leave him there until you get everything ready to go. Then take him through here fast, with his face covered."

Jerry was sitting on the snowy step outside the door, his fingers coiled in Major's thick coat. Jessica dropped down beside him.

"All right, Jerry," she said. "Here's what we have to do." When she finished speaking, he stared at her a moment, then rose and started toward the barn. Then he paused. "What do you need, the buggy or the sleigh?"

She smiled. "I hadn't gotten that far. I guess it will have to be the sleigh."

Nothing went right. At the Logans, they learned that Mary Huffman was staying with the Ryan child who was "like to die" with pneumonia. Mrs. Logan herself, with a house full of little children, had turned as white as a sheet at Jessica's report.

"There's no call to panic," Mr. Logan said, pulling on his pipe and frowning. "My hand and I can cover the feeding of Patrick's stock and do the milking if you don't mind our leaving it outside the door. You can't take that baby back in there," he added, looking at Jimson.

As Jessica nodded, he looked at Jerry. "And your mother can't be left there by herself, you know."

"I can stay with her," Jerry said. "I can do fuel and chickens and all. I can even milk."

"That's how it has to be," Mrs. Logan said.

"But. . . ." Jessica began, appalled at the thought of being away when Melanie and Tad needed her.

"This boy has already been exposed," Mrs. Logan said flatly. "He was in school with that girl and rode home with that child against his chest."

"And he's more than half a man," Mr. Logan added, "being his father's son."

It was dark when Jerry left the Reynolds dugout in the steadily falling snow. How small he looked, crouched in the seat of the sleigh, his muffler wound around his face clear up to his eyes.

Jessica watched him disappear into the whiteness and turned back to the dugout, furious at her helplessness. Jimson, catching her eyes, spread his fingers in front of his face and peeked out at her, smothering a giggle.

"Stop that," she shouted at him. "You've spent half of your life getting between me and what I needed to do. I should have been teaching school. Instead, I sat around while you sucked on a lamp wick and got myself all mixed up by falling in love with the wrong man. Now, when I should be home with my mother, comforting her and fixing her hot meals and taking turns with my baby brother, I'm stuck off here in this mud hole, and you want to play games."

The baby stared at her. She was instantly repentant. It wasn't his fault.

Just knowing that he would cry the way her brothers always had when she yelled at them, she crossed the room to comfort him, to tease him into forgetting her tantrum. Instead of crying, he stared at her as she approached, looking at her just like his father had so many times. Then, as she knelt before him smiling, he turned his head away, refusing to look at her, acting for all in the world as if she were invisible. Like Will always did.

Jerry came the next day as he had promised. When she heard the snowball hit the door, she ran to open it. He stood a few feet back and grinned at her.

"Mama said not to come in because I'm exposed."

"How's Tad?" Jessica asked. "And Melanie?"

"Tad's really sick. He chokes up, and Mama sticks a feather in him with turpentine. Mama holds Tad all the time, so I'm learning to cook. She told me how to make cornbread, and it wasn't half bad."

Jessica tried to swallow her tears. How manly he looked there in the snow, how proud and capable. "How are you doing with Daisy and Brindle?"

He grinned. "Finally, I just whacked Daisy in the hip and yelled at her like Papa does. The milk comes easier now."

"Jerry, you are quite the fellow."

"I wish Papa would come," he told her. "Mr. Logan says the snowstorm slowed them down. They say it's lots deeper south and west of here."

"He'll be along," she assured him. "Thanks a lot for coming."

"We'll play dominoes when you come home?" he asked, his voice wistful.

"Sure thing," she told him. "And I'll do the milking again."

"Hug old Jimson for me," he called as he started off.

She was glad he didn't ask for an answer to that. The last thing that Jimson would take from her was any affection.

But she hadn't given up yet. She grinned at the baby.

"If you were a dog, you'd bite me, wouldn't you?" she asked.

He turned his head away and stared at the corner to avoid her eyes.

Chapter
Twenty-four

FOR weeks, Jessica had wakened before dawn to drive the wagon to the far pasture, feed the cattle, and be with Hawk. Not even the darkness of the Reynolds dugout was enough to break that habit. It took her a moment even to remember where she was and to realize that the child breathing beside her was not Tad but Jimson.

Tad. His name was enough to shock her awake. After a couple of restless turns, she sat upright in the bed, her arms around her knees, listening to the barking of coyotes carried on the wind.

Jerry had told her more than he realized. If Melanie was having to cut the diphtheria membrane in Tad's throat with the harsh poison of turpentine, the child was desperately ill.

Once up and dressed, she sat in the deep

windowsill to watch the sun rise. Hawk would wait for her, and she would never come. Would he be gone by the time Logan went to feed the stock? There, she had given herself another thing to worry about, as if she didn't have enough.

At least the snow had finally stopped.

The baby finally stirred awake. He let her feed him but stared at her warily as she spooned diluted porridge into his mouth.

"Sooner or later, we have to be friends again," she told him.

She began to watch for Jerry in midmorning, between the completion of the chores and lunch. By the time the sun, a bleak, glimmering circle, reached the top of the gray sky, Jessica wanted to scream. Noon and Jerry still wasn't there. All sorts of terrors rose in her mind. Tad was too ill for Melanie to handle alone. Jerry himself had been stricken with the disease. Melanie, exhausted by nursing and frantic with worry, had broken under the strain and was sick herself.

Having done everything she could find to do in the house, she tried to read a book from Will's shelf. It was about raising crops, and a good deal of it was wrong, for Kansas.

By late afternoon, the baby, having eaten and slept, wakened fretful. He consented to sit on Jessica's lap and be sung to. She was closer to singing herself to sleep than him when she heard the hoofbeats of horses and saw a dark movement outside the window.

She had leaped to her feet with Jimson on her hip when the door of the dugout flew open. The Indian in the doorway was so tall that he stooped to enter. Before she could challenge him, three others crowded in behind him, filling the small room.

"What do you want?" she asked. "Why are you here?"

The oldest of them, a woman with a face as seamed as a dry creek bank, studied her with dark metallic eyes. Then, turning away, she began to move around the room, examining everything that fell to her hand. She lifted Rosemary Reynolds' Haviland teapot at such an angle that Jessica feared the delicate lid would fall and break. She picked up the basket of letters Mrs. Hogan had saved since Will left and dumped them on the rug. Then she pulled the canvas drape away from the wall to peer into that darkness. As she did this, the old man, who had balanced himself on a polished staff, stared steadily at Jessica.

The tall Indian who had entered first walked silently to the stove where he stood examining the cutlery and tools.

"What do you want?" Jessica repeated, hoping that her voice didn't reveal her terror. The fear that she had held for all Indians, before knowing Hawk, rushed in on her in a shivering torrent. The young girl, like the ancient man, seemed content to stand and stare. She was pretty in a wild, burnished way, and her mouth tightened in a tidy smile as she stared back at Jimson. Only when two of them moved toward her at once did Jessica lose her control and raise her voice.

The old man, mumbling something aloud, staggered toward her on his unsteady legs and reached out for her hair. Even as she shrank from his touch, the girl stepped forward and reached out for Jimson.

"No," Jessica said firmly, holding the baby tight against her. "No."

The girl's face contorted with fury. She seized Jimson under the arms, trying to wrest him from Jessica's grasp. They were all talking now, not shouting but talking swiftly to each other, nodding as if in a conspiracy with the old man, who clung to her hair as the girl fought for the child.

There was no point in screaming for help. No one would hear. "Go," she said to them. "Go from this place and leave me be."

Though her words apparently meant nothing to them, the old man shrugged, released her braid, and was backing off as Hawk appeared in the door.

With his name quick to her lips, Jessica was silent. This was not the Hawk she knew. Straightening from the doorway, his eyes swept the room, seeming to diminish each of the intruders in size. His soft, musical voice had become the singing of a whip. The old woman would have protested, but he turned away from her. Seizing the young girl by the shoulder, he spun her around and shoved her toward the door.

Then, motioning the old man to follow her,

he strode across the room to face the tall young man behind Jessica. Without understanding a word that he said, Jessica knew Hawk had saved his harshest words for this man.

Stunned and gripping Jimson tightly, Jessica watched them leave as quietly as they had come, the young girl first, the old man behind her, and then the young man, stumbling a little in his haste.

The old woman was the last to go. She stood in the doorway with those dark, unblinking eyes fixed on Jessica until Hawk went to her side, turned her gently, and pushed her out the doorway.

If there had been a bolt, she would have shot it at that moment; if a lock, she would have sealed it. Instead, she leaned weakly against the edge of the table, reminding herself that Hawk was there. Hawk. But even as she repeated his name, she shivered at the memory of his passionate fury.

Jimson, tired of being twisted in her arms, puckered toward a wail. She began to walk the room with him against her shoulder, murmuring a reassurance she didn't feel. Passing the door, she saw them moving **aw**ay, the two women sharing a pony, the young man on a larger horse, dragging behind him a travois in which the old man rode. Hawk, his back as straight as a plumb line, stood watching them go.

When he turned to see her in the doorway, he reached her in quick steps.

"Why?" she asked. "Who are they? What did they want?"

She had never seen his face so somber. He reached out, took Jimson from her arms, and turned her around as he had the young girl, only gently. "Come," he said, his voice heavy as if with great fatigue. "We must talk."

Setting Jimson against the bed, Hawk reached for a spoon, shook it to get Jimson's attention, then put it into Jimson's hands.

Then, without hesitation, he rose, walked to Jessica, and took her in his arms. What he crooned to her was in his own language, like the song of his flute, a message of love and comfort. How could she feel his grief so painfully when she didn't know its cause?

When he released her, he set her down at the table with himself across from her and took both her hands in his.

"Why?" he repeated. "They wanted to see the Wihio who had snared me with the webs of love until I forgot the hour or the season." He shook his head, those dark eyes pleading for her understanding.

"Who are they? They are Swift Runner, my mother; Bent Willow, her brother; Spring Rain, my sister; and White Fox, a member of my warrior society but no friend." He paused. "As to what they wanted, a chill about my heart tells me that they achieved it."

"To scare me to death?" she asked, trying to coax that darkness from his face.

He shook his head. "Not your death, Jessica, but mine."

She stared at him, her heart pounding. What did he mean? What was he saying?

He turned her fingers in his hand, staring at them before folding them down gently, one by one, until he had made closed fists of both of her hands, tight, white fists, gripping nothing. These he enclosed in his own strong, brown hands and clasped the two of them together.

Glancing up at her, he forced a smile that did not reach his eyes. "I knew there was little time, but I didn't know *how* little time there was. I told myself that we could grow our love strong enough for you to make the journey from your people to mine. But the family had voted to move on. I alone held back. They wanted to see this woman with the hair like ripe grain who had made a child of a warrior. They wanted you to see what family you would become a part of. But most of all, they wanted you to hate and fear me, so that you would send me back to them as a man and a warrior."

Jessica stared at his hands, knowing that her own were hidden within them, lost in his strength but held by his gentleness.

"If that is what they wanted, they have failed," she told him slowly, only knowing what was true when she heard her own words in air. "I do not hate you. I do not fear you. I love you, Hawk, and I cannot imagine that I will love anyone this same way ever."

He studied her, then pressed her hands warmly. "But today is not the day?"

"There can never be that day," she told him. "If I went with you to be one with your people, the Hawk I love would have to become the Hawk they need. You yourself have told me how great this need is. You have told me how many battles stand between your people and mine before justice is done. As you grew as warrior, our love would shrivel to fear and hate. It was all in this room today."

He looked at her and shook his head. "How can a maiden with eyes the color of the sky be as wise as a shaman? I dreamed, and now I waken." He released her hands and rose. Her hands were cold without that gentle covering. But he came around, lifted her, and held her against him, his lips in her hair, whispering.

"But let me teach you about death, my Jessica. The Cheyenne knows what a Wihio does not know. There is no death, there is only change. The bones of the buffalo crumble to feed new corn. The water burned away by sun is given again in snow. Our love will not die but change, Jessica. It will change both of us and every life we touch."

She was weeping, and he touched her cheek the way he had before, with the flat of his hand pressed against her tears. Then he kissed her gently a long time.

"I could leave you the flute, Jessica, but it is silenced now. Did I leave you the song?"

"Yes," she whispered. "That at least won't change."

They moved toward the door with his arm

around her. There he stopped and touched her lips again. He walked away a few steps and then came back. He smiled at her in the same way he had smiled that first time, when she had caught only that glimpse of him under the buffalo robe that sheltered them both from the fury of the storm.

"Stop here," he warned. "My people are famous with your people for taking what they want. What is to prevent me from seizing you this minute, throwing you across my saddle, and riding away?" Now he was openly laughing. "Oh, Jessica, I am more warrior than you know. You are the conquest that my arms ache for. How easy it would be, Jessica. This night my tribe moves under cover of darkness to keep the blue coats from knowing where we go. We will fade into the mountains like a day going into night. They will search until their horses are lamed and their rifles empty, and find nothing. And no one." He touched her cheek. "I am a warrior but no fool. I will take from you only what I already have. And be grateful through all the long nights."

She stood at the door and watched him go, looking back only once before striking the pony's flanks with furious blows, so that the beast thundered away in a cloud of snow. The wind was rising. It swept the snow around the corner of the dugout, over the trail of the travois and the hooves of the horses that had dragged it away.

She turned to see the child, the spoon sideways in his mouth, watching her from the floor. When he tried to smile around that spoon, his face twisted all out of shape with happiness.

The dullness stayed, the pain coming and going, as if a part of her had been torn away and fought against healing. Her mind leaped from pain to pain like something pursued. Tad. Why hadn't Jerry come? Hawk. She restored the spilled letters to their basket, put the teapot back in its place, and fixed food that wouldn't go down her throat.

By the time she lay down, still in her clothes, she was tired even past weeping.

But not past thinking. "I am changed," she told herself. "This must be how it feels to come back from a long journey to find your landscape changed." What had really changed? Herself, her world, or the eyes she saw it through? The thinking didn't work. She wanted to scream, needed to release her pain.

"How could I have let him go?" she wailed to the empty room. Then she remembered and tried with her voice to recapture the song he had left with her.

She almost had Hawk's song so that she could imitate the tones of that plaintive flute perfectly. She would have had it perfectly if the earth had not begun to vibrate around the dugout.

Leaping to her feet, she ran to the door. The sun that had set behind Hawk had been replaced by a pale moon. A moving river of silver stirred on the backs of the cattle flowing along the road from the west. Mounted men rode at either side, as the animals veered and trotted along.

As she watched, one of the cowboys galloped to the front of the herd and began to cut the cattle off, driving them toward the house. The sound was thunderous, the lowing of the cattle, the cries of the men, the cadence of those hooves barely muffled by the snow.

With awkward fingers, she trimmed the wick and blew the lamp to flame. They were home. That had to be her father and Will. She filled the pot and dumped the basket of buffalo chips in on the coals to speed the fire.

By the time she reached the door with the lamp, the men had driven the cattle into the Reynolds corral and were walking toward the house in the staggering gait of men too long in the saddle.

"Papa," she cried, unable to contain herself. "Papa, you're back."

He was just within the circle of that lamp when she called to him. He stopped short, staggering a little on those high-heeled boots. She couldn't see his face under the shadow of his hat brim, but she read his fury in the lines of his body.

"Jessica," he roared. "How dare you be here? By what right have you defied my orders?"

She drew back into the room, her stomach heaving. How could she have forgotten?

She had no place to hide. She could only

wait there inside the door with the coffee behind her, scenting the room with its fragrant welcome. He came in as roughly as White Fox had, shoving the door open, standing to stare at her, his face bearded from the drive and stiff with anger.

"Where's Mrs. Hogan?" Will asked from behind her father.

"The baby came," she said carefully. "Mrs. Hogan left."

"But here," Patrick Findlay said roughly, only tempering his volume to the sleeping child in the cradle. "By what right are you here?"

"Tad," she said slowly. "Tad is sick, and Melanie sent me."

"Tad sick?" the words came swiftly, rising. "How sick?"

"I haven't heard today," she told him. "Jerry didn't come to tell me."

He forgot the child and raised his voice again, cursing her. She registered his words with shock. This was something he had never done in all her life.

"Can't you do anything right?" His tone was rough with disdain. "I don't mean how sick is he, I mean what's the matter with my son?"

Jessica knew that this was not the real Patrick Findlay standing there with clenched fists shouting at her. She knew this was a man transformed by fear for his child and worn past endurance by the weeks past.

But neither was she Jessica Findlay, a

child to be blamed and shouted at for doing the best she could, the best she knew how.

She stiffened to the last inch she could muster against his height. "Tad has diphtheria," she said hotly. "I came here to try to protect this child."

Once that moment of defiance was past, she felt herself crumple into weakness. Turning away, she covered her face with her hands and began to cry helplessly. Even as she stood there, blinded by her own tears and sick with anguish, she felt warm, strong hands take her by the shoulders and guide her to the bench. Needing the comfort she felt in their touch, she clung gratefully to those warm hands that held her. Not until she caught her breath enough to control her sobbing did she realize that it was Will's gentle touch that supported her. Her father still stood inside the door, his face slack with shock.

Will looked no more like his usual arrogant self than her father had behaved like himself. Instead, he leaned to her, patting her shoulder with tenderness, comforting her. As she looked up at him, she saw his eyes full on her face, looking at her, really seeing her. She knew that Will felt only gratitude for what she had done, but his expression, so tender and intense, reminded her of her father's lost love, and the tears began to flow even more freely.

"Thank you, Miss Findlay," he kept repeating, his voice breaking with emotion. "Thank you. Oh, thank you."

Chapter
Twenty-five

AFTER staring at her for that long moment, Patrick Findlay turned and plunged from the dugout into the darkness.

Will was after him swiftly, leaving the door ajar so that the wind swept snow in a fan across the floor.

"Patrick, Patrick," he called. It was useless. Jessica knew how fast her father could mount and be off.

She was grateful that Will didn't return at once. She wiped her eyes, pulled herself together, and set a tray of bread and butter on the table. She frowned at so little food for a man who had ridden all day. Then, remembering the basket Mrs. Logan had sent as she and Jerry left their house, she pulled it from the shelf.

"What are you doing?" Will asked suddenly from the doorway.

"Cutting side meat," she explained, slicing

the hard, salted pork on the breadboard.

"But it's the middle of the night."

"Have you eaten?" she asked. The moment the meat touched the hot skillet, the room filled with a smoky, mouthwatering fragrance.

"Only some hardtack," he admitted. "Being so close, we decided to push on."

She nodded. "That is Papa's way." Then, seeing him standing hesitant, she said, "Sit. The coffee is there and bread to start."

He sat silently as she lifted the bacon out, moved the skillet, and broke two eggs with a single, sharp blow on the edge of the pan. "Two or four?" she asked, looking around.

He was watching her with such a strange expression on his face that she turned again swiftly to hide the flush she felt rising in her cheeks.

"Four," he said. "I wasn't hungry until I smelled that meat. Have you eaten?"

She shook her head. "I guess I forgot."

"Then cook six at least," he said. "And come and eat with me." Then, after a pause, "Where did those eggs come from?"

"The Logans," she told him, lifting them to slide onto his plate.

"Tell me how all of this came about," he asked.

It was as if a truce had been established between them. They sat and ate together like old and comfortable friends. Sometimes he had a question. More often, he only shook his head.

"That little guy," he said affectionately when she told about Jerry bringing his delirious brother home from school in the snowstorm and hitching the sleigh to go looking for help.

When she told him that Mr. Logan was tending the Findlay cattle, he sighed. "I'll never get over you Kansans," he murmured.

She was refilling their coffee cups when he said, "Your father was awfully tired."

"You don't have to explain Papa to me," she told him.

He looked at her. "Do you realize how much you are like him?" he asked.

She shrugged. "Only once in a while."

"He's my best friend in this world," he said.

Jessica looked at him, puzzled. She had the feeling that he was saying more than his words told her. She was too tired for games; too much had been crammed into the day just past.

"You could do worse," she said.

"I will never be able in a single life to repay him and you for what you have done for me," he told her, his eyes steady on her own.

What could she say to that? She had protested his thanks too many times. Too many times she had done things for this man and his child because she *had* to instead of because she wanted to.

When she looked over at him, she realized that he had sat there across from her, eaten her cooking, and talked to her like a human

310

being, only to end up furious at her again. His face was stiff with that cold anger that she seemed to be able to provoke without doing or saying a thing.

"Listen, Miss Findlay," he said. "I am in debt to you and your father, singly and together. Sometimes I find myself trapped between these loyalties until I don't know which way to turn."

When she only looked at him, puzzled, he rose and began to pace the room.

"All right, all right. If I have to say it right out, I will. I came here eight months ago as green a city boy as you'd hope to find. But I've learned a lot. I not only know a snakeskin from a pile of dirt, I can track a wolf and recognize the trail of a Cheyenne travois dragged through fresh snow."

She felt the color drain from her face. She did not even try to meet his eyes.

"When I went after your father, I missed him. Thank God he didn't have time to see what I saw in the snow outside my door. You see, Miss Findlay, I know the cause of his anger at you. No one has told me, but I know. Floss sometimes gives more away than she means to. I was there, if you remember, when you found your Indian lover's gift on Christmas Eve. See how my loyalty is split, Miss Findlay?"

"No," she told him. "I don't see any split in your loyalty. What you are talking about is none of your business."

He shook his head. "You can't have it both

ways. In one moment you make my problems your problems. Then, when I see my best friend frantic with fear over you and that Indian, I'm suddenly not minding my own business." His tone was scathing again, as it had been that first day and so many times since.

Two could play at his game. After all, he was the one who had taught her this one. She stood up very straight, her eyes level on his. "If you are quite through, Mr. Reynolds, I would appreciate your leaving so that I can get some rest."

She would not have been surprised if he had hit her. He swelled with fury, his fists tight at his side. "You," he said in a low, furious tone, "are the most bullheaded, infuriating woman I have ever met."

She stared him down deliberately. "Goodnight, Mr. Reynolds," she said quietly.

It was a wonder that he didn't wake Jimson with the slamming of that door. Rosemary Reynolds' teapot dancing on the shelf, and the snow inside the doorway blew halfway across the room.

Jessica should have fallen to sleep the moment her head touched her pillow. Instead, she thought of the scene just past. Before, she always had fought Will on principle or for someone else, for his wife crouching behind the canvas flaps of that wagon, for the baby's safety in that snake pit he was cleaning out, for Floss's right to have their letters kept confidential.

This had been different. This time she had been fighting for herself. "I am changed," she realized with wonder. Hawk had said that their love would change and affect other people. Had it affected her with this new courage to confront her father, then Will, and hold the ground she felt she owned?

She could put an end to Will's problem of loyalty fast enough. She would simply tell her father all about Hawk. Her father couldn't have it both ways, either. He had raised her to work beside him like a man. He had braced her arm when she was too small to support the rifle he was teaching her to shoot. He had forced her to make decisions and act on them when he was not around to counsel her. He couldn't raise that kind of a frontier daughter and then expect her to turn into a simpering ninny at the drop of his command.

Jessica was awakened by men's voices and the lowing of cattle. She leaped into her clothes, splashed her face with water, and pulled on her bonnet without even untangling her hair.

Her father turned as she ran toward him across the snow. "How are they?" she called, barely within shouting distance.

He caught her in his arms like the old days. "Good news," he said. Then he frowned. "Jerry is down with it, but he's a strong boy with a lot of fight."

"Tad?" she pressed, remembering his wild eyes and babbling voice.

Her father grinned ruefully. "You won't know him at first. He's as bald as his grandpa was those last years."

"Papa," she cried.

"Fever," he explained. "He liked to burn himself up with it. Mary Huffman says people with fevers like that often lose their hair."

"Mary Huffman?" Jessica asked.

"She's there now, giving Melanie a lot of support."

"Oh," Jessica sighed. "I wish —"

"You wish you could be there to help," her father finished for her. "We know that, and so does Will here. But the best place for you is where you are, you and that baby. That's all Melanie needs, to have her daughter go down like her sons have."

Jessica nudged the snow with her boot. "There's got to be *something* I can do," she mused aloud.

"Cook," Will said suddenly. "It must take all the strength those women have to nurse two sick boys. Maybe. . . ."

Jessica stared at him. "You're right," she cried. "Look, Papa, if you can bring me goods, my bread isn't as fine as Melanie's, but nobody's choked on it yet. And there's that beef. With some vegetables from the cellar and homemade noodles, you could have a really nourishing stew."

Will laughed. "It makes me hungry to listen to you."

"Give me a half hour and I'll have breakfast," she told them, slipping from under her father's arm.

"I wouldn't fight breakfast," her father grinned. "I let myself out of a sleeping house, knowing you'd want to hear." His eyes held something like an appeal, maybe an apology. Jessica caught his hand and squeezed it hard.

"I did," she said, "and thank you."

Mary Huffman made the rules about Jessica's return. "It will be eight days after Jerry's infectious period before we know about Melanie," she told them. "Then you can talk about bringing your girl home."

Twice each day, Jessica sat with Will to eat. That last confrontation about Hawk had changed their relationship. Instead of the spit and fire of their earlier confrontations, they mutually retreated to stiff civility.

"I hope you slept well, Miss Findlay."

"Thank you, I did, Mr. Reynolds. And yourself?

"More coffee, Mr. Reynolds?"

"If you please, Miss Findlay."

Jessica thought about Hawk as much as she ever had, but differently. While she cherished her memories and was constantly reminded of things they had shared, she was increasingly eager to talk to her father and get that behind her. He had been gentle with her since his return, but a distance still lay between them. She would risk losing him all the way rather than go through life with that shadow between them.

Jerry regained strength steadily. Tad had a fine down of hair coming in curly. Rachel was due home from the honeymoon that Jessica had followed through a blizzard of postcards.

When Jimson wakened from his nap one afternoon, Jessica took him out into the sun. With Will off in town on an errand and her father not quite due for his daily visit, she carried the baby to the corral and propped him on a fencepost to watch the cattle.

She saw the buggy coming from a long way away and watched it idly, expecting it to pass. Instead, it slowed and drew in by the dugout.

Jessica saw Roy Blanding leap down from the driver's seat and help an older woman to the ground. Two older men, dressed as handsomely as the woman was, joined her.

"Jessica," Roy called imperiously.

When she only nodded, he softened his tone. "We're looking for Will Reynolds," he said a little more civilly.

Given that, she walked toward them, Jimson staring curiously from her hip.

"I'm sorry," she said. "Mr. Reynolds is off on business and won't be in until after dark. I would be happy to give him a message."

She might as well have spoken into the wind. The woman, really a handsome woman with glistening black feathers on a satin bonnet and a tippet of fur trimming her jacket, clasped her hands together and burst into tears.

"Oh, the dear love," she cried. "Jonathan, that face. And his hair."

To Jessica's horror, the woman reached for Jimson to take him from her arms. Even as Jessica stepped back, Jimson clutched Jessica around the neck and bawled in protest.

"Now, dear," the woman cooed, following with gloved hands outstretched. "Come to Grandma."

Ray was smiling like a carved pumpkin. "Give her the kid, Jessica. She's his grandmother. Jessica Findlay, Mr. and Mrs. Jonathan Parker. From Chicago," he added importantly. "And this is their lawyer, Frank Quiggens."

"He's afraid of strangers," Jessica said, nodding but tightening her arms around Jimson. "You have to wait until Mr. Reynolds comes home."

"My dear child," the woman said from what seemed a greater height than she stood. "I have no desire to see my dead daughter's husband now or at any time. We have come for her child."

"No," Jessica said, feeling as bleak and helpless as she had when the house had been crowded with Hawk's kinsmen. "I'm responsible for Jimson, and I won't give him to anyone."

"Don't be such a stubborn fool, Jessica," Roy said. "These people came all the way from Chicago for that child, and they have every right to him. They are his grandparents."

"I don't care who they are," she told him. "And I don't know how you got mixed up in this. I only know that this is Will Reynolds' son, and I won't hand him over to anyone but his father."

The attorney kept clearing his throat to speak, but Roy didn't give him a chance. "All right," he said, his voice patronizing. "Let's try to make some sense. These people have come for their grandchild with full legal papers. You have no right to stand in their way."

Jimson, who had only whimpered when the woman clutched at him, now broke into a full, wailing bawl. "No," he gasped. "No. No. *No.*"

"He's talking," the woman cried, grabbing for him again. "Listen, Jonathan, the little dear is talking."

Step by step, they had backed Jessica almost to the door of the dugout. She panicked. Against four of them, she had no chance if they trapped her. She was conscious of nothing but this fear and Jimson's wailing as she ducked and ran from them toward the open prairie.

They shouted after her. She heard Roy curse, and his footsteps hard on her heels.

Then the shot rang out. She gasped and wheeled to see her father, rifle in hand, on his bay horse just beyond the dugout.

The woman screamed, covering her mouth and turning to her husband. Roy froze where he stood.

"Jessica," her father said. "What's going on here?"

"These people —" Roy began.

"I am speaking to my daughter," Patrick Findlay broke in. "Jessica?"

Her father had always said she could run as fast as a weasel. Even carrying that sturdy, screaming child, she made very good time getting to his side.

"These people," she echoed Roy, "claim to be Jimson's grandparents. They tried to take him away from me."

"Claim to be," the lawyer spoke up. "There is no doubt that they are the grandparents of this child and have every legal right —"

"Sir," Patrick Findlay interrupted. "As a man of the law, you must certainly grasp that your words do not establish the identities of these people. Even if they did, in this state, seizure of a citizen is kidnapping, which is punishable by law."

"Now, Mr. Findlay —" Roy began.

"Also," Jessica's father went on, "our laws protect private property. I would advise you to leave this property until Mr. Reynolds is here to allow you trespass."

In that moment of stunned silence, Jessica heard the faint click of her father's rifle being cocked.

"Maybe you should take the baby inside, Jessica," he said genially. "Just in case there is further unpleasantness out here."

Chapter Twenty-six

PATRICK waited with Jessica for Will to return that night. Even though Jessica was busy at the stove and her father was reading quietly at the table when the young man entered, Will sensed the tension in the room before he was through the doorway. With a quick nod at each of them, he crossed the room to stare into his son's cradle.

"Well," Will said, lifting the child against his shoulder. "I had the worst feeling when I walked in here." Then, quickly to Jessica's father, "Jerry is all right, isn't he? Melanie?"

"Everybody's all right, Will," Patrick told him. "Now sit down. We need to talk."

Will's waiting was more intense than any question.

"Some people came here today," Patrick began. "People name of Parker, claiming to be Jimson's grandparents."

Will's fist hit the table with a crash that set the plates to dancing. "I knew it," he cried. "The minute I walked in here off that cattle drive and found that bunch of letters stacked up, I smelled trouble coming from those people."

He rose and shoved three envelopes toward Patrick. "See those? I never thought about those letters coming during the cattle drive. Before Rosemary and I left Chicago, when we were hiding out with one friend after another, her parents never gave up. They hired private investigators, they paid people bribe money, they did everything in their power to get their hands on Rosemary. See there? Those are lawyers, Carpenter, Quiggens, and Grant."

"Quiggens was with them today," Jessica told him, setting bowls of stew before both of the men.

"But why did they do all this?" Jessica's father asked. "Why were your wife's folks so anxious to get hold of her?"

Will slumped wearily. "We eloped without their permission when Rosemary was under age. They had sworn to separate us, and it was our only course. She was their only child, and their high hopes for her didn't include me. We thought we would be safe once we were out here. They can buy any court in Chicago, so we didn't dare stay there. When the letters started coming out here, I sent them back so they wouldn't know where we were."

Addressee unknown, Jessica thought, remembering Floss's agitation when Rachel had handed her that letter.

"Rachel mentioned your sending those letters back. If she had been running her post office instead of being off on that honeymoon, this would never have happened," Jessica said.

Will shook his head. "It had to happen sometime. I put it off, dreading to face them after losing Rosemary. No matter what the truth is, they are going to blame me for the loss of their beautiful child."

In that pause, Patrick Findlay met his daughter's eyes and sighed.

"I hate to tell them," Will went on. "As much trouble as they made us, they loved her, too. They would have thrown me in prison in Chicago if they had caught me. I'd still be afraid to go back, and yet I hate to tell them that Rosemary is dead."

"Will," Patrick Findlay said heavily. "They know their daughter is dead. They have come for your child."

Will stiffened and stared first at Patrick and then at Jessica, who nodded slowly.

"Papa drove them off with a gun," she said quietly.

More than once, Jessica had been astonished at how quickly the expressions changed on Will's face. Not even he had ever gone from despair to disbelief as fast as that.

"With a gun?" he repeated. "You drove the Parkers off my place with a gun? The

Parkers of Ashland Avenue and State Street? The Parkers of the eight matched horses to a gold-and-white carriage and the summer house in France?

"They can't have Jimson. There's no way they can take Jimson, is there, Pat?"

"I'm no lawyer," Patrick reminded him, "but I can't figure any way they could get that done."

"But they'll try," he added after a minute. "They clearly didn't come out here from Chicago with that lawyer just to turn around and go back home. Mrs. Parker was trying to grab Jimson away from Jessica when I rode up."

"Miss Findlay," Will said, turning to her and shaking his head.

"Oh, Jessica was all right." Patrick smiled at Will. "She had lit off across the field, running with them chasing. It was a pretty good run, considering the weight of that boy. But one rifle shot in the air and it was all over."

"But it's not all over," Will said, staring at the table gloomily. "What will they try next, after kidnapping?"

"From the looks of that lawyer, Quiggens, they didn't bring him along for company. I've been trying to figure out their next move."

Jessica, seeing their untouched plates, took them up again. "I am going to put this stew back on the fire and heat it up again," she told them firmly. "I will do that as many times as you men let it get cold. Getting weak from starvation isn't going to make either one of you think better."

Her father grinned before turning back to Will. "My best guess is that they'll claim you can't take proper care of a child out here without a woman. I figure they'll say that he will grow up without schooling and culture and whatever else people have to have to be comfortable in a summer house in France."

"But he couldn't have had better care," Will protested.

"You don't have to convince me," Jessica's father laughed. "You have to convince them or the court. Anyway, that's only my guess."

"The court," Will repeated thoughtfully. "I can't afford a lawyer."

"*Hot stew*," Jessica said, setting the plates in front of them again. Her father grinned and lifted his spoon before looking over at Will.

"A lawyer could do you more harm than good out here," he said. "A lot of people figure you only hire a lawyer if you need somebody to lie for you."

"But what happens when they challenge me on making a good steady home for Jimson?" Will pressed.

"You tell them that you're prepared to pay a fine Kansas woman to care for that child every day you can, and when such is not to be had, that Mrs. Patrick Findlay and her daughter Jessica Findlay will fill in like they have since he was born. While you're at it, ask the crowd there how many of them were raised by kin and neighbors out of love. Now eat your stew. It's not going to improve by being heated up another time."

When Jessica joined them, her father grinned over at her. "I came with good news, which those folks knocked right out of my head. Mary Huffman and Melanie have scrubbed up every single thread in that house and dried it in the sun. Mary was packing up to leave and said I could bring you and the boy home anytime."

It was flattering to see Will's face fall. "I know it's the right thing," he said. "But I'm sure going to miss that little boy."

Invisible Jessica, she thought crossly, wishing she had thought to add a couple of extra tablespoons of pepper to his stew.

"What if the Parkers and that Quiggens try something at your place?" Will asked with sudden concern.

"They're welcome." Patrick Findlay laughed. "I wouldn't want you to quote this to my son Jerry, but the only two people around here who are better shots than I am are Jessica here, and my wife. Dead-shot aims, both of them. And then there's Major."

Soon, they were notified that there was to be a hearing about Jimson's custody.

Melanie suggested that Will take Jimson along with him to the hearing in Justice Schoenbrun's saloon. "One look at that little fellow will convince any judge that he's had the best of care from the word go."

After all the stories Jessica had heard
about Justice Schoenbrun's court, she would
have loved to attend the hearing. She knew
better than even to ask her father. Louis
Schoenbrun, who was justice of the peace,
owned the saloon on the northwest corner of
North Main and Fort streets. To keep his
trials and judicial procedures from interfer-
ing with his business, he held his court in
front of the bar in the saloon. Jessica had
heard her father joke about how many times
the court had to be adjourned for Justice
Schoenbrun to serve out another round of
drinks. It was bad enough, in Patrick Findlay's opinion, for an innocent baby to be
carried in there, but he did agree with Melanie that Jimson would win the day for Will.

The minute Patrick Findlay and Will
walked into the Landers store, Jessica knew
Will had won his case. She would have con-
gratulated him like all the others who
crowded around, but she would have had to
fight her way through a crowd.

In the buggy going home, he turned from
where he sat by her father and said, "Miss
Findlay, I think you're the only person in
town who hasn't had something to say about
the hearing today."

"You must know what I think," she said

He shook his head without even smiling.
"Miss Findlay, I can't imagine that anyone
could ever predict how you were going to
feel about anything." Then he turned back
to her father.

All of the things he had ever said about her to her face tumbled back into her mind: bullheaded, trying, infuriating. As much as that list angered her, she was amused to realize that if he ever looked at himself in the mirror and saw himself as she saw him, he would be reciting all those charges against himself.

That was all right. The crises were all past but one. Will could keep his son. Tad and Jerry would be back on their feet within a few weeks. The snows that had made winter so miserable had brought Melanie's garden leaping from the earth in elegant rows of verdant green. There remained only one hurdle. She must take her father through her relationship with Hawk and let him know that although it was over, she had no regrets.

She quickly changed from her town clothes and into her working boots. She sang as she checked the nest of eggs beneath the brooding hens.

When she heard her father calling, she thought Melanie had supper ready. Instead, he had come to look for her, his face as solemn as it had been before the trial.

"What's the matter?" she asked.

"The Parkers," he said bitterly. "Apparently they were just laying a trap for Will."

"What do you mean? What kind of a trap?"

"They presented the charge on a paper before we got out of town."

"What charge?" she asked. "What possible charge?"

Not since the evening that he confronted her about Wheeling Hawk had she seen such anguish in his face. This time he couldn't even meet her eyes. "Monday," he said. "On Monday, you have to be there before Justice Schoenbrun. The Parkers claim to have witnesses to prove you morally unfit to care for Will's child."

"Papa," she said, "I don't believe this."

"I don't know what to believe anymore," he said, turning away.

"She doesn't have to go to church," Melanie announced.

"She does too have to go to church," Patrick Findlay said. "It's the same as admitting to guilt not to face up to her friends and neighbors at church."

"But the pain," Melanie insisted, fighting back tears.

"Sometimes," Patrick Findlay said slowly, "I think pain is what life is all about."

During the two days following, Jessica didn't feel any pain at all. There was just numbness and a startled disbelief that this was really happening.

Melanie was right, of course. Church was the worst. It was so bad that by the time Jessica could escape to the family buggy to go home, she was fighting herself not to laugh hysterically.

Rachel, her best friend through all of her life, stood with her arm through Walt's, nodding like a toy. "Don't you worry one minute," she commanded in a whisper. "You have more friends than you know, and they all know more than you think they do." Could Rachel really think that was comforting?

The worst, of course, was Will. He did not meet her eye during that interminable Sunday dinner. Melanie turned herself inside out to make the dinner light and friendly the way it usually was.

The first moment Jessica could get out of the house, she did. She didn't even put a saddle on Dancie. She simply led her from the barn and leaped on her back, Indian-style, the way she had taught herself to do on the sly the year she was Jerry's age.

"Now go," she whispered fiercely in Dancie's ear. Dancie went, beyond the burying ground and across the hillock, east of the pasture where the cattle had wintered. The pony huffed and blew at the rise of the ridge but made it to the top where Jessica slid off.

As Dancie cropped among the trees, Jessica lay on her stomach, staring at the curled growth of new grass. She smelled a fox, an acrid, sharp scent borne on the wind. She rolled over, hoping to see him with his delicate, sly face and glorious ears.

Instead she saw a rider, his horse straining at the rise of the ridge. Will. She turned back on her stomach and willed him not to see her. For once, let being invisible work her way.

She heard the horse stop, and the sound of his dismounting.

"Miss Findlay," he said.

"Yes, Mr. Reynolds," she replied, not turning over, not looking at him, not caring what he thought about any of that.

"I had something I wanted to say to you," he said. The nearness of his voice startled her. It was so close, as if he were kneeling beside here there on the grass. She felt her heart hammer. This was ridiculous. She wasn't afraid of him; why should his being so near affect her like this?

"Help yourself," she said. "Everyone else has."

"You're not making this very easy for me," he said suddenly, that cold anger coming back into his voice.

His tone stunned her. Why did it always have to be like this? There had been those brief moments between them when it seemed that they could be friends, sometimes even warm and understanding friends, like that night he returned from the cattle drive. But no! Every time she had felt warmly drawn to him, he had come back like that, with coldness and anger.

And now! What arrogance that he dared to act like that now! No matter what happened, whether he kept Jimson or lost him, didn't he realize that she would go through life as a woman branded with scandal, even though nothing was proved against her?

She rolled over, rose to her feet, and stood looking down at him. "Is this easier?" she asked in a syrupy tone as unlike her ordinary voice as she could make it.

He had been kneeling on one knee. He flushed with color as he rose to face her. Then, without warning, he reached out, caught her arm, and pulled her against him. Before she could protest, he cupped her face in his hand and pressed his lips to hers. His kiss, which had begun roughly, ended in such tenderness that she forgot to pull away. How could she be doing this? How could she be letting this man who had used her so badly and treated her with such scorn hold her lips in such a kiss and love every moment.

When he released her, it was only to hold her tight against him, his lips against her hair as he groaned. "Forgive me for taking that liberty, Miss Findlay. I'm not sorry, not for a minute, but forgive me for losing my control like that."

He held her close, shaking his head. "I swear, Miss Findlay. You are a trial to me. I have been tricked by people, and betrayed by people. I have been stolen from, cheated, and humiliated. But never in my life, Miss Findlay, have I ever been tempted to murder anyone as many times as you've tempted me."

She could have pushed him away, but she didn't. She waited, feeling the thundering of his heart so close to hers. Suddenly, she was terribly confused by her own feeling for him. Maybe it was just that together they had gone through so much. Maybe it was how empty her own life was of love, with Hawk gone. For whatever reason, his arms were so warm and comforting around her that she didn't want him to ever let her go.

Of course, he did. He loosened his grip until she was free, and he was looking at her, his face tender and questioning. He wanted the forgiveness he had asked for. How could she forgive him for warming her life for that brief moment in such a loving way? Instead, she turned to jest.

"Murder," she repeated thoughtfully. "Now there's a solution to my problem that I hadn't thought of."

He stared at her a long moment before a slow smile lit his face. "Okay, you win again, Miss Findlay. Come on. We'll ride back together."

"You have to look the other way while I get on," she told him.

He glanced at Dancie, then stared again. "Good Lord, woman, where is your saddle?"

"Hanging in the barn," she said. He looked down the valley in the opposite direction, laughing as she leaped onto Dancie's back.

The pace was fast going back. Only as they approached the burying ground did he speak again. Then he caught her reins and pulled Dancie in.

"You don't have to listen, but I have to speak," he said. "Nothing that happens tomorrow can keep me from being grateful to you all of my life, Miss Findlay."

"Thank you," she said, not able to look up into his face.

Chapter
Twenty-seven

JESSICA had never been inside a saloon until the day of her hearing. Later, when she tried to remember that place, she could only recall a confusion of bottles, mirrors, and colored glass. Behind her, as she faced Justice Schoenbrun, was a large, dark room crowded with tables and staring men's faces, floating in a haze of tobacco smoke. On her right, a bar of polished wood ran the length of the room.

Justice Schoenbrun was a solid man, heavy-set with a stiff military carriage, and brilliant blue eyes. It took a few moments for her to understand what he was saying in his thick Austrian accent.

Mr. Quiggens read the charge that she, Jessica Findlay, daughter of Patrick Findlay, and wife, deceased, was a woman of moral turpitude, unfit to care for a child.

"Turpitude," the justice interrupted. "Vat do you mean, that she's not a good girl?"

At Quiggens' nod, the justice stared at Jessica. "You *look* like a good girl. Vat did you do?"

"I haven't heard the charges," Jessica told him.

He chuckled. "How old are you?"

"Sixteen, your honor."

"You're not much grown for that," he observed.

"Her mother was little like that, too," someone called from the back of the room.

"I object, your honor," Quiggens said nervously.

"Nothing for you to make objection to," the justice rebuked him. "What haff you to do with her mama's size?"

Jessica's heart fell. This court was as bad as all the stories she had heard. But this was her life they were discussing. If this strange judge was playing for the entertainment of his saloon crowd, she was at his mercy as much as Quiggens was.

"Tell me what she did you don't like," the justice directed.

Rattling his papers, Quiggens began to read. "Said Jessica Findlay habitually behaves in an unladylike manner with young men, luring them into amorous relationships."

Jessica stared at the attorney in disbelief.

The justice laughed at her. "You still don't know what he's talking about. We hear him out, then we'll see."

Quiggins produced witnesses to the charge.

Agatha Williams, with an absolutely straight face, said the defendant "behaved immodestly," "walked out alone with," and "led on," a certain Geoffrey Montgomery of Oxford, England.

Roy Blanding, with his mother at his side, claimed he was jilted by the defendant after she lured him by accepting his attentions, handsome gifts, and encouraging him to build her a handsome house.

On behalf of Mr. and Mrs. Parker of Chicago, Mr. Quiggens presented statements from local citizens that the "said defendant Jessica Findlay, a single woman, stayed for two months in the dugout of Will Reynolds, a widower, without chaperone. The irregular nature of this arrangement was made more obvious when Jane Hogan, a widow from Ellis, came to care for the child. Said Reynolds then built quarters for himself outside the dugout where he stayed at night."

"I have a further charge to present," Mr. Quiggens said.

"You haff made your point," the justice told him. "If you just have more men's names, we go to defense's witness."

Quiggens blushed. "This may be the most damaging charge of all, sir. It is public knowledge that said defendant has carried on, over a period of months, a relationship with a member of a warrior society of the Northern Cheyenne Indian tribe, an enemy of our people."

A moment of stunned silence was followed by ugly muttering.

"Well, now." The justice looked at Jessica strangely. She felt the color drain from her face. "What do you say to this?"

Mr. Quiggens was quick on his feet. "Defendant must testify under oath, your honor."

"Make her tell about the Indian first," someone called from the back of the saloon.

"I run this court," Schoenbrun said. "We take in order. Is what this Agatha Williams say about the Britisher the truth?"

"No, sir," Jessica told him.

"You tell me about this Geoffrey Montgomery?"

"I met him at his parents' house. We talked a lot and enjoyed each other's company. He wanted to immigrate to Kansas and we talked about that."

"Did he immigrate?"

"Not that I know of."

"Then you didn't lure him very good, did you? Next charge. What about this Blanding? Did you jilt him?"

"I couldn't jilt him. I was never engaged to him. We just went together."

"Did you ever tell him you would marry him?"

"He never asked me. He just presumed it."

"Did you ever consider marrying him?"

"Yes, sir, but I decided against it."

"Why?"

Jessica felt her color rise and dropped her eyes. "I didn't love him. I thought he had a mean streak, and I was afraid of him and his mother."

"He was big in here with these Chicago people about taking that man's baby. That makes him a prejudiced witness. Now, about staying there with Reynolds?" the judge asked.

"After his wife died, I went as a neighbor to tend the baby until his relative came from Chicago. My father took me in the morning, and Mr. Reynolds rode me home after he returned from work."

"He never stayed in there with you?"

"No."

"Not to bring water? A bucket of chips?"

Jessica shook her head. "I've been carrying chips and water since I was eight — why would he do that?"

"But she rode with him, double on a horse in intimacy every day," Quiggens put in.

"You did that?"

"There was only one horse, sir. I ride like that with my father and brothers, too."

Quiggens made an ugly little smile. "Now don't tell us it wasn't different to ride with this young man."

"Of course, it was," Jessica said. "Mr. Reynolds was a better rider than my brother but not so good as my father." Jessica groaned inwardly the moment her words were out. She didn't intend to send that room full of men into gales of laughter.

The justice scratched his neck and refilled his glass. "To my mind, no immoral woman would choose to stay alone in a dugout with a baby all day. As for the charge of intimacy, I think of two on a horse as economy, given the price of a good horse in this country. Now tell us about that Indian."

Jessica could feel a moment of panic. Now she was truly alone. Carefully, she told about the flood, the wall of water against the dugout door, her rescue and ride home by Wheeling Hawk.

The justice nodded. "But you saw him again?"

"He often passed going from work as I rode to bring my brothers from school. We rode along together and talked."

"Talked," a voice hooted. "What Indian can talk?"

"Then there was a cow killed," Quiggens prompted.

"Who killed the cow?" the justice asked.

"Coyotes," Jessica said swiftly. "The calf was newly dropped and the cow defended it from them. My friend came by, shot the coyotes, and helped me build a travois to drag it home, hoping to save it. We lost the cow, but the calf lived. This happened while my father was on a cattle drive."

The silence in the room remained ominous through all this.

"Where is this man now?"

"Somewhere in the mountains with his people."

The justice groaned, poured himself a half-glass of whiskey, and downed it in a gulp.

"Some citizens have come forward to testify in this girl's defense." He peered at the list in his hand.

"Lady Montgomery," he said.

Agatha blanched as her former employer stepped forward. Hats swept from heads in the back of the room. In her elegant accent, Lady Montgomery told of Jessica's visit, of her nephew's attraction to this charming and intelligent young lady, and of Miss Findlay's wise counsel to the young man "on life decisions he was considering."

"Has this widow from Ellis anything ugly to say about this girl?" the justice asked.

Jane Hogan, rising from beside Will, took offense at the very suggestion of wrong on either Jessica's or Will's part.

"We keep coming back to this Indian," the justice reminded Jessica. "With him gone, how can we learn about him?"

The man who came forward was a stranger to Jessica. But once he stood under the bright lights by the bar, a ripple of talk stirred among the spectators. He introduced himself as Hamlin Fairchild, a merchant in horses. The room fell silent when he began to speak.

"Wheeling Hawk is indeed a member of the warrior society of the Northern Cheyenne. He is of the followers of Dull Knife, a group that has long worked for peace. To this end, Wheeling Hawk was taught English as a child to be his tribe's advocate.

"He is a kindly, intelligent, and proficient man. When he left, I lost the best horseman I have ever known. Her story rings true.

Wheeling Hawk would save a drowning white woman and a child, help her with injured cattle, and be a friend without threat. He will also be a deadly enemy if his tribe is forced to turn against us, because he is a man of honor."

The justice studied Jessica. "You make good friends," he told her. "You make bad enemies, too. How do you explain this?"

She looked at him, confused.

"I asked an important question," he prodded her.

"I object," Quiggens said.

"Objection denied," the justice said without taking his eyes from Jessica's face.

"Maybe I don't pay enough attention to how things look," she told him, thinking aloud. "I go more by what I think is fair. Maybe that bothers people." She hesitated and grinned at him. "Maybe other people like it."

"I like it," Justice Schoenbrun decided. "I think that baby is better off with somebody fair than with somebody worrying about the looks of things. Case dismissed. Gentlemen, what do you take?"

"We will appeal," Quiggens cried.

"Drink orders only," the justice told him.

Out in the sunshine, Jessica felt unsteady on her legs, blinded by the light and giddy from the pure air. She felt a firm hand at her elbow and saw Will smiling down at her.

"Magnificent," he whispered.

All of those unexpected friends gathered around her, smiling — Mrs. Montgomery, Jane Hogan, Mr. Fairchild, and Rachel.

"How did you all come here?" she asked, overwhelmed by what they had done for her.

Rachel laughed. "I told the Montgomerys what Agatha and Roy were up to. Walt and I drove over and got Mrs. Hogan."

Mr. Fairchild smiled at Jessica. "I have trained horses for the Montgomerys. When his Lordship told me what you had told them about the Cheyenne, I knew it had to have come from Wheeling Hawk. We miss him."

"I do, too," she told him.

"Let's hope they find rest in the mountains," he told her. "If they are driven into banding with fiercer tribes, like the Sioux, things could turn ugly for all of us."

As the crowd thinned, Jessica's father took her aside.

"Thank God it went so well," he said. "He's gone then?"

She nodded.

"I didn't give him his due," he admitted. "Or you forgive me."

She stood on tiptoe and kissed his cheek.

"Now," he said briskly, "I told Walt Brannon I'd drive Mrs. Hogan by to see Melanie and then take her home. Will will give you a ride."

"And start a scandal?" she asked, able to tease him again after so long.

"Get along with you," he said, chuckling.

Chapter
Twenty-eight

I T is very nice of you to take me home, Mr. Reynolds," Jessica said, seated in the buggy beside him.

"I have no intention of taking you home," he told her.

She looked over to see him grinning at her. "You see, I have a lot to say to you. I figured the best way was to take you somewhere that you couldn't outrun me, outshoot me, ride off on a pony, or slam my own door in my face."

She was too exhausted to protest. The sun and the horse's easy pace made her drowsy. Not until the buggy stopped did she look around. She saw a grove of trees, taller in the middle like the pitch of a house.

He was quick to her side of the buggy, offering her his hand to help her step down. Without releasing her hand, he led her to the side of a stream that ran over pebbles washed as silvery clean as moonlight.

"Come and sit," he said, leading her to a smooth stone on the bank. She sat stiffly on the stone beside him because he was so near.

His soft chuckle startled her. "I'm not a dangerous man, you know," he told her. "You could lean back without fear of being eaten alive. After such a day, even you must be tired."

"I am tired," she agreed, leaning back gingerly against his shoulder. *What am I doing?* she asked herself. *Why am I behaving like this?* And he *was* a dangerous man. How many times had she been stirred with strange responses when he had turned that charm of his on her? Even without those other times, the way his kiss had haunted her made him dangerous.

He reached over and loosened her bonnet strings, smiling at her. Lifting her bonnet off, he laid it on the grass and said, "Here. Let me show you how to be comfortable." Shifting, he looped his arms around her loosely so that his chin rested lightly on her hair as she leaned against him.

"You are absolutely sure that you aren't dangerous?" she asked, startled by how warm and natural it felt to be there against him.

"I might be," he said lightly. "Look at how small you are here against me. I could tighten my arms and crush you." He hugged her, stopping her breath for a second. Before she could protest his roughness, he spoke again, his words coming slowly as if his thoughts formed only as they fell from his lips.

". . . And there have been times I have been so tempted to do just that. I didn't want to fall in love with you the way I did. I fought it every way I knew how, with rudeness and anger and turning away so that your golden head didn't glow in my eyes. But all the time I knew I was losing. I kept falling more in love with you, and deeper into your debt."

When he sighed, she felt the rise of his chest against her. "And now you've done it again, you know. Just today, you took the debt I owed you and doubled it a million times. But strangely enough, I'm even grateful for that debt because my love always manages to grow with it." His tone turned light. "I haven't always enjoyed your lessons, Miss Findlay, but I've profited mightily by them."

A dragonfly arrived to hover, brilliant in the sun, above the moving water. Why had he brought her here? She wished she could forget that tender kiss on the hill, how warm and joyful it had been to cook and eat and talk with him that night in the dugout. The last thing she needed was to have the love she had already begun to feel for him stirred to flame. It had been a living death to give up Hawk; she couldn't face that level of pain again. Yet here she was, leaning against him and loving it. Had she lost her mind from the strain of the days past, or had she become a wanton woman simply by being accused of it in open court?

"About those lessons," he said. "You have a mannerism of speech that I noticed from the first. You put everything into a single word. Your father is masterful; Melanie is regal. I am rude."

"Jessica," he went on. She felt a shiver of something like recognition at the sound of her name on his lips. "Jessica," he repeated, "I look at life out here, a place that began by killing my dream and has thwarted me over and over ever since. I wonder how you can love Kansas as you do. You must have a single word for Kansas, too, a word that sums it all up for you, that catches this endless, driving wind, this sky that is wider than a man can see with a single pair of eyes, the storms that come every season like a beast from a fable. Name Kansas for me, Jessica."

"Home," she said swiftly. "It's all of a piece. Even as Jimson is to me, and Papa, and Melanie. You don't love because an object of love is perfect but for what it is, all of a piece."

He slid his hands to her shoulders and turned her to face him. Usually, when he had studied her this way, intently, he had ended in anger or by looking away. Why did she keep remembering the only time that such a glance had ended in that rough kiss, which had turned so gentle? This time his mouth softened into a smile. He leaned and pressed his lips on hers tenderly, the way she pressed

345

her own on Jimson's fragrant flesh.

"You don't know," he said softly, "how many times I have wanted to do that, how many times I have dreamed of the last time our lips met." Then, briskly, "All right, then, name a Kansan for me. What does it take to call a place like this home?"

What a crazy man he was. He melted her with a kiss and then tugged her mind away when all she wanted was his arms around her again, tight like they had been. She recognized her father's laughter in the chuckle that rose in her throat as she dragged her mind back to answering his question. "Defiant," she told him. "Just plain old bullheaded defiant. That may not be a pretty trait, but it's what Kansans are made of. Everything you attempt on the frontier is a fight. Nothing comes easy. You've learned that. The earth fights the plow, and the sky fights the seed you plant. After a while, you quit trusting anything that comes easy. Who wants to win easy? What's the glory in beating a nothing? You show me a Kansan who gives up and turns his wagon back East and I'll show you a man without defiance."

She felt the long exhalation of his sigh. "Dreams die painfully," he reminded her. She knew he was thinking of his beautiful Rosemary and the white stone where she had slept away these seasons. She thought of her own mother's grave.

Jessica leaned her head against his chest. "Dreams don't die," she told him. "They change. Like love." She thought of Hawk, leaving that dugout to go follow his people. A lesser man would have been angry. A lesser man would have rebelled against his destiny. Not Hawk. He had whipped his pony to a gallop and left like the warrior he was. Somewhere in the mountains, as hidden as mist, his tribe had gathered. She wished him the peace she felt with Will. She wished him love. Not their love but a new love that would bring him a child he could enjoy.

Will tightened his arms around her, burying her face in his shirt, which smelled of sunshine and the harsh lye soap that Melanie had boiled behind the garden. "You are right, of course. Dreams do change. But what they change to will have new enemies springing from the ground."

"What do you mean by that?" she challenged, struggling to free herself so she could look into his face. She didn't succeed. He held her too tightly, keeping his eyes hidden from her.

"That's not hard to tell, Jessica. It's just hard to take. More than anything in this world, I want you beside me, all the days of my life. I want to waken beside you and watch you drift off to sleep. I want to see Jimson on your knee and later his brothers and sisters."

"And what enemy rises against this dream?"

"A legion of enemies," he said. "The way we met. The debts I owe you. The dirty, ugly things that were suggested today in that courtroom. Even if it had never come to that, I've heard the way people talk. They say your father married Melanie to have someone to keep the house and raise you. I've heard them say that a man in Kansas without a woman is a farmer without a plow. Your father and his friends saved me from failure. Your neighborliness saved me my child. Do you think I can ask you to marry me and start everybody in this county to nodding like crows on a fence?"

"What a lot of silliness," she cried. "Do you think I'm the sort of person to tailor her life to the cut of a gossip's tongue? If I had been, Will Reynolds, I certainly would never have been hauled into that court today. Let them say what they want to. What we feel is our own business."

He sighed and tightened his arms around her. "I love you, Jessica. I was already more in love with you than I could admit when Floss came. Floss doesn't always know how much she tells. She said you were a woman in love, a woman with a romantic, perfect love that no ordinary man could compete with. What a bolt that was! I was in love with you and falling more deeply in love with you every time we crossed swords and I lost. And all this time I knew you belonged to someone else." He shrugged. "Now, just today, when I hear that your young man is gone, my hands are still tied. Even if you would have me, I could go around the countryside on a galloping horse and shout everybody out of doors. I could yell, 'Hear ye. Hear ye, Jessica Findlay is my heart of hearts, all that I love in this world aside from my son.' Who would believe me?"

Jessica shivered at the splendor of his words, at the thunder of his voice rising from the warm chest against which she was held so firmly. "If I believed you, the others wouldn't matter," she told him softly.

"I can't do it," he whispered, his voice breaking. "Loving you as I do, I can't ask you to marry me and bring you all that shame and hurt."

When she finally drew breath enough, she shoved him hard and suddenly, so that she could look up into his face.

"Will Reynolds," she said, not wanting the words to come out sounding as angry as they did. "How can you say you love me and then stand back for reasons like that? You don't even care whether I care about all that. You have become a true Kansan in some kind of record time. Talk about defiance. You'd kill your own dream if nobody came along to give you a fight." She knew her tears were going to start spilling any minute. She didn't know whether they were tears of love or pain or anger. It didn't matter. Will was, and always had been, the kind of man you had to straighten out.

"And you listen here," she went on. "It just so happens that when you talk like that, it's not just your own dream that you're smashing. It's mine, too. I was a Kansan before you ever saw a stretch of prairie. You may give in if you want to, but I am not going to."

He stared at her, clearly puzzled.

She frowned. "Leap year was last year, so I can't use that. Okay. I say that a man who sneaks around and sends a girl a pair of wedding slippers for Christmas and pretends they are from someone else has compromised her and better marry her before he gets into even deeper trouble."

The laughter that swept across his face instantly turned to tenderness. He gently cupped her face in his hands.

"Jessica, Jessica," he whispered. "All this time I have turned away and walked away, trying not to reveal my growing love for you. Now I really have to walk on eggs, don't I? How can I let you win this fight when I know from your own words that you don't trust what comes easy?"

She felt that wonderful warmth of laughter start deep in her chest. She ought to be able to see rainbows with her tears still running. But if a girl can come right out and propose, she can certainly take other liberties, too. She grabbed him hard around the waist and held her lips up to his.

"If you call what we've gone through finding each other easy, Will Reynolds, you are Kansan enough for me."

She knew she was dampening his cheeks as he kissed her. That was all right. This time she knew they were tears of joy.

SUNFIRE™ ROMANCES

Spirited historical romances about the lives and times of young women who boldly faced their world and dared to be different.

From the people who brought you WILDFIRE®...

An exciting look at a NEW romance line!

Imagine a turbulent time long ago when America was young and bursting with energy and passion...

When daring young women defied traditions to live their own lives...

When heart-stirring romance and thrilling adventure went hand in hand...

When the world was lit by *SUNFIRE*...

SUSANNAH by Candice F. Ransom $2.95

Not since young Scarlett O'Hara has there been a heroine so spirited. SUSANNAH Dellinger had lived her sixteen years as a proper Virginia girl. But when her brother and her fiancé are called on to defend the South, she must fight for her own life, for her family, and for the secret love born in the flames of war.

ELIZABETH by Willo Davis Roberts $2.95

The Salem witch hunts of the 1600's is the frightening setting for ELIZABETH's story. When her friend Nell is accused of being a witch, ELIZABETH has to decide whether to risk her own life and defend Nell, or to remain silent and watch her friend die. Silence will win ELIZABETH wealthy Troy and safety. Crying out will bring her reckless Johnny and love.

DANIELLE by Vivian Schurfranz $2.95

It is the War of 1812, and the city is New Orleans. Beautiful DANIELLE is a headstrong, young girl, who must choose between an exciting but frightening pirate and the quiet understanding boy she grew up with. As the war engulfs her, DANIELLE's choice is no longer a matter of the heart. It is a decision that will determine her destiny.

JOANNA by Jane Claypool Miner $2.95

After her sweetheart has shipped out to sea, lovely JOANNA leaves her farm to find mill work in Lowell, Massachusetts. What she really finds are dangerous working conditions, a romance with the mill owner's nephew Theo, and the challenge to join other women at the mill in a strike that could cost JOANNA everything she has gained.

An exciting excerpt from the first chapter of
CAROLINE follows.

CAROLINE

by Willo Davis Roberts

Chapter One

CAROLINE could tell immediately, before her brothers entered the house, that something was up. Something had happened, something that had them both excited and secretive, for they didn't blurt it out at once. Billy, especially, had trouble keeping secrets. For all that he was nearly seventeen, Caroline thought he often seemed younger than her own fifteen years.

He brought in the bag of flour and lowered it to the floor, where it gave off a faint white cloud. "What're we having? Stew and dumplings? Boy, I'm famished. How long before it's ready?"

"You have time to wash up after you un- load the wagon," Grandma Rose informed him. "Put that in the pantry instead of where we'll trip over it, why don't you?"

Billy grinned at his sister and reshouldered the bag. "All right." His eyes were blue, his unruly thatch of hair the same shade of pale gold as Caroline's. He winked at her. "Dish me up a double helping of everything when it's ready. I'm about to starve."

Dying of hunger was a daily thing with Billy; nobody paid much attention to him. Caroline followed him into the tiny pantry, lowering her voice. "What is it? What's hap- pened?"

He gave her an exaggeratedly innocent stare. "What do you mean?"

She reached out to pinch one of his mus- cular arms. "I mean what are you bursting to talk about?"

He laughed and dodged around her. "Frank'll tell everybody at supper," he said, and went back to the wagon for another load.

She wanted to smack him, but the excite- ment was contagious, even though she didn't know what it was all about. Her brothers teased her, spoiled her, defended her; most of all, they were her friends, the best friends she had except for Nancy Shorey. Usually they let her in on whatever they were plan- ning or doing, so why not now?

Frank was nineteen, and Caroline had al- ways thought him the best-looking of her six brothers. He was the oldest still at home, tall, muscular, darkly handsome. When he came into the house, carrying supplies, he, too, grinned at her with that underlying tension that she was certain was excitement.

He stowed rice and corn meal on the pantry shelves, then washed up in the basin on the bench beside the door; he was toweling himself dry when Andrew Hoxie came through the door with the evening's milk.

"Here, Pa, I'll take that," Caroline offered, relieving him of the pail. How could he not see, Caroline wondered, that something important was afoot?

It wasn't until they'd eaten and she'd risen to serve out the rhubarb pie onto each plate that her curiosity was finally satisfied. She knew it was coming when she saw that Frank did not pick up his fork at once to plunge it into the flaky crust but leaned his forearms on the table and cleared his throat.

Frank, hesitant to speak?

"Billy and I have some news," he said, finally. Frank hesitated just long enough to be sure that he had everyone's attention.

"We're going to California," he said. "To the gold fields."

"California?" Caroline echoed.

Frank glanced at his younger brother, and it was clear that they'd talked it all out and made up their minds, that this time they would allow no one to talk them out of this dream. "We're leaving day after tomorrow," he said, "for Independence. The wagon trains will start pulling out by the end of next week,

355

and we aim to go with them. And we are going to find gold."

Andrew Hoxie had forgotten his dessert. "Now look, boys, we've been all over this before —"

"And we're going over it again," Frank said. There was a note in his voice Caroline had never heard there before, of determination, strength, conviction. Frank was no longer a boy, he was a man, she thought, and what he said he'd do, he'd do. A tremor ran through her, and she finally remembered the pie and dished up the rest of it. Even when she took her own place again, however, nobody ate.

Ever since they'd heard about the gold rush, they'd been talking about going to California.

Caroline understood how they felt. But she knew that if they went, they would leave her behind. The thought made her chest ache and her eyes sting with unshed tears.

All through that first winter, when the snow drifted to the eaves and they were only warm when within a few yards of the stove or the fireplace, Caroline dreamed of the romance that would surely come in the spring. She could have John Wilkins if she wanted him, she knew she could. He had kissed her once, and it had made her feel quite peculiar. She'd liked kissing him, yet she was fairly certain — no, she *was* certain — that she didn't love John. She enjoyed dancing with him, and she *liked* him, but she didn't think this was enough to build a future on. She couldn't ever seriously imagine *marrying* him.

Somewhere, Caroline was convinced, there was a young man, handsome and strong like Frank, who would stir her emotions and capture her heart.

While Caroline dreamed, her brothers poured over the newspapers that reported the latest finds in California. Nuggets the size of a man's fist, enough to make a man wealthy, were found in every creekbed, hidden in tree roots, or lying freely on the ground just for the taking by the first man who saw them.

And then, in late March, Andrew had fallen from the haymow and broken his leg.

It was Billy who found him, stunned and in pain, and he and Frank had carried their father to the house. Frank had gone to town for Doctor Hansen. They all watched as the leg was set, Frank pulling with his hands under Andrew's arms while Doc Hansen gripped the foot, stretching out the muscles that had contracted when the bone snapped, until the broken shards were correctly aligned and could be held in place with splints. They had all been sweating, suffering along with Andrew. Caroline had stood by with the strips of cloth to hold the splint in place.

There was no more talk of California or gold. It was clear even to Billy that they could not walk away and leave the farm with no one at all to run it. Caroline could milk the cow and feed the chickens, but she couldn't do the heavy work, the plowing and seeding and harvesting, all by herself, and the older boys had all they could do to manage their own farm work.

Caroline worked outside as much as she could. She enjoyed the sun and the wind on her face and arms, and only her grandmother thought her tan unbecoming in a young woman. Grandma always made it clear that she felt Caroline's upbringing had been inappropriate for a female. She did too many things with the boys, like fishing and riding and racing, and even, occasionally, wrestling, although the latter had pretty well come to an end now, for she *was* growing up.

By the time Andrew's leg had healed enough so that he began to limp around the house and to venture outside, it was too late in the year for the boys to consider California.

Through this past winter, however, the boys had begun to talk again of California, though more guardedly, when Andrew was not around. And Caroline had continued to dream of a special young man. He hadn't come last spring, nor during the summer or fall, but now spring had come again. What better time for him to arrive than when she turned sixteen?

And then today the boys had gone to town and heard again that rich veins had not yet run out; there were still fortunes to be found in California.

Andrew had kept them home for two summers, but this time Caroline thought, it would be different. They would really go.

Her own emotions, considering this, were turbulent. Frank and Billy were her brothers and her best friends. She could hardly bear to think of life without them, and she suspected that her father was right in believing that if they ever went so far away, they would never return home.

The idea began as a tiny seed, then sprouted and grew like the corn she'd helped to plant as soon as the frost was out of the ground.

Caroline gathered her courage, determined to ask the boys to take her with them. She had a fleeting thought of John Wilkins — was it possible that if she allowed him to see her home from the dances, a romance could blossom between them, after all? But to stay and find out would mean losing Billy and Frank, and that she didn't think she could bear to do.

No, John was not the man of her dreams. But somewhere out on the prairie, as she traveled with her brothers on the trail to distant California, there might be the very man she'd been waiting for. Perhaps she had to leave home to find him.

It made her heart beat faster, thinking about it.

She thought about it throughout the evening, covertly watching the faces of the other members of the family to read their thoughts.

She had to wait until the household had settled down for the night. Then Caroline prepared for bed as usual, in the flannel gown her grandmother had made for her, and brushed out her hair. She was not a vain person, but she knew her hair was lovely, long and silky and pale. If only it had waved a bit more, instead of so faintly, it would have been perfect.

Tonight she gave little thought to her hair or her looks. She strained to interpret the small sounds in the house: the falling of a log in the fireplace, a cough, and finally her father's gentle snoring. It was time to seek out Billy.

He and Frank both slept in the loft, but she knew Frank was not there now. He'd gone out, just when the others retired, to check on a heifer about to calve for the first time, and he had not yet returned.

The wood floor was cool under her bare feet as Caroline crept out of her own small cubicle and across the main room of the house toward the ladder that led to the loft. There was enough light from the dying fire to enable her to find her way and she climbed quickly, speaking in a whisper when she'd gained the top.

"Billy?"

He sat up and peered at her through the near darkness. "Come on up."

She scrambled onto the loft floor and then to the bed that Billy shared with Frank, tucking her feet under her long gown. "Take me with you, Billy. Don't leave me behind."

"Hey! Caro, you know we can't do that," Billy began.

She leaned forward and clamped a hand on his arm. "Billy, please! You've never left me out of anything you and Frank did, and this is the most imporant thing ever! You know neither one of you can cook or sew, and you'll need somebody to do those things —"

"Pa's furious about us going. He'd kill us both if we even suggested taking you along —"

"Then don't tell him. Just take me, and I'll leave a note telling him I've gone."

"He'd come after you so quick, and probably take the horsewhip to all three of us, before he'd drag you back by your hair."

"I'll tell him I'm going to stay in town a few days with Nancy. He won't know until it's too late to catch up with us, and if he did he wouldn't do anything to anybody but me. Please, Bill, I was counting on you to understand why I have to go!"

"You're too young, Caroline, and besides you're a girl."

"Why do girls have to be left out of everything interesting?" Caroline heatedly demanded. "Besides, I'm not an ordinary girl. I can do just about everything a boy can do, except lift a hundred-pound sack of meal."

He didn't deny that. He sounded a lot like his father in a reluctant mood, though. "But you are a girl, Caro. And this is going to be a rough trip."

It might have been more convincing if his tone hadn't shown so clearly how thrilled he was at the prospect of the adventure.

Caroline argued for a few minutes longer, until she heard the door open below. She didn't want to confront Frank now, not until she'd had time to think up some more convincing arguments than those that had failed to sway Billy. She half slid down the ladder, nearly colliding with Frank at the bottom.

He only bid her good-night; he was used to his younger brother and sister having frequent conferences and private conversations, and he was not curious as to why she had been in the loft.

In her own bed, Caroline lay awake for some time, plotting her strategy. It wasn't fair that only boys had any say about what they got to do, she thought. If she told her father and her grandmother that she wanted to marry John Wilkins, they'd probably allow her that decision. Yet her conviction had grown that it was not John she wanted, and she knew as well that they would never think it proper for her to go with her brothers.

Somehow, she had to persuade Frank that she would be an asset on the trip to California, and she only had two days to do it in.

The next day her best friend Nancy stopped by to see her. Nancy had heard Frank and Billy were leaving and had to talk about it with Caroline.

Nancy was a few months older than Caroline. She was rather plain, but after a few moments in her company everyone forgot that because Nancy was such fun.

"You'll miss the boys a lot," Nancy said, and Caroline made up her mind. She didn't dare tell Nancy she was going to go, too, because Nancy might mention it somewhere, and it would get back to Pa and complicate things. Nancy was a good friend, but sometimes she forgot and talked about things better kept secret.

"Did you hear about Hal Buxton's gold nuggets?" Nancy demanded, suddenly. "He and Harriet are getting married on Saturday, and they're going to move onto his grandfather's farm. Don't you just envy her?"

"No," Caroline said bluntly. "Hal may have gold nuggets, but he's so — so silly!"

Nancy laughed. "Well, yes, but he's *nice*, Caro. He treats her very well, and she adores him."

Caroline gave her a sidelong look. "Their children will have those ears that stick out like wings, the way all the Buxtons do. I'd never marry him."

"John Wilkins really likes you, Caro. He'd marry you in a second. If you just *smiled* at him, you'd have a slave for life."

"I don't want a slave," Caroline said crisply. "When the time comes, I want a man."

And maybe, she thought, she would find this man in California.

SUNFIRE®

**Read all about the fascinating young women who lived
and loved during America's most turbulent times!**

☐ 32774-7		**AMANDA** Candice F. Ransom	**$2.95**
☐ 33064-0		**SUSANNAH** Candice F. Ransom	**$2.95**
☐ 33156-6		**DANIELLE** Vivian Schurfranz	**$2.95**
☐ 33241-4	#5	**JOANNA** Jane Claypool Miner	**$2.95**
☐ 33242-2	#6	**JESSICA** Mary Francis Shura	**$2.95**
☐ 33239-2	#7	**CAROLINE** Willo Davis Roberts	**$2.95**
☐ 33688-6	#14	**CASSIE** Vivian Schurfranz	**$2.95**
☐ 33686-X	#15	**ROXANNE** Jane Claypool Miner	**$2.95**
☐ 41468-2	#16	**MEGAN** Vivian Schurfranz	**$2.75**
☐ 41438-0	#17	**SABRINA** Candice F. Ransom	**$2.75**
☐ 33933-8	#18	**VERONICA** Jane Claypool Miner	**$2.25**
☐ 40049-5	#19	**NICOLE** Candice F. Ransom	**$2.25**
☐ 40268-4	#20	**JULIE** Vivian Schurfranz	**$2.25**
☐ 40394-X	#21	**RACHEL** Vivian Schurfranz	**$2.50**
☐ 40395-8	#22	**COREY** Jane Claypool Miner	**$2.50**
☐ 40717-1	#23	**HEATHER** Vivian Schurfranz	**$2.50**
☐ 40716-3	#24	**GABRIELLE** Mary Francis Shura	**$2.50**
☐ 41000-8	#25	**MERRIE** Vivian Schurfranz	**$2.75**
☐ 41012-1	#26	**NORA** Jeffie Ross Gordon	**$2.75**
☐ 41191-8	#27	**MARGARET** Jane Claypool Miner	**$2.75**

Complete series available wherever you buy books.
